last kiss
of the
Butterfly

last kiss of the Butterfly

JILL HUCKLESBY

ORCHARD BOOKS

ORCHARD BOOKS
338 Euston Road, London NW1 3BH
Orchard Books Australia
Level 17/207 Kent Street, Sydney, NSW 2000

First published in paperback in Great Britain in 2008 by Orchard Books
A paperback original

ISBN 978 1 84616 343 2

A CIP catalogue record for this book is available from the British Library.

1 3 5 7 9 10 8 6 4 2

Printed in Great Britain by
CPI Cox & Wyman, Reading, RG1 8EX

Orchard Books is a division of Hachette Children's Books,
an Hachette Livre UK company.
www.hachettelivre.co.uk

To Chris and Maddy
And in loving memory of my mother and my brother

My thanks to Christine Lo, my editor Catherine Coe and the team at Orchard Books; Rosemary Canter and Jane Willis at United Agents; Chief Instructor Rachel Innes and the inspiring Vo's 2 tae kwon do school in Rottingdean; Deborah Jeffreys for sharing her *dojang* experiences; the RSPB Dungeness Nature Reserve; my lovely friends Debbie, Viv, Sue, Polly and Elaine and Bernard Clifford for prolific kindness during all the storms; Jonathan Poole, for being my ITU buddy. And thanks always to Chris and Maddy for the journey through the marshes on a spring day in 2006, which led to a discovery and a beginning.

1

Here with me.

I would give anything – my breath, my body, my soul, my life, to reverse time; to hold the world with both my hands and spin it gently backwards on its journey round the sun. I would stop it on its axis at the time I am tiny, curled up on your lap while you read me stories about heroines and happy endings in the heat of the day. You hold me until my eyes close, lulled by the rise and fall of your words on the warm summer winds under the shade of the apple tree.

I want to be your heroine now. I would do anything – walk a tightrope over an abyss of fire, wander in frozen wastes without hope of reaching home, sail through unending storms with waves skyscraper high, leap from the Empire State Building, crawl through trenches of mud and blood, allow doctors to dismantle me to donate my organs, immerse myself in liquid nitrogen, drink a potion like Juliet, to change the clock, to disable its momentum.

We're moving slowly through traffic and I'm not taking my eyes off you. On the other side of the glass, which is separating me from the normal world, pedestrians, kids in buggies, dogs, toddlers, stiff mannequins in shop windows, a man slumped in a doorway, half in a sleeping bag, pass by in the soft focus of my outer vision. Some people stare in our direction. Others look away, not wanting to intrude. Many don't see us at all, their faces vacant, minds on a mission to avoid body contact with anyone else.

Only you are in focus, a short distance ahead, smiling at me, throwing your head back, laughing, surrounded by lavender and sunflowers. The sound of your voice in my ears takes me by surprise, makes me catch my breath. The heavy thing that sits inside my chest, as solid as tree bark with twisted roots, is suddenly pushed up my throat, through my mouth and out into the world. Shards of pain shoot down my abdomen and up my spine.

'Jaz, it's OK.' Dad is holding me tight, trying to soothe me. I am rigid, like a feral creature, trapped in an alien environment, barely breathing, my heart at the point of explosion. My body softens under Dad's touch. The dam behind my eyes breaks and my tear ducts are pumping pure sea water.

'Cry Me A River' is one of your favourite songs. I remember that humans have the same water-to-salt ratio as the sea – nine parts to one. Today, I am your river flowing into an ocean, washed away by the pull of the tide.

I thought if I were strong, strong enough for two, even three, we would win. The brave and valiant Ballantynes. Dad calls us 'the Three Musketeers'. No matter what confronts us, we always 'ride out to face another day'. We're the three permanent sides of the triangle, but the damaged angles have skewed and flexed and changed the shape of us.

Dad must think of a new name now.

We've driven down this road so often, you and me. We usually turn left just ahead and pull into the pay-and-display car park, the start of a shop-fest (if I have my way) or a book-fest (if you have yours). If I close my eyes, I can hear our indicator ticking, like a metronome, keeping time with *The Lark Ascending* on our CD player – your favourite classical piece. I'm longing to feel a swerve as the wheels change direction, to hear you hum the melody, but today we continue onwards, past the round sign displaying a capital P and two more sets of traffic lights. The engine is so quiet, it feels as if we're in a bubble, blowing through other people's lives. Unreal, surreal and real relentlessly entwined.

'Nearly there,' says Dad softly, kissing my forehead. The thorn from the yellow rose I am holding is scraping my skin. The flower is from our garden, freshly picked.

Time is moving us forwards, Mum. There is something else I want to tell you before the bubble bursts and it's no longer just the three of us. When I close my eyes, I am standing in your marshes, under a wide, sun-streaked sky, singing a single note for all eternity.

I am calling you. And you are here with me.

2

'You could stay here with me,' says Mum softly.

'I have to go and let my aggressive tendencies out – and, by the way, I can't breathe,' I reply, my voice muffled by her fluffy, short-sleeved top. Mum wraps her arms around me even more tightly and squeezes.

'I could give that Lioness a run for her money,' she says, pleased with herself.

The Lioness is Sarah, my tae kwon do instructor. She who must be obeyed.

'Er, I don't think so,' I respond, disentangling myself reluctantly from Mum's embrace.

'Rubbish!' declares Mum, flexing a small bicep at me.

'She's a Third Dan,' I sigh, picking up my kit bag.

'That's a strange name for a girl,' quips Mum, pulling a face at me.

For two pins, I would happily curl up with Mum on the sofa and chat some more about my day at school – she loves all the gossip about my mates, 'the Urban Chicks', but I'm supposed to train at least twice a week. And I know that if I go out, Mum will do some more cello practice. She's trying so hard to get back up to standard for the orchestra's next concert. And now she's so much stronger, Dad says I have to 'hang up my angel's wings' and get back to doing my own stuff.

I don't like leaving her, even so.

'Gotta go,' I say, kissing her on the forehead. She wraps her arms around her slender body, in that way which makes her look so young and vulnerable. But then she snarls like a wild cat and reaches out as if to claw me.

'Very funny,' I say. 'See ya later.' I give her a Korean bow, a mark of respect, which she copies. She's in a funny mood today – mischievous, with a sparkle in her hazel-green eyes.

'Love you,' she mouths through our tall windows as I jog past. She looks beautiful and serene, in a blaze of late afternoon sunshine – like a portrait in the space between the struts of freshly painted white wood.

I wave back and quicken my pace. The Lioness doesn't accept lateness and I'm not in the mood for an extra fifty press-ups – her usual punishment for crimes against courtesy.

'*Hana, dool, set, net…*' I count to try to get my legs into a rhythm, but there's something about the stillness of the afternoon, the lazy hum of the cars near the Heath, the long shadows under the trees, the warm air scented with mown grass, that is intercepting the message from my brain to my muscles.

And the image of Mum in the window is filling my head, superimposed over other memories of her in bed in a room with pink curtains at the end of a long, carpeted hospital corridor, wired up to tubes and monitors, battling to recover from hours of surgery. And a few weeks before that, holding my hand on our sofa, telling me things which felt like someone was turning out all the lights, one by one.

'Can you be strong, Jaz?' she asked. She should have known that fighting would come naturally to me. When it's a question of survival, your mind and body become your strongest weapons. But in Mum's case, the enemy was within, unseen, hidden in the lining of her stomach wall, her own cells mutating and cloning themselves, forming a malignant mass with a mindset for murder. In terms of launching a counteroffensive, Mum didn't know where to begin. She couldn't even call it by its name.

She told me she hoped it was just a Krispy Kreme doughnut that had got stuck. Dad even managed a small smile at this, but I saw that he was gripping her hand in his so hard that it was leaving white marks on her skin.

That was the day I came face to face with cancer – a year ago this week.

It was also the start of some mega-strops on my part. When I took the tae kwon do oath, I promised to 'build a more peaceful world'. That doesn't include yelling at doctors and kicking bedpans about. I've done both of those things. The trouble is, they told Dad and me to 'accept the things we can't change'. But Mum asked me to be strong, so, from day one, I decided to fight and not to accept. I would grip her hand and order her to squeeze mine really hard, with all her might, and to keep that feeling running through her body.

Dad's approach has been slightly different. He reads her poetry – all her favourite Shakespeare sonnets, and T.S. Eliot's *Old Possum's Book of Practical Cats*. Mum knows them off by heart now. And we loaded her favourite music onto a new iPod – a mixture of orchestral work, soulful jazz solos and those terrible country and western songs she loves, whose lyrics centre on lovers dying of broken hearts, or murdering their rivals, or suffering unbearable loneliness in some desolate town surrounded by desert and one cactus plant.

People say that going through rough times makes you stronger. I'm not sure about that. You wouldn't say that cows benefit from a trip to the abattoir or that war-torn countries recover completely from their wounds. I think I've turned inwards, rooting around for anything that could stop the feeling of freefall. And in some ways, I've become a model student in one specific area.

To the amazement of Bella, Olly and Tasha – the 'Chicks' – I'm a disciple of perseverance, one of tae kwon do's five tenets. I've stayed up late researching cancer treatments on the internet, everything from bathing in kelp and walking over hot coals holding hands with a shaman, to adopting a total detox diet in far-flung private medical centres in America. Dad sometimes appeared in my doorway, bleary-eyed, woken from a deep sleep by me phoning experts from all over the world in the early hours, explaining my mum's symptoms, asking for information and advice.

'Mr Kenwood is considered to be the top man here for Mum's type of cancer,' Dad assured me, more than once.

'That's what most of the Yanks said too,' I agree. 'Everyone seems to have heard of him.' It was only when Mum said she wanted us all to put our faith in him that I relented.

'We're in the best hands,' said Mum, stroking my forehead, the night before her operation. And fifty-two weeks, one gastrectomy and gallons of chemotherapy drugs later, we still have her with us. And I can stop dreaming about needles filled with epirubicin and cisplatin and tubes dripping fluorouracil into her small frame, stop imagining them pouring like liquid fire through her veins, like phials of Merlin's ancient potions, vanquishing a faceless foe.

Her tests came back clear last month. There is no sign of cancer. That doesn't mean it won't reappear, but Mr Kenwood was 'cautiously optimistic'. So we're not hanging out the bunting, just taking each day at a time, and as the weight of the worry begins to lift slowly, all that's happened is starting to feel like a bad dream. The faster I run, the more positive I feel and the quicker it seems to recede.

I check my mobile. It's 6.20. I have ten minutes to reach the Fitness Factory, change into my *dobok* and join my class. There's just one more road to cross and a fifty metre sprint and I should just do it. The Green Man is flashing, so here goes.

'*Hana, dool, set, net, tasut, yausut, ilgope, yauldul, ahope, yaul!*' I say out loud. And suddenly, a smile spreads across my face. Bella, my best mate, gets fed up with my outbursts of Korean. But I tell her, as a blue belt, I am a plant which is maturing into a towering tree, growing towards Heaven.

I won't tell you what she says in reply.

3

'*Charyot, kyung-ye!*' cries the Lioness. We move to the edge of the *dojang*, the training space marked out by blue rubber matting. There are four of us and we take up positions, two behind two in the square, ready for the practice of patterns, the sequence of moves which form the basis of tae kwon do.

I should be focused on her commands, but I'm feeling weak with hunger and my mind is drifting to the thought of Dad cooking up a feast in our kitchen, which he manages to do most nights of the week, and especially on Fridays. He has a real affinity with food, claiming it's due to years in charge of camping rations as a young Venture Scout. I tease him that it's his feminine side craving fulfilment. Either way, he's brilliant at it. As if in agreement, my stomach emits a mahousive gurgle and Jo, the red-stripe black belt next to me, stifles a giggle.

'*Taeguk oh chang!*' orders the Lioness, referring to the particular patterns we are to perform, according to our belt status. '*Taeguk oh chang*, Ma'am,' we reply, obediently. Her eyes are searing into me. She misses nothing. I'm glad Emma and Cally, the twelve-year-old black belt prodigies, are in front, screening me. I'm the least senior in this group and the other students, a mixture of white, yellow and green belts, are sitting in silent anticipation, hoping to learn from us. I must concentrate.

'Remember, Jaz. Tae kwon do makes you strong in your life. You will never be crushed.' The Lioness's words from a year ago echo in my head. I was explaining to her the reason for my kamikaze attack on the punchbag during training, just after Mum's diagnosis. There were times, like when the consultant told us Mum had only a thirty per cent chance of making a full recovery, that I doubted Sarah's wisdom.

'The tenets and the oath will be your backbone,' she encouraged, and she sounded so sure that for a few minutes I felt invincible, like Superman and Buffy rolled into one, ready to take on Mum's disease and smash it into dust.

'*Si-jak!*' the Lioness shrieks and we begin, punching, kicking, turning, retracting, pausing in the air, every movement precise and strong, like a flow of physical poetry. It has taken me two years to get to grips with the patterns. I know it will take a lifetime of practice to perfect them.

I'm not exactly an ideal student, so the five rules of courtesy, integrity, perseverance, self-control and indomitable spirit have brought their own challenges, too. Even before Mum got ill, I was a kid with a short fuse and a mahousive temper. For this, I blame the terrible twins dyslexia and dyspraxia, which were diagnosed (category 'mild') after I sat some special tests when I was ten. I was sent to an educational assessment centre after it was clear my school exam papers looked like a dumb rhino had written them. The teachers said my anger was due to frustration. I was very bright but couldn't articulate well under pressure. They also thought dyspraxia could account for my occasional concentration lapses and clumsy phases.

Shortly after I was labelled with the 'D' words, my frustrations spilled over and my piano's lid shut itself on my teacher's fingers. (Mum confided she always thought him 'too highly strung'. She also grounded me for a week.)

Strange how things turn out. Without the piano incident, I wouldn't be here now. The school suggested to Mum and Dad that my 'aggressive tendencies' might be tamed by a contact sport, so after a little family chat, I was getting kitted out in a white suit with a white belt and attending my first session in this *dojang*.

It worked a treat. Within a month, the kids who had sniggered at me for my school work or for knocking my books off my desk (a fairly regular occurrence) had zipped it as news spread about my combat capabilities. A couple of the 'tough' boys even asked me to teach them some moves. I just made them do press-ups while I put my foot on their backs, enjoying a new feeling – something close to confidence.

'*Kihap!*' we cry victoriously. We finish in synchronicity, standing with weight down into our knees, one arm extended strongly, the other gripped to our bodies. The outburst sounds like 'ketchup' and my stomach gurgles again.

'Louder!' shouts the Lioness. 'Express yourselves with passion.'

Passion fruit sorbet, passion cake, passion fruit soda... Oh God!

'*KIHAP!*' I utter, the sound exploding from my lungs. As a team, we create a huge roar. Maybe Sarah isn't the only big cat in these parts.

I'm out of my *dobok* and into my trackie bums, T-shirt and trainers in no time, pushing through the glass swing doors of the reception, back onto the pavement in Hampstead High Road, setting off at a comfortable jog. My phone is making sneezing noises, telling me I have two text messages.

The first is from Mum. It's just a row of smiley faces and a kiss. Aw.

The second is from Bella:

'The sun'll come out 2morrow, but only in the Kalahari Desert'

Ever since assembly, when the Head gave us his 'stuff happens and sometimes it's no one's fault' spiel and Miss Simmons waved her baton at us during the final chorus from the musical *Annie*, Bella has been sending me mad 'tomorrow'-related texts — about everything from *Macbeth* to the Beatles.

Idiot. Now I've read this, I've got to stop jogging and send her a reply. Bell says I've got obsessive compulsive disorder. I have to do things in a certain way — like fold up my sweet wrappers neatly before I throw them in the bin and brush my hair in multiples of three (my lucky number). And I always arrange Mum's tablets – a mixture of enzymes for digestion and vitamins – in size order in the morning. I don't think that's weird. It just helps me to remember all eight. If I don't get them out, Mum forgets. She's useless until about eleven am, so I have to nag.

Bella, who will probably be a psychologist one day, has a few theories about my relationship with Mum. She teases me that I may be envious of Mum's cello because of her 'special relationship' with it. It was her 'first born', according to my demented friend, and so I feel 'displaced' and 'less worthy of her love'. Bell thinks that's why I'm skinny and tall with a long neck and a wide bum. I am trying to 'emulate' the instrument.

I dismiss my genetic freakery by reminding her I'm 'emulating' my Nana Jane, who was a model in the 1960s. If Bell ever wants to wind me up, though, she just has to draw a cello in the air.

Bell's teasing is never serious. Most of the time, she tells me I'm lucky. My mum doesn't put any pressure on me to take up music professionally. She says she wants me to do my own thing, whatever it is, and be happy. Bell's mum, who is a brilliant hat designer, has aspirations for Bella to be an opera singer and go to the Royal College of Music, like her grandmother. Bell's not sure it's for her – this 'chance of a lifetime'.

She knows her mum just wants the best for her, but the pressure to keep getting top grades and to turn up for choral and orchestral practices is a strain. Bell's just happy playing the flute and prancing about in a tutu in her spare time. Her older brother, Adam, is a dancer, too – Bell's whole family is impossibly arty. Her dad Meredith is a historical novelist who thinks he is the incarnation of King Arthur. He calls me the Lady of the Lake because I live near Hampstead Heath. Bonkers, the lot of them!

I'm texting Bella. 'Factor 1000 Desert Cream, because you're worth it,' is all I can be bothered to say. I'm not that quick at it so tend to keep my texts short. We learned about the Kalahari bushmen today in Geography. They can survive temperatures way above scorching. Their skin is tough like an iguana's. Bell wondered if we would all turn into iguanas because of global warming. Our teacher, Mr Cradditch, just looked at her and sighed. And the pathetic boys poked their tongues in and out at her for the rest of the lesson.

No reply. Bell is lost for words, or doing music practice. I love the text frenzies we have. They've kept me sane during the whole cancer scare. She's like a sister, only better, because there's no rivalry between us – except at lunch, when we see who can eat the inedible concoctions in the fastest time. And Bell can burp for England, no contest.

I'm feeling light-headed now, the result of intense exertion and starvation. Usually after training, I feel energised and ready to take on the world. It's been a brilliant battery that has kept me charged up, even in the dark days of winter when we weren't sure if Mum would make it to Christmas, and in the early weeks of March, when her face was as white as the snow that fell and froze the lake on the Heath.

We've come through it. Luck? A miracle? It doesn't seem to matter. It's June. The evenings are long and light. Mum is into her music again. (I even heard her singing 'Don't Leave Me, Eloise' in the shower this morning.) Dad is his old, chirpy self. He's reverted to galloping out of the flat in the morning, declaring, 'The Three Musketeers ride out to face another day!'

As I jog back up Willow Road I can see Possum sitting on our gate post, washing his face with a white-edged paw. He often waits for me to return from training. His eyes are heavy from all his sunbathing, like a bee drowsy with nectar. He purrs loudly as I reach up and stroke his head. He nuzzles my fingers and arches his sleek, brown back.

'Hey, mog,' I say, rubbing his chest. A moment later, he leaps into the air, trying to pinion a white and blue butterfly, which flutters away evasively, narrowly escaping a grisly end.

Our Head is right. Stuff happens. Two small words which could explain everything, from the meltdown in the Middle East, to why really nice people get sick. I watch the butterfly flitting onto one of our yellow roses and restrain Possum from a further attack. I'm very sensitive about saving lives these days.

And trying to make sure of a happy ending.

4

I'm sitting at our big pine table in the kitchen, glugging down a glass of elderflower cordial with sprigs of mint on top. I'm still breathing hard after the jog home. Dad is busy creating chicken in a mushroom and sherry sauce with crispy fried potatoes. My tongue is doing gymnastics just thinking about the flavour. He's wearing the apron I bought him for Christmas, with 'Food Dude' embroidered across the top in red.

I think Dad's wasted as an accountant. He says a career as a celebrity chef wasn't part of the equation after doing a Maths degree in the 80s. He's an organic oracle now, though. His night-time reading of thrillers with 'Dead' in the title has been replaced with volumes by the gastric gurus Gordon, Jamie and Nigella. The other week, I caught him teaching Bella how to chop a mango.

Mum is practising in the back room, which has been rather grandly named the music room. When we moved here, when I was three, it was a dining room with dusty old orange velvet curtains and a huge mirror over the stone fireplace. Now it's painted cream – there are no curtains at the full-length windows, and the polished wooden floor is home to a grand piano, piles of sheet music, a saxophone, various percussion instruments, an old red sofa which

Possum thinks is his property, Mum's practice stool and, of course, her beloved cello.

The room looks out onto our garden, which has a long, rectangular lawn framed by tall trees. It's a bit wild, as it has moved down Mum and Dad's priority list lately, but the butterflies are happy, flapping between the big daisies that are taking over the borders, doing their best to avoid Killer Claws.

The music room is next to the kitchen. Everything is on one floor, as we own the bottom part of Number Six, a three-storey Edwardian house. There are two flats above us; the top one is owned by Max, a theatre director with bleached blond hair and a yappy white terrier called Finkie. I feel sorry that Finkie doesn't have a garden. He barks at Possum from the roof terrace, and when Max isn't looking, Dad pretends to shoot 'the mutt from Hell' with a bow and arrow. Possum just arches his back and flicks his fluffy brown tail, before stretching out on the warm, sweet grass.

'Does Finkie Winkie want his salmony walmony, does he, does he?' oozes Max, holding a bowl with Finkie's name on above his head. It's the same ritual every afternoon and it's the only thing that shuts Finkie up. Dad crossed his fingers once and asked the universe for plenty of bones in the fish.

The middle flat is owned by Mr and Mrs Dobbs, who are old but still hold hands when they toddle off to the shops. Luckily, the Dobbses only have a chinchilla called Roxy, who is a total vandal but doesn't make any noise. It's my job to feed her when they go on holiday. She always stares at the wall when I fill up her food tray and goes totally rigid if I try to pick her up. I haven't mentioned this personality disorder to the Dobbses as they think she is an A-list pet with top cute appeal.

'She sings!' Mr Dobbs tells me, nearly every time I visit them.

'She does, like this!' says Mrs Dobbs, clearing her throat and making half-strangled, half-musical noises. Mr Dobbs nods and beams.

'Amazing!' I say, to humour them. They really are very sweet.

'She'd give that dog who says "sausages" a run for its money,' adds Mr Dobbs.

I have no idea what he's on about, so I agree wholeheartedly.

'Sausages!' warbles Mrs Dobbs, in a chinchilla voice.

That's usually the time to leave.

Anyway, being on the ground floor is cool, because it's the biggest pad and there are steps with mosaics up to our front door. Dad says it's like being the bottom tier of a wedding cake. 'Each tier above us is more full of nuts,' he sighs, when he sees Max dancing with Finkie in his arms on the roof terrace to some soft jazz late at night.

Mum isn't fazed by the neighbours. The only thing that gets her riled is if she breaks a string on the cello. Or runs out of energy when she's practising. She knows it'll take several more weeks before she feels strong again. She's impatient to make all our lives 'normal' once more.

And sitting here, watching Dad chop herbs and turn potatoes over in the frying pan, the deep, sad sound of Brahms's cello concerto in the background, the evening sun lighting up our lemon-coloured walls covered in black-and-white prints of me doing various embarrassing things in nappies, the air full of fantastic foodie smells mixed with the scent of fragrant jasmine, which curls around a frame by the open door to the garden (planted when I was born), it feels as close to normal as I remember.

'Hey you,' says Dad, turning to see Mum in the doorway. He always senses when she's there.

'Smells great,' she smiles, sitting down at the table next to me and inhaling deeply.

It's a job to get Mum to eat a full meal these days on account of her reduced capacity for digestion. Dad and I do our best to keep meals interesting, though. Dad often arranges food horizontally, like they do in restaurants, and drizzles a special sauce around the outside. Last week, he made her a new dish – the Leaning Tower of Peas – and she got the giggles like I've never seen before. She and Dad were gasping for breath by the end of it. Even the sight of peas set her off for a few days afterwards.

'A little peas offering,' Dad whispered, giving her mashed peas on toast in the shape of a heart one evening.

'Your father is suffering from PSS,' she whispered, seriously. '*Pisum sativum*, or garden pea, syndrome. He will need a lot of support.'

She's funny, Mum. Not in the way Dad is, with his terrible puns that make me groan. She often says something with a straight face, and it'll crack us up. Even after her surgery, when she was in the recovery area and still fuzzy with anaesthetic, she nodded to all the lines attached to her body, delivering fluid and painkillers, and said, 'You know what they say. It's quicker by Tube.'

I'm giving Mum her enzyme tablets with some iced water. I put a paper parasol in the glass.

'Party time,' she sighs, eyeing the tablets. She gives me a grin as she swallows the capsules, one by one. 'How was training?'

'Good,' I reply.

'Wish I could say the same for my concerto,' says Mum. 'It felt like I had six fingers today.'

'Like Anne Boleyn,' I say.

'Let's hope Stephen doesn't want to cut my head off,' she responds, pulling a face.

Stephen is the orchestra's conductor – a complete perfectionist when it comes to music, but someone who is likely to turn up for dinner in unfashionably ripped jeans and a T-shirt with John Travolta on it. He has unofficially adopted us as his family, which is great, because he's a laugh and really kind. He even buys Possum a present at Christmas (and Possum always writes to say thank you).

'Jaz?' asks Mum, as she replaces the glass on the table.

'You know our walk tonight?'

I can feel what's coming. Mum's trying to wheedle out of her exercise.

'It's just a mile, Mum. Half an hour, tops,' I say.

'Can we do it tomorrow? I feel I just want to…be,' she explains, smiling at Dad.

'Don't bully your mother,' says Dad, taking her side. He always takes her side.

'Yes, don't bully your mother,' echoes Mum, waving an elegant index finger at me.

I'm outnumbered. So much for Dad's description of us as a 'sacred triangle, with equal lengths'. Mum and Dad have this secret language of looks and smiles which they shared before I was born.

'You are very naughty,' I say, putting my arms round Mum and giving her a squeeze.

'Yes,' she agrees, kissing my forehead. 'I love you.'

'I love you,' I reply. Mum knows she's won and puts her feet up on the opposite kitchen chair and shuts her eyes for a moment. In the sunlight, her skin looks the colour of cream marble, smooth and slightly shiny, like the statues of the Virgin Mary in St Paul's Cathedral.

Possum jumps up onto Mum's lap, purring. He curls himself into a ball and starts to wash his feet, splaying out his claws and poking a pink tongue in between each one. Mum tickles his belly and Possum rolls onto his back, in bliss.

'Dinner is served!' announces Dad, throwing a tea towel over one shoulder and placing two plates before us. He's made wigwams out of grilled courgette. Inside each is a fried shallot, which looks like an eyeball. Mum breathes in the aromatic steam happily, at the same time lifting a disgruntled Possum onto the floor.

'This is quite a good restaurant, you know,' she says. 'And the staff are lovely.' She catches Dad's hand as he sits down and holds it a moment. 'Thank you,' she mouths at him.

'Would madam like some wine?' he asks, holding her gaze.

'Yes please!' I interject. Mum and Dad have let me have wine since I turned thirteen – just a small glass on special occasions. The taste is growing on me, although red wine makes my ears go red.

Dad raises his eyebrows at Mum in silent consultation and she nods. Yay!

'A little one for me, too,' agrees Mum, stretching. Dad gets up and takes a bottle of Chardonnay from the fridge, opening it with the slick, professional gadget Possum bought him for Christmas. Gloop, gloop, gloop goes the wine as it fills three glasses.

We chink them together. Mum says, 'To life, love and lipstick.' It's the toast Nana Jane always used to make.

'Life, love and lipstick,' say Dad and I. Our glasses connect and beams of sunlight shaft across the space between us.

5

Saturday morning and Bella and I are on Oxford Street, shopping. This entails zigzagging in and out of our fave stores, trying on piles of jeans, tops and more tops, hogging the long mirror in the changing rooms and, in Bella's case, twirling about in each outfit like the Sugar Plum Fairy.

Bella's got some birthday money and she wants to get 'Urban Chicks' T-shirts printed for Olly, Tash and me. Her Dad came up with the name when we started meeting in town at the weekend and having sleepovers on Saturday nights. When he says it, it's with a glint in his eye and a smile around his lips. With his white beard and bushy eyebrows, he looks a bit like Merlin. When you look into his eyes, you can almost see the past, where he lives in his imagination. The pale blue half-moons are doors to ancient Britain, to battles fought for honour and kingdoms, to knights vanquishing the forces of evil, to Excalibur, the sword in the stone.

When Mum's cancer was diagnosed, he put his heavy hands on my shoulders and fixed me with a stare that sent my fears scurrying into the shadows. 'Miracles happen every day,' he told me quietly. 'Remember, the Lady of the Lake has special powers.'

I thought he was probably making that up. But I hoped he was right.

'Is there anyone home?' asks Bella, two millimetres away from my face, her eyes so close to mine that they fuse into one.

'You don't look nice with one eye,' I reply, blinking.

'We're programmed to like two, that's all,' she shrugs. 'When you think about them, two fluid-filled, wet blobs that swivel about on either side of our noses, they're disgusting.'

There's a long queue at the shop that prints T-shirts, so Bella and I decide to buy juices from the stall near the Tube station while we wait. We sit on a low wall off the main road, drinking through straws, our faces turned up to the sun. Crowds of students pass us from every direction, all jabbering excitedly in their own language. The smell of garlic mixes with exhaust fumes from passing buses and taxis. Sweetness from a cookie shop wafts like a sugar-veil across our noses before winding skywards, carried on the summer wind. Wherever you look there are splashes of colour – shop fronts, passers-by, dogs with crazy collars and, above the tall, impressive white buildings, a bright blue stratosphere.

'I love London,' I say out loud. A flock of pigeons takes off from a high ledge nearby, wings beating like applause.

'I love pizza,' says Bella, with her eyes closed. She noisily sucks up the last froth from the bottom of her cardboard cup through the straw. 'The T-shirts could wait till next weekend,' she adds, already moving in the direction of the open-fronted Italian restaurant with takeaway section nearby.

Ten minutes later, we are chomping into a slice of the best Margarita I have ever tasted. The tomatoes are so fresh their fragrance is tickling my nose.

'Wachoo!' I sneeze. I look around for the true culprit. Yes, there, at the bottom of the pedestrianised area, is a tree. A couple of years ago, Mum got me tested by a homeopath for reactions to tree pollen and I showed up for at least ten types of allergy. I'm supposed to take a course of special capsules before the hay fever season, but my red eyes and explosions, which always begin in June and last a few weeks, aren't exactly a medical emergency.

'Cheer up. Might never 'appen!' says a man in a stripy jumpsuit, juggling skittles, as we walk past. He has mistaken the post-sneezing snail tracks on my cheeks for sadness.

'You could take that two ways,' says Bella, thoughtfully. 'You could be pleased, or the thought of something you wanted to happen never happening might make you very depressed. Either way, it's a stupid thing to say.'

'He was just being friendly,' I reply, my mouth chewing the last piece of pizza. Bella always analyses what people come out with and is often the last person to get the joke. If she doesn't become a psychologist, I'll eat one of her mum's hats. Not one with feathers, though.

It's half past two and we hop on a bus that will take us up

Edgware Road, through Maida Vale and back to West Hampstead. We sit upstairs in the front seats and wave like maniacs at people in other buses going in the opposite direction. (Who says you can't be friendly in the city?) Lots of individuals wave back: an old woman in a pink jacket with two round blobs of red blusher on her cheeks; a little girl with blonde pigtails and chocolate round her mouth; a man with a circular cap on his head; and a Japanese boy with his arm in a sling.

Bella smells of mangoes. I'm not sure if it's from the juice she was drinking, or the perfume she sprayed over her stomach in Top Shop.

I look at the size eight orange strappy top I've bought for Mum as a surprise. 'Do you think she'll like it?' I ask Bella, for the tenth time.

'She'll love it,' she reassures me, resting her head on my shoulder for a moment. I wish I hadn't said I would stay with Bell tonight. I want to go home and give Mum her present. I'll settle for texting her. Bell watches my thumbs fly over the keys.

'There's no "z" in "surprise",' she comments.

'I know,' I retort, cross with myself. I correct the spelling, add a row of kisses to my message, and press send. The reply comes almost instantly:

'There's a surprise for you 2. Have fun. C u 2morrow ☺☺☺☺☺☺ xxxxxx'

'What do you think it is?' asks Bell, her tongue pushing gum into stretchy shapes.

'Holiday, maybe. To celebrate and stuff. God, hope it's the Maldives.' I grab Bell's arm in a frenzy of excitement. 'Or Hawaii.'

'Wow!' says Bella. 'Do you think?'

'Mum's always talking about thatched beach huts on stilts,' I reply, my voice almost an octave above its normal pitch.

I cross all my fingers and let warm, turquoise waves of anticipation wash over me as I float off the bus and follow Bell onto the pavement, which has become a white-sand spit fringed with tropical palms.

I'm in such a good mood now that I even agree to Bell's usual suggestion/pathetic dare that we do this ridiculous skipping thing from the stop all the way to her house in Belsize Park Gardens. Well, I look ridiculous. Bell is always graceful when she moves. It's her ballet training and her small, arched feet. She's laughing now because, despite my blue belt status, I've managed to get a stitch and am doubled up on her front path.

'Shall I get Adam to carry you in?' she teases. Her brother is looking out of the long dining room window and seems pleased to see us. He's wearing a black vest over jeans and I notice his biceps are looking like tennis balls. His straw-blond hair is gelled and upright. I'm taking a mental picture. He's grinning as he opens the window.

'Hey, Ballantyne,' he says to me. We always call each other by our surnames.

'Hey, Farrell,' I respond, wincing with the pain in my belly. And blushing, worst luck.

'Let me guess. Skipping contest?' he asks.

'She was rubbish,' replies Bella, triumphantly twirling and bowing.

'My sister was a kangaroo in a past life. You didn't stand a chance,' he says kindly.

The pain is easing now. Bell and I walk up the stone steps to a huge, pale blue front door. Adam is opening it and gesturing for us to enter with a theatrical sweep of his tanned arm.

'Is that Bella and Jaz?' calls Tara, Bell's mum, through lips which are pursed, holding pins. She is adding final bits of fluff to a red and black hat that is balanced on a stand in her work room, off the long hallway. We poke our heads round the door and her face breaks into a smile.

Tara, who is only five feet two, has long brown hair, usually wound up and secured with a brightly coloured clip. She hardly ever wears make-up, but even though she is in her late forties, she has a young, unlined face which is always bright with enthusiasm. Often, when she hugs you, you get an electric shock. She's that sort of person.

She gives both Bella and me an air kiss, pins still in her mouth, and motions to the hat stand.

'What do you think?' she asks, removing the pins. 'It's for Lady Foxton, who is throwing a lunch to celebrate her divorce. That's why she asked for red and black — "a suitable combination of mourning and celebration".'

'Great!' I say.

'Try it on,' encourages Tara. Gingerly, I lift the creation and place it on my head. It sits on top, like an elaborate lampshade, the fluff and feathers doubling the size of my head. I glimpse myself in the mirror on the wall. I look like a mutant ostrich.

'You have a great neckline,' says Tara, appraising me.

'Don't say it,' I hiss at Bella, who is giggling and mouthing 'cello' at me. 'I'm not really into hats,' I explain, replacing Tara's work of art on its stand. 'Mum's the hatty one in the family. She looks great in everything. She picked me up from school once wearing a tea cosy that Nana Jane gave us. She'd sewn a band round the bottom and added some sparkly bits. One of the other mums asked her which designer she'd bought it from.'

'I should get her working with me,' smiles Tara, putting pins back into a box on her work table. 'Bella says she had good news. The tests? Fantastic!' she exclaims, giving me an enthusiastic squeeze which makes my spine tingle. 'Well, I'm nearly done. It's just you two and Adam for dinner. Meredith and I have to go to some literary thing. He's speaking and signing. I've no idea what to wear and he's no help. He just says "wear whatever you like", but I'm guessing that PJs and dressing gowns are out, so I'll have to blow the dust off a dress.'

Tara says all this at great speed with lots of hand gestures. She's quite eccentric, but lovely. Whenever I'm at Bell's house, I feel like I'm in a play, swept up in the Farrells' world of publishing parties and celebrity clients. It's normal to them that rock stars' girlfriends and politicians pop in for a hat fitting. They are likely to be offered tea from the pot with the cracked spout, or biscuits on the plate that Bell painted with daisies when she was five. I've noticed that they treat everyone the same, whether it's Bell's thirteen-year-old mates, or a Middle Eastern princess who arrives with two security guards in dark glasses.

Actually, that's not quite true. Their dog, Mowgli, a King Charles spaniel who is fifteen and almost completely blind, gets totally spoiled. He has his own chair at the kitchen table and a specially cooked diet of organic chicken liver. And several times I've heard Meredith singing him lullabies whilst cuddling him like a baby.

'Have you done your practice, Bella?' asks Tara, as we leave her work room.

'Yup,' answers my friend, crossing her eyes at me. Bella is taking her grade six flute and singing exams next week. She and Adam are effortlessly musical, with perfect pitch, which is very unusual. No wonder Tara has high hopes for them.

'Mum keeps on about me singing *Carmen* at Covent Garden,' whispers Bella as we head for the kitchen. 'But I'm not Granny Phoebe. I'm not even the right shape for opera. Big hair. Big boobs. Mahousive bum! Phoebe was a size eighteen!'

'There's still time to fill out,' I comfort her, puffing out my cheeks. 'It might be in your genes.'

'Remind me why we're friends?' Bella says, pinching my arm.

'Hmm. Get back to you on that,' I reply, plunging my hand into the bowl of nachos Adam has just put on the long pine table in the kitchen. 'I love 'or family,' I tell her, my cheeks full of fantastic, crunchy chips. 'Even him,' I add, pointing to Mowgli, who is snoring loudly on his dog bed.

Adam is holding the edge of the sink, raising his left leg behind him until it is almost as high as his head.

'Show off,' scoffs Bella. 'We can do that, can't we Jaz?' She grips the back of a kitchen chair and extends her right leg behind. I do the same. We all get the giggles. Meredith appears in the doorway, clutching a mug with a picture of Adam and Bella on it when they were toddlers. He takes in the scene and weaves around us all to get to the kettle.

'Take care. You might turn to wood and spend the rest of your lives dancing to the chimes of a cuckoo clock,' he says, quietly, his eyes wrinkling in a wicked smile.

'Aren't you going to some literary thing?' asks Adam, taking up fifth position.

'I am informed by my social secretary that this is, unfortunately, true,' replies his dad.

'Don't you think you should get ready, Pops?' suggests Bella, giving him a hug.

'You fear they won't appreciate my cardigan with the hole in the elbow?' asks Meredith.

'It's only cute in young guys,' explains Bella.

'No, you're right. It won't do for an old fart.' He switches on the kettle and sees Bella looking at the clock on the wall. 'Panic not. I've got fifteen minutes. A universe of time.'

I love the way Meredith talks. He's like something out of Old England – his sentences sound like poetry.

'Mowgli's the old fart,' says Bella, ruffling her dad's hair. 'You're cool.' She kisses his cheek and he looks pleased.

'That's a relief,' he says, pouring boiling water into his mug. 'Chin chin!' he grins, and saunters out of the room.

'He forgot the tea bag,' comments Adam, shaking his head.

'*Abiit, excessit, evasit, erupit,*' calls Meredith from the hallway.

Bell and I look at Adam for a translation. He has just taken his GCSE Latin.

'He is gone, he is off, he has escaped, he has broken away,' Adam obliges, bending in fifth position, one hand above his left brow, as if scanning the horizon. From this angle, backlit by the sun, he looks like a film star. He catches my eye and pulls a face before I can look away.

'Shotgun I'm not cooking,' says Bell suddenly.

'Shotgun neither am I,' I add. We beam at Adam, who frowns and sighs.

'You are on salad duty then, Bell the Barbarian, and you, Jaz the Jellyfish, with the fatal sting, can cut up the French stick,' orders Adam, who is always making up names for us. Last time, I was Jaz the Jezebel because my T-shirt was up above my navel. And when I stayed over once and had pillow creases in my face, I was Jaz the Jurassic.

Older brothers can be cool. When Mum was in hospital and we were having one of our heart to hearts, she told me that she had lost a baby two years before having me. He was just three months old inside her and something went wrong and Mum's immune system rejected him. It's funny to think that he would be fifteen now. Mum says that things work out the way they are supposed to, but I wonder if she thinks about him much and feels sad. And if my brother had lived, would I be here now?

And if so, would it be the same me? Or a me with a different collection of genes, facial features and personality traits?

I might have inherited Dad's big nose, or Mum's pixie ears and elfin feet. I could have been the next Einstein with Dad's computer brain or a musical prodigy with Mum's gift for cello.

None of those things have passed down to me, although people say I have Dad's smile and Mum's expressions. In truth, I'm a random product of their X and Y chromosomes.

A slightly damaged product, I reckon – with design faults resulting in whole sentences and lines of numbers dancing in my head, words leap-frogging on the page, full stops cascading in fountains down margins and figures flying in formation like the ducks on the lake.

Turns out dyslexia passes down the male line to offspring. (Mum says at least it isn't distemper, because we could be put down for that.)

I can't complain. The 'D' words don't dominate my life. They tend to make an appearance on bad days, when I'm stressed or very tired. Those are usually the times when I catch my jumper on door handles and walk into walls and trees.

I'm learning to handle them better (when my hormones aren't turning me into a werewolf – Dad's description). Trying to stay calm is the key and the best way to do that is to jog, practice my patterns or to hang upside down from the branch of the oak tree in the garden. It's something I've done since I was young. Papa Tom used to say I had inherited bat genes. I would whisper in his ear that the world looks better from that angle and he always nodded and said it was the best way for a saggy mouth to become a smile.

Compared to Bella and Adam, who remind me of sunflowers, their vibrant faces turned up to the light, I feel like I am somehow in shadow, a strange, gangly flower with its petals still furled. I know that gangly things *sometimes* turn into beauties; cygnets, caterpillars, giraffes, even frogspawn. So I'm hoping.

The Lioness wouldn't approve of my insecurity. But to be sure of yourself, and to make your spirit indomitable, don't you first need a self of which to be sure? Maybe now Mum's on the up, I can explore new possibilities; Jaz the joyful and jubilant. That sounds a good start.

'Nachos?' asks Bell, beaming, passing me the bowl of spicy corn chips. I take three and begin to bite the corners off each in rotation. I drop two on the table. 'Knew you'd do that,' she says, putting three in her mouth together and licking her fingers at the same time.

'Jaz the Jackass,' I shrug, grinning.

6

'Do you see it?' enthuses Bell.

'What?' I ask, sleepily.

'The comet,' she replies, almost breathless. 'Look!'

We are both huddled under a green tartan rug in Bell's back garden, our knees curled over our chests to minimise contact with the damp grass, and we are staring at stars.

'That's a plane,' I state.

'Isn't.'

'Is. That's its tail light flashing.'

Bell doesn't like being wrong. She is pulling out blades of grass from the wet ground as if she couldn't care less.

'The universe is an illusion,' I tell her. 'Papa Tom told me that some of those stars exploded zillions of years ago and it's taken that long for the light to reach earth.'

'If they're not really there, maybe we're not really here,' she replies cryptically, yawning.

'I need the loo – so I must exist,' I say, pulling a pained face.

'You can't go, you'll miss the comet,' she warns, scrunching up her eyes and scanning the endless darkness, sprinkled with luminous glitter.

The grandfather clock in Bell's hallway is chiming twelve. A bat swoops past our noses and makes Bell shriek.

'Bat's don't bite, do they?' she asks.

'Dunno,' I say, pulling the blanket up to my eyes, just in case it went to tell its bat mates that there are two tasty snacks on the lawn. Papa Tom would have known. My stomach tenses as a tingling sense of loss spreads through my body and into my chest. A moment later, it is gone, vanished into the indigo sky, already a memory.

The air smells sweet with summer fragrances. It's wafting through the bamboo wind chimes Bell bought for her mum on Mother's Day. Meredith says they sound like a tone-deaf fairy playing a xylophone. Tara put them up anyway, near the kitchen door, just to annoy him.

Low laughter tumbles from the open doors to the lounge. Tara is recounting a tale about the 'terribly boring man' she sat next to at the literary dinner, who insisted on referring to her as 'Ta-ra-ra-boom-di-ay'. Meredith is finding her indignation very funny. I can only hear snatches of the conversation, according to whether Tara raises her voice or not. She is getting increasingly aerated and high-pitched.

'And then he did the most appalling thing and actually TOOK OUT HIS LEFT EYE, put it on the tablecloth, and said – "I have my eye on you!"'

There is an explosion of chortling and wheezing from Meredith, who is banging the side of his chair with his hand.

'Excellent!' he tells Tara.

'It wasn't excellent at all,' she sulks. 'It was moist and disgusting.'

At this, Meredith laughs even louder, holding his stomach. Tara is joining in now. If I didn't know better, I would say that Bell's parents are having a fit of the giggles. Bell and I exchange glances. Then she yawns extravagantly, her exhaled breath spiralling up into the night sky.

'You can find the face of the person you're going to fall in love with in the stars,' she announces, sleepily.

'Yeah. I see him. Mahousive head, black hair and a million spots,' I reply. Bella is sticking her tongue out at me.

'Pops says the ancients believed it,' she says defensively. 'It would be good if we could, wouldn't it?'

'I'd rather it was a surprise,' I reply, trying to block out images of Adam dancing in the gaps between the twinkling lights. Bell lets out a disgruntled sigh. Then she sits up, holding my gaze. She looks as if she's going to tell me a huge secret, like the location of the Holy Grail.

'We've got stardust in our bodies,' she whispers slowly.

'You're making that up,' I reply, giving her a long look.

'Nope. Adam said. He did it in Chemistry,' she replies, lying flat again and closing her eyes.

I feel a shiver down my spine. It comes with this revelation that we have the secrets of the universe locked in our cells. The how, when and why. The answer to questions we don't have the imagination to ask. The stars are so far away, though – the connection between us seems so distant. Maybe that's an illusion, too. Maybe it's like the feelings you have when someone you love dies. You hold them in your heart, in the deep chambers of your memory, but their unique energy has gone forever, dispersed by the winds, diluted out of existence.

When you stare at a photograph, you see only ghosts. It is the same with stars.

'Elvis has left the building,' Papa Tom used to say, tapping his nose. I used to think it meant someone was a sandwich short of a picnic. But Mum told me about the King of Rock 'n' Roll and how, when he died, women across every continent mourned. I suppose my granddad meant that something had been lost, never to be retrieved.

I feel that way without him. My chest tightens at the sudden memory of being enveloped in his baggy jumpers, which smelled of wood smoke and furniture varnish, held tight in his arms, safely locked in, even if I tried to wriggle out from under his strong, weather-beaten fingers.

The stars look extra bright through my watering eyes – their light pierces through into my skull, which is throbbing with thoughts of loss. The soft lamps in Bell's lounge look suddenly inviting and safe. I am longing for the softness of the deep, floral sofas and some hot chocolate. And for Meredith to recite a poem in Elvish. And for Mowgli to chase his tail and make us laugh.

Out here, there is only a black, huge, forever nothingness which reminds us we are as small as atoms and as unimportant as dust. And suddenly, travelling across it, what looks like a small ball of white fire, leaving a trail of sparks in its wake.

'Bell, look!' I whisper, but her breathing is deep and regular. She is asleep.

I prop myself up on my elbows and follow the bright trajectory across the inky vastness, like the sweep of a flaming pen down a dark page.

'Wow!' I say, out loud. I'm texting Mum:

'Look at the sky!'

'Not bad for a bunch of icy chunks of water and rubble, eh?' says a voice close to me. Meredith is standing in the open doorway to the lounge. His eyes, which are gazing upwards, are almost liquid behind luminous glasses caught in the beam from the terrace light.

'It's a sign,' he adds, more quietly. 'Or so it's believed. The wrath of the gods. The beginning of an apocalypse. A portent of doom,' he chuckles.

'Do you think that's true?' I ask.

Meredith pauses before he answers. He is looking at me over the steel rims of his glasses.

'People are preposterously superstitious,' he tells me. 'It is part of the human condition. Our word "disaster" is derived from the Latin word "astre", meaning "star".'

I hope you're right, I'm thinking, as more shivers pass up my spine. Damp has seeped through my jeans and stiffened my joints. The chimes give an eerie tinkle of discordant sounds as a chill breeze disturbs them.

My phone is sneezing in the damp, cold air. 'I see it! Let's make a wish,' reads the text from Mum. So I do, with all my heart. I'm hoping that the second part of the wish, involving certain islands in the Indian Ocean and the acquisition of a spectacular pair of designer sunglasses, won't be considered too selfish by the universe.

7

'Six weeks off, yay!' Bella exclaims, quite loudly. My brain can't quite engage with the fact that the last week of term is upon us. It's Sunday morning and I've had four hours' sleep. After Bell woke up in the garden, she was in the mood for a midnight feast followed by dancing on the bed. I heard the clock chime four before we crashed out. I'm glad Tara had to visit a client for an emergency alteration this morning. It means I'm getting a lift home, which has saved me the jog back and will speed up the unveiling of Mum's surprise.

'I can't wait. We can do stuff every day,' continues Bella. 'Swimming, tennis, picnics, sunbathing, shopping, cinema, pizza, *band practice*...' Tara is raising her eyebrows. I think it might be the first she's heard of this. 'Put your hands together for the Urban Chicks!' Bella is giving us a premature round of applause.

'I'm not sure about the singing bit,' I tell her. I know it's the only option if I want to join in, as I don't play zillions of instruments like the others.

'But you've got the best legs,' says Bella. I don't think the two are related, unfortunately. Whenever I warble in the shower, Finkie goes into manic bark mode. He's probably trying to put his paws in his ears. It's a shame Mum's musical gene passed me by.

Whatever happens behind the microphone, the hols are going to be great. No more essays, algebra and the constant struggle to maintain above-average-effort grades. Mum and I can do all the things we had to postpone last summer – painting plates at the pottery café, picking strawberries at the fruit farm. And hopefully, with Dad, heading to the airport with suitcases full of sarongs and suntan lotion…

The Heath is golden today, bathed in warm morning light. A little kid with glasses is trying to make a bright blue kite fly, but despite his efforts to run down a bank, the small triangle is bumping along the ground unhelpfully. He sits down with a grumpy thud, legs crossed, head resting on his fist.

I want to open the window and shout out 'the wind has no master', which is what Papa Tom used to tell me when gusts of salt air popped my bubbles blown so patiently through a plastic hoop. But I hear Mum's voice telling me it's rude to yell, especially at strangers, so curb my desire.

Today, the wind is having a siesta, or it's somewhere else in the world, ruffling the skirts of salsa dancers in market squares, or blowing dry clumps of vegetation across desert plains. The scent of freshly mown grass tingles in my nose. Two seconds later, I am sneezing. Bella passes me a tissue from the box on the car floor.

'Bless you,' says Tara. Funny how people still do that, even though no one has the plague any more.

We are pulling onto the kerb by my flat and Bell is giving me a big hug.

'Thank you very much,' I say to Tara. 'Good luck with the hat.'

'She said the Alsatian savaged it, but reading between the lines, I think it was sat on,' sighs Tara. 'One will do what one can,' she shrugs, like a doctor faced with a multiple trauma. Bell is ballooning out her face in the back seat, indicating that the client is a little on the large side. 'Love to all indoors, kiss kiss,' Tara adds, pulling away and waving at the same time. I watch Bell's hand doing mad things in the air as the car recedes down Willow Road, taking my best mate to help resuscitate a fragile, feathered creation, flat and lifeless, somewhere in deepest Fulham.

As I put my key in the lock, Finkie emits what sounds like a strangled yelp on the top floor. I will say one thing for him. He is a good guard dog. Or he would be, if he were ten times the size he actually is.

Mum is in the hallway looking like the cat that got the cream. She gives me a mahousive squeeze and then takes my hand and leads me into the kitchen, where Dad is on the phone, grinning from ear to ear.

Something is going on. These two are up to something. Mum motions for me to sit down next to her and she intertwines her hands — something she always does when she is about to make an announcement or give me a pep talk.

Dad has replaced the receiver and is beaming at Mum. 'It's all sorted,' he says.

'What's all sorted?' I ask, making an excited gasping noise as I breathe in, mentally crossing all my fingers and toes. Dad nods to Mum. She beams at him and then at me.

Maldives, here we come…

'We're going to the Rainbow Marshes for the summer. To Papa Tom's cottage,' says Mum.

I think I just heard my jaw hit the wooden floor and shatter into a hundred pieces.

'The *whole* summer?' I ask, my voice a thin, wavering whine. This news is so unexpected, I just stare at the table and push a breadcrumb round with the tip of my index finger. No Urban Chicks, no pottery café, no tae kwon do, definitely no Indian Ocean and, worse than everything, no broadband.

'The letting agent is going to get the services reconnected over the next week and we can move in at the weekend,' explains Mum, exchanging glances with Dad. 'Jaz, we can spend the whole holiday together, going for walks, riding bikes, exploring…'

I can feel my throat tightening. That always happens when I'm about to cry. It's so pathetic of me to be upset. I really don't want to burst Mum's balloon, but this is not my idea of a great summer, marooned in Papa Tom's creaky old house in the middle of the flat, frog-infested, foggy marshes of Kent.

'Dad'll be there at weekends,' enthuses Mum. 'But during the week it'll be just girl time. You and me. I'm so excited!'

'Wow,' I manage to say at last. Mum reads me like a book. She's exchanging looks with Dad, who is putting the kettle on. Come on, I'm not the bad guy here. I can't think of any teenager who'd leap up and down at the prospect of enforced exile.

'I think the peace will be amazing,' says Mum, less exuberantly. 'It'll be a chance to really get my strength back and be a proper mum.'

'You *are* a proper mum,' I say, taking her hand. She shakes her head.

'I want to look after you for a change,' she says, a bit emotionally. 'It'll be great – no noise, no hassle, fresh air in our lungs, seeing the ocean every day, you used to love splashing about on the sand...'

Yes, Mum, when I was three. I look to Dad for support. 'What sarong, Jasmeen?' he asks, in a silly mock-Oriental voice. This is no time for puns.

'Nothing. It's all good,' I lie, taking Mum's face in my hands and kissing her nose.

So it's settled. The day after school breaks up, I'm going to Nothingsville-on-Sea to be under house arrest until September. And my ears are hot with guilt for thinking like this. Mum's only trying to make up for all I've been through. But I can see how it will be – long afternoons of silence while Mum has a nap, or practices the cello; grass and sky and sheep wherever I look; endless cooking and washing up; and the biggest ever mobile phone bill because I have to stay in daily contact with Bella and the Chicks so that I don't go completely loopy.

And for most of the time, not even Dad to shore up the sides of the triangle. Without him, we'll just be two lines, joined at one end – a compass without a direction.

I hear myself making some excuse about needing a shower so that I can leave the room and shut myself in a cubicle of steam. Presenting Mum with her new orange top has suddenly gone down the list of priorities.

I turn the key in the lock inside the bathroom and reach for the silver handle in the shower, pulling it clockwise and feeling the pelt of cold water on my arm as I try to retract it quickly. The water soon becomes hot and I start to get undressed, but end up sitting on the closed loo seat, my knees up, bunching my body as tightly as possible. The room is filling with moist, warm air and there are tears coming out of my eyes and rolling down my cheeks in silent cascades – self-pity with the volume turned right down.

And I feel suddenly afraid – of not being at home, where everything is familiar and Bella and her kooky family are just a few minutes away; of being in a strange bed with only the sound of the marsh wind at night; of being without Dad, who is like an anchor in our storms; of being with Mum in a new way, not as a carer but more as a friend; of not having enough to say to her that she will find interesting; of being bored out of my brain and a complete disappointment to her.

Double D kids like me don't thrive on change. That's what the educational psychologist told Mum and Dad when I was diagnosed. We like structure and certainty. Surprises, like balloons bursting near our ears, can upset us for several hours.

Water is splashing out of the shower tray onto the floor. I get up reluctantly and close the screen to contain it. As I do so, I catch sight of my hazy reflection in the mirror above the basin. I am indistinct, covered in mist, my features a blur. 'Chicks rule OK' I write with my finger, to cheer myself up, dispersing the layer of water on the glass. I step back into a warm pool on the stone tiles, parts of my streaked face visible in the dissolving lettering. And I blink as I read the words facing me, a testament to my brain's disobedience.

'Chicks rule KO.'

There's a soft knock on my bedroom door. Mum pokes her head round and gives me a little wave. I'm lying on top of my duvet listening to my iPod's compilation of 'anarchic teen scream', as Dad calls it. I'm still wrapped in a towel and my hair is damp on my shoulders. I motion for Mum to sit on my bed. Sometimes we share ear pieces. Looking at her serious face, I don't think Mum will be up for the

Rude Boys' manic yelling about global warming and dead polar bears so I turn the iPod off.

'Jaz, I'm really sorry,' says Mum, pushing strands of wet hair off my forehead. 'I got so fired up about Frog Cottage and having this adventure with you – I didn't stop to think how you would feel, away from your friends. It's all happened a bit suddenly, hasn't it? Me and my mad ideas, eh?'

'It's not as mad as the long drive and night walk through the New Forest without a torch, in the rain,' I say. Mum smiles.

'That's one winter solstice we won't forget,' she agrees. 'Only Dad could get his foot stuck in a rabbit hole and be attacked by a cross-eyed horse at the same time.'

We both giggle at the memory of Dad trying to shoo the inquisitive wild pony away whilst trying to prise his left welly out of the deep tunnel in a muddy bank. The image unlocks another thought. Until now, I had forgotten Mum's occasional spontaneous plans to travel and arrive somewhere new. Her illness smothered her fire for sudden change and slowly ground us all down into a routine of daily survival. But now her eyes are bright again and her hands are moving animatedly, full of life.

'It's just that I've got plans, too,' I tell her, trying not to sound petulant. 'But that doesn't mean I don't want to be with you as well.'

'Mums have to learn to let go,' she says. 'First timer.' She shrugs. 'You could trade me in on eBay for a more experienced one.'

'Never!' I reassure her.

'We'll work it out,' she promises. 'Maybe Bella can come later on, or you can stay with her. But I would really, really, really like to have you to myself for a little while. Deal?' she asks, giving me a big squeeze.

'Deal,' I reply, feeling a mahousive wave of relief coursing through my body, tinged with a nervousness about accepting a different routine.

Dad is calling us, letting us know lunch is on the table. I've just got time to give Mum her top. She holds it against herself, grinning from ear to ear.

'Jaz, it's fab!' she says. 'I'll go and try it on. Tell Dad I'll be there in a mo.' In two skips, she is gone. But then her head reappears round my door and she blows me a kiss and mouths, 'Thank you.'

I should be throwing some clothes on, but I've got a sudden compulsion to reach for my mobile and text Bella.

'Gd news and bad news. Hope u like frogs…'

8

'To the Urban Chicks,' says Bella, raising her glass of Coke and chinking it against mine, Olly's and Tasha's.

We're in our local Italian restaurant, Guido's, celebrating the end of term. Olly's mum and dad, Liz and Doug, are at another table, pretending they are nothing to do with us. It was their idea to treat us all to dinner, especially when they found out I was going away for the whole summer (minus as many escapes back to London as I can manage). When Olly told them there was no internet connection her mum pretended to faint with shock.

'Got you something,' announces Olly, producing a medium-sized box wrapped in bright pink paper and tied with a pink ribbon. She is grinning from ear to ear, displaying the brace on her upper teeth. It's not great as she has red pepper stuck behind some of it.

My ears have gone hot. I didn't think to get my mates end-of-term presents. I've been in a bit of a strop since the bombshell dropped, despite Mum's offer of time out for good behaviour. Bella has tried to make me laugh with mad texts and lots of hugs and the promise to come and see me, or abduct me back to London.

I think I'm depressed. I've missed all my training sessions this week because of a headache and pains in my stomach.

I'm never ill normally. I've tried to hide all this from Mum, unsuccessfully. She and Dad have been making me honey and lemon drinks and taking my temperature, which has remained normal. They only let me go out for pizza after Stephen called us today and confirmed that there is a nasty three-day bug going round. Half the orchestra has it. Mum, who was threatening to take me straight to the A and E department, was reassured by this, especially as it's day four for me and I'm looking 'less like a grim gargoyle' (Dad's words).

Possum has been eyeing his cat transport – a basket with a rectangular peep hole at the front – with the greatest suspicion. It usually signifies a trip to the vet and a scrabble to avoid the sharp needle. Taking him with us was a last-minute decision. He wouldn't enjoy weekends on his own, Dad said, and cats like travelling. He cited Dick Whittington's sidekick and the Siamese from the film *The Incredible Journey* as proof.

I've had a recurring dream that Possum gets carried away by an eagle. Mum said that's impossible because a) he's much too fat and b) there are no scary birds of prey living in the marshes. She hasn't been there for a long time, though, and climate change brings unexpected developments, so I'm going to scan the horizon very carefully.

'Go on,' says Tasha. 'Open it! It's from all of us, by the way…'

I'm guessing she chose the wrapping as Tasha's life is full

of pink things. She's half Japanese and has a beautiful pink kimono for special occasions when they go and visit her mum's family in Kyoto.

I push my glass across the table to prevent clumsy accidents, untie the soft pink bow and pull at the securely stuck end of the box. The flap responds and I peek inside, hoping for a clue.

'Toys 'R' Us,' I read from the label on the side of the container.

'This is torture,' sighs Olly, her red head in her freckly hands.

I slide the box out of its wrapping and begin to fold the paper neatly.

'Nope!' admonishes Bella, snatching it out of my hand. 'You're not allowed to do that weird folding thing tonight and keep us all waiting.'

'OK.' I smile sheepishly and take a deep breath, lifting the lid a little. There is a mass of orange string tissue paper, scrunched up.

'I'm going to explode!' announces Olly, reaching into the box and dumping the orange worms on my head.

'Oh, wow!' I say, as I see a big card with 'Sorry you're leaving' on it and the words 'for the summer' scribbled underneath. They have all signed it. Tash has done a cartoon of me on my bike, stuck in mud with a seagull on my head.

'Aw, thanks guys,' I say.

'Pressies!' hisses Olly, pulling her lower eyelids down so that we can see her bloodshot eyeballs.

'Sorry. I know I'm rubbish at this,' I apologise. It feels awkward being the focus of attention when it's not my birthday.

'Close your eyes,' says Bella, coming to my rescue. 'I'll give them to you. Ready? Right. First one.'

I feel the familiar texture of cotton on my hands. When I look, I see a white T-shirt with 'Urban Chicks' in black lettering across the front.

'It's fab!' I tell them, hugging it to me.

'Ta da!' they reply, producing their own T-shirts from their handbags (apart from Olly, who had hidden hers down her trousers – she wouldn't be seen dead with a handbag).

'Put it on!' instructs Bella enthusiastically, and twenty seconds later, the four of us are wearing our new girl-band uniform and giggling like idiots.

'Next present,' says Tasha and I close my eyes again. This time, I can feel heavy plastic and there's a strong smell of rubber.

'Oh my God!' I gasp, when my gaze is greeted by the sight of fluorescent yellow wellies with big pink flowers on them.

'We thought the marshes sounded, well, kind of wet,' shrugs Olivia, 'so we got these in case you didn't want to get your trainers muddy.'

I try them on and stride up and down the aisle by our table, as if on a catwalk. Bella, Olly and Tasha are clapping. We have a group hug and Doug takes a photo. I remember that the last time I had wellies, I was about two. They were so sweet, once my feet had grown Mum still kept them, along with other bits of my 'growing up' memorabilia, like my wind-up bear-in-the-moon lullaby player – the only thing that would get me to have an afternoon nap.

An hour and four big chocolate cheesecake desserts later, the Ollies are dropping me outside my flat. Bell gets out to give me a last squeeze. She looks quite tearful.

'I'll see you soooooon,' she promises. 'Text me as soon as you're there, and every five minutes.'

'Yeah,' I answer, not wanting to let her go.

'Byeeeeee!' they all yell, as the car pulls away. Olly is leaning half out of the open back window, waving like a lunatic. 'Watch out for water rats!' she shouts, doing a rodent impression. Hers is the last face I see as the Olly-mobile turns left at the end of Willow Road.

I realise I'm still waving – which is a bit sad. I drop my arm down to my side and let out a sigh that spirals up into the deep, Tasha-pink July sky.

'Red sky at night, shepherds' delight,' Papa Tom always said. I wonder how many shepherds there are in the marshes and whether, when they see streaks of rose, salmon and purple above their heads, they break into an ancient dance of joy, or whether they simply lean on their crooks and smile.

In less than twenty-four hours, I'll have my answer.

'Hello, Roxy. Dinner time.'

It's the Dobbses' wedding anniversary tonight and they've gone to see *The Sound of Music* in the West End, so I'm on chinchilla duty and have let myself in with the spare key.

The flat is in darkness. Mr Dobbs booked a pre-theatre supper for two at the Savoy Hotel as a surprise. I flick on the light in the hallway and see an envelope with my name on it, propped against a huge vase of Mrs Dobbs's favourite pink roses. Inside is a card with a cat on it and a ten pound note. The words read, 'Have a wonderful holiday, Jasmine, and thank you for looking after Roxy for us.'

They are so lovely, Mr and Mrs Dobbs. I tuck the card and note into my jeans pocket. I can hear scuffling in the lounge. When I turn on the lamp, there is silence. Roxy is in the corner of her chinchilla house, with her back to me, as always.

'Nice to see you too, Rox,' I say, opening the metre-high cage carefully. Inside are pieces of furniture – a four-poster bed with a tiny duvet, a chair and a hollowed-out wooden tube, all chinchilla-sized and hand-made by Mr Dobbs, who used to be a carpenter. There's even a small grandfather clock, identical to the one ticking in the hall. This one has teeth marks down both sides, though.

I'm very careful about not letting her escape. The Dobbses have told me that Roxy can jump several metres into the air. Her ancestors came from mountain ledges in South America, apparently. I'm not sure what I'd do if she were to leap over my head and climb the curtains, so I keep my eye on her.

I reach in and stroke her grey and brown back. She feels incredibly soft, but stiff at the same time.

Mrs Dobbs told me it takes one hundred chinchilla skins to make a fur coat. I'm glad most women go for fake fur these days.

'Hey,' I coax, touching her head. Roxy flinches and continues to stare at the wooden wall in front of her, unblinking. 'You've been busy, I see,' I tell her, noticing the pieces of pine wood strewn across the floor of her cage.

'It wasn't me,' replies her body language.

I take her empty earthenware bowl and fill it up from the packet next door to her home. 'Look, Roxy, sunflower seeds and grainy things and yummy stuff. Mmm. Delicious,' I enthuse, trying to tempt her. There is no response, so I put the bowl back in its place, check the water level in her auto-feeder and close the mesh metal door.

There is something about her stillness that stops me wanting to leave. I switch off the lamp, which has frills around its cream shade, and sit down cross-legged in front of her cage. The street lights send a gentle glow through the flowery net curtains hanging at the long windows. I can still see Roxy in the shadows of her home.

'Maybe you're lonely,' I say. 'Maybe chinchillas aren't happy being on their own, like cats and dogs.' Roxy makes a strange noise in her throat. I feel I'm making progress.

'I'm an only child too, so I know how you feel. And Mr Dobbs told me chinchillas can live for up to twenty years and you're just five, so if your brain can analyse things, you must be quite depressed. I've never really thought about you properly before, Roxy, and how you might be happier if you had a friend. I'll speak to Mr and Mrs Dobbs when I get back and see if we can't fix you up with a mate.'

Roxy turns round and stares at me with her saucer-wide eyes. Her big ears are tilted forwards, attuned to the rubbish tumbling from my mouth.

'We have quite a lot in common, you and me,' I continue. Roxy blinks. 'You should be scurrying about high up on Machu Pichu, where you belong. From tomorrow, I'm going to be taken out of my natural habitat to a place in the marshes, which are flat and wet. I'm used to pavements and concrete. There is no cable for the television and no internet, just grass and sky wherever you look. It used to be OK when my granddad was there. But he died ages ago.'

Roxy blinks again.

'I know, I know. It's not for ever and it's making Mum really happy, going back to where she grew up. She's all bouncy and smiley, like a happy fairy, so I'm going to try really hard to have a good time.'

Roxy tilts her head to one side, her eyes downcast.

'Jaz, listen to yourself. You're talking to a rodent whose idea of fun is running through a tunnel and throwing bits of wood about. OK, Roxy, I'm off now. Have a good summer. I'll bring you back something nice.'

I stand up slowly. I'm just leaving the lounge when there is a sudden high-pitched noise from the direction of Roxy's cage, one which sounds a lot like a recognisable English word. She is up on her back legs, looking at me through the mesh door.

'Oh my God. Did you just say "sausages"?'

9

'OK, mental check list,' I say to Mum, who is laying her cello into its case in the music room. 'Tablets.'

'Yes,' she says.

'Clothes and food,' I state. I have to ask. Mum can be quite vague about both. 'Mum?' When I poke my head round the door, she is wiping the neck of the instrument with a soft cloth, something approaching adoration in her eyes.

'Yes and yes, including cat munchies,' she answers, smiling when she notices me.

'Bedding, tea towels, bath towels…?'

'Not yet,' says Mum. 'But you could get the sheets out ready. We'll just take the duvets in the morning.'

'Poor Dad!' I exclaim, imagining my father, left here shivering under the one blanket we possess, all alone in the double bed.

'There's a spare one in the cupboard,' explains Mum. 'I can have that.'

'Bikes,' I remind her. 'Shall I get them out of the shed?'

'Good idea,' says Mum, closing the cello case softly and fastening the silver latches. 'On second thoughts, leave it till the morning. We don't want them in the hallway, cluttering everything up.'

Our hall is already crammed with cases and plastic boxes full of detergent and washing-up liquid, cling-film, silver foil, rubber gloves. Anyone would think the marshes were completely uncivilised.

'How far is the nearest shop to Frog Cottage?' I ask Mum.

'Ooh,' she says thoughtfully, standing up. 'Must be three or four miles.'

That wasn't quite the answer I was hoping for. Well, hey, we've got a car and the bikes and I can run that distance in twenty minutes, with the wind behind me. I walk into my bedroom and turn on the light. Possum blinks at me crossly from the bed, surrounded by all my stuffed animals. I know it's a bit sad, but I can't decide which of them to take. I want something that smells of home, so it will have to be either Ron the three-legged polar bear or Isaiah the crocodile (who has one eye higher than the other). Tasha thinks my taste in cuddlies is completely weird and can't understand why any parent would give their kid a disabled bear or a reptile famed for eating humans.

We Ballantynes like things which are a bit different. Dad's favourite-ever present is a plastic frog that sings when you walk past it. I got it online from a garden catalogue. In the end Mum took the batteries out and hid them, because she said 'the joke had worn thin'. When Dad wants to wind her up, he just says 'rivet'. She goes from nought to ballistic in about two seconds. Brilliant! We've been careful not to mention the frog since she's been ill, though.

Mum has two favourite-ever presents. The first is a wooden seagull that hangs from a light fitting and flaps its wings up and down. It was something Dad bought her because they had both read a book about a seagull called Jonathan when they were students. At Christmas, we always put a tinsel bow on his head.

The second is a dish I made for her at school when I was eight. It's blue on the outside and yellow in the middle. I wrote 'To my lovely Mummy' on it. The edges are a bit wonky, but I remember being dead proud of it at the time. Mum cried when I gave it to her and said she would always treasure it. The bowl sits on her dressing table, on a crocheted circle made by Nana Jane, and she keeps her rings in it.

I'm not sure what my favourite-ever present is. Probably the silver heart bracelet Mum and Dad bought me for my tenth birthday. It would surprise them to hear me say that, I expect, because I don't wear it. They've made a point of giving me 'outdoor' stuff since then – a fantastic bike, roller blades, snowboarding lessons when we went to the Alps for my birthday. The bracelet hung on my bedroom mirror for two years, a reminder of their love for me. When Mum became ill, I started to keep it under my pillow, so that our hearts were joined. It sounds stupid, but I hoped it would help keep her safe.

I'm going to take it with me to the marshes and am

wrapping it in a tissue to put inside my wash bag. Usually, when we go away, I have butterflies in my stomach, filling me with excitement. And they would be doing loop-the-loops if we were off to the Maldives. But right now, I'm sitting down on my bed, with Possum giving me the evil eye, staring at the bags stuffed with my possessions, and I feel as if I have a rock inside me, anchoring me to the ground.

Dad pokes his head round the door and grins at me. 'You're a case,' he says camply. When I don't respond, he tries another tack. 'Hot chocolate and cookies will be served in approximately five minutes.' His face screws up in a giant yawn and he pretends to fall asleep against my door. When I glance at my clock, it reads eleven pm. I clap my hands and Dad stands to attention and gives me a salute.

He can be very silly sometimes. His dad was in the army so maybe military gestures are in his genes.

'Possum's upset,' I tell him. 'And I had that eagle dream again last night.'

Dad takes this in, hunches his neck forwards, raises his arms and comes flapping into my bedroom, half-tripping over my suitcase, making a mad bird noise. He swoops down on Possum, who is cowering on my duvet, picks him up with one arm, twirls him round and exits with exaggerated leaps.

'That's really helped him feel better!' I yell. Dad, who normally keeps things pretty level, is being a complete idiot, but it's quite sweet. It must be holiday fever. I'm sad he can only stay for weekends in the marshes. He used up so much leave while Mum was getting over her operation that he's got to work right through the summer.

I wander out of my room into the kitchen, where the milk is steaming gently on the stove, ready to be poured over the organic chocolate flakes Dad buys from a specialist shop in Hampstead. When you walk in, you are almost knocked out by the pungent smell of cocoa and other fragrances – chilli, lavender, vanilla. You could stand there all day with your eyes closed. At least, Dad and I could, because we are total chocoholics. Mum, on the other hand, would kill for crisps and peanuts, and can often be found scouring the cupboards for savoury snacks in the middle of the night.

The doors to the garden are still open. It's very warm and airless, a bit oppressive, with low clouds shielding the stars. Honeysuckle and scented stock fill my nose as I step outside. It's great to be able to breathe them in without exploding. Mum bought me a new antihistamine from the chemist this week and it seems to be working. My eyes are still quite itchy, but at last I can make friends with trees!

I move up the three stone steps and across the damp grass towards my favourite branch and ten seconds later I'm observing an upturned dark world. The blood-rush to my head is a welcome distraction from the thoughts of leaving here in the morning. I let my arms dangle and a familiar peace fills my body. I spot Dad's favourite-ever present lurking in the undergrowth near the path and my saggy mouth responds with a smile.

'Hoppity hop, little frog,' I hear Papa Tom say. I have a mental picture of him sitting on the wooden veranda of Frog Cottage, watching me jump about obligingly in the long grass, his knees covered by a thick wool rug. His chuckle would become a wheeze as he clapped his hands to the beat of my antics.

I miss him telling me stories all about the local wildlife. He liked real accounts more than fiction. 'You know where you are with the truth,' he used to say.

Mum's a lot like him in that way. I think that's why she and Dad were so honest with me about her illness. Openness can be good and bad, though. Shivers ripple up my spine when I remember Dad sobbing as Mr Kenwood told us he believed he had successfully taken out all the cancer, together with over half of Mum's stomach. I felt helpless and scared, holding his heaving frame. I realised then I hadn't allowed myself to go down the route of 'what if she doesn't come through the surgery?' even though I knew the risks.

Just over a year ago, I was hanging here, a kid worrying about every spot on her chin. In the space of twenty-four hours, I was self-appointed Team Coach, talking tactics, strategy, options, with a cure as the goal, probably being a pain, with my tick-lists and pieces of paper.

And now, Mum's three-week chemo cycles are history.

The days when she was so sick I missed school just to sit with her have become a blur. I've thrown away my lists of chores and time-plans. The only real reminder of our collision with cancer is the exercise chart on our kitchen wall, the pots of pills – and the scar on Mum's belly.

It was like a bad dream, but it's over now.

In no time, I will be here again, my mind full of summer memories, and life will carry on the way it always has. In the blink of an eye, or the trail of a comet. The thought is comforting and makes me feel secure.

Sometimes, being upside down helps you see things clearly, eh, Papa Tom? Perhaps bats have got it right after all.

Two half-bare legs are approaching. Backlit from the kitchen, I can tell they belong to Dad because a) they are very hairy and b) they are topped off with a pair of horrible old flip-flops and c) they bend like a cowboy's when he walks.

Dad doesn't say anything, just unhooks me from the branch, places my knees over his shoulders and takes gentle steps towards the waiting hot chocolate. I'm so big now that I can tickle his ankles as we go. He responds by pinching my waist and threatening to reduce my cookie ration.

It's a total bluff. My dad is completely soft. And he needs someone to share his bad munchie habits with to make his conscience feel better. Judging by the little muffin top appearing over the edge of his shorts, I should be reducing *his* cookie ration. Maybe, in the marshes, I'll make him an exercise programme and he can do press-ups with me.

'Will you come running with me, then?' I ask, squeezing the soft flesh of his belly.

'I wouldn't want to beat you,' he sighs.

'You think exercise is doing the crossword.'

'You have to be an intellectual athlete, that's true,' he nods.

'I wish you could stay with us the whole time,' I tell him and I can see he's chuffed. 'We might starve to death if Mum cooks.'

'Hey!' she shouts, from inside the flat. She's got super-human hearing, that woman.

Dad looks thoughtful for a moment and then deposits me carefully on the kitchen floor.

'Death by baked beans. Horrible way to go.' He shudders. And with a grin, he squirts cream from a can onto the two mugs of chocolate.

'Shall we?' he asks.

'Go on, then,' I reply. Dad reaches into the cupboard near the door and produces a box with small Flakes in it. He pops one on top of each cream swirl and after a count of three, we each investigate the delicious white mountains with our tongues.

'Mmm,' we are both saying, very loudly, as Mum walks in and puts her hands on her hips in mock shock.

'Outrageous!' she exclaims. 'You great pair of babies.'

10

'Have arrived at world's end. Nothing here but seagulls and oxygen. Hoping giant windmills will phynoties me for whole summer. How r u? ☺ xxxxxxx'

I am standing on Papa Tom's wooden veranda, leaning against the solid strut that holds up the arch over the plum-painted, half-glazed front door, and I'm texting Bella. The word 'phynoties' doesn't look right. I rewrite it, moving the 'p' and changing the end to 'se'. The letters keep jumbling in my head and the end product looks completely foreign.

I press 'send' anyway – Bell is used to my brain's tantrums. My phone sneezes to let me know the message is on its way to London.

My nose is taking in the smell of air heavy with the dampness of vegetation and my eyes absorb the varieties of grasses whose names I don't know, drenched after a recent downpour. A film of mist is rising from the stream at the end of the garden like strands of old man's beard. Balls of tiny midges cluster above the water, like dancing dandelion seed heads.

Possum is staring at me through the peep-hole in his cat basket. He makes a low, yowling noise, which is a plaintive begging to be liberated. I open the wicker door carefully and reach in for him. He is stiff and unyielding. I wonder if he and Roxy have had a chat.

'Out you come, mog,' I say, lifting his heavy weight gently and cradling him in my arms. His eyes are like two full moons and the tip of his tail is twitching. 'There, look. It's cat paradise.'

A seagull lands on the ledge of the tiled roof above us, throws its head up, and emits a raucous 'e-e-e' sound. Possum looks up at it, startled. His tail arches and fluffs up. I can feel his heart beating like a hammer.

'You'll get used to it,' I tell him, stroking him under his jaw. He swallows hard and watches the bird intently as it launches itself into the air, swooping in a tight, effortless circle on invisible currents.

Possum probably needs feline Rescue Remedy. I sit on the top step and cuddle him closer, gazing out on a soft, wide landscape. After a few minutes, his body relaxes and he starts to purr. Warm sun is bathing the marsh grasses, blending into a low shingle bank far on the horizon, which melts into a cloudless sky, which in turn merges into a mirror-flat, languid sea.

To the west, about a kilometre away, I count thirty-six wind turbines clustered like soldiers on parade. They remind me of the King's Troop, who wear the tall busby hats and sit very still for hours on their gleaming mounts outside Buckingham Palace and Horse Guards Parade.

The turbines are poised for action, but there is no wind, and their massive sails are motionless.

'Change blows in when you least expect it,' I hear Papa Tom say. I turn to my left and see only an empty space where his wooden rocking chair used to sit. Mum bought it for him when he reached eighty – the result of a long-running joke relating to *The Little House on the Prairie*, which he used to read to her when she was small. His ability to make authentic rocking-chair noises at the same time as narrating the text had become legendary amongst us.

I remember that when he pulled off the sheet covering the rocker, he laughed so much, he wheezed himself breathless and needed his puffer. And he squeezed Mum so hard it made her cough.

'You're a wily weasel,' he half-scolded her. 'I'm not creaking yet.'

'I know,' she replied, pinched his craggy cheeks and gave him a kiss. 'Happy eightieth birthday, Dad.'

I wonder what has happened to the chair? After Papa Tom died, when I was nine, Mum and Dad let the cottage to an artist called Esme, who painted bees on hand-thrown pots which she fired in a kiln in the shed. She rented it furnished, so maybe the rocker is still here somewhere, covered in a protective sheet.

About eighteen months ago, when Esme went to Spain on holiday and never came back, Mum decided to close everything up. She told us she stacked Esme's bee pots and plates neatly in the garage, in case the errant artist turned up one day to reclaim them.

'Why did she stay in Spain?' I had asked when Mum returned to London, hung up Papa Tom's door keys and poured herself a big glass of wine, telling us in an upset torrent about the turbines that were being erected on the marshes. It was a while before she had calmed down enough to answer my question.

'Esme fell in love with an olive farmer,' Mum replied simply, without any irritation or regret in her voice.

Love, in Mum's book, explains everything and is always indisputable. Whether it's the reason for a terrible crime (e.g. mad wife kills unfaithful husband with carving knife) or a crazy gesture (e.g. divorced man with fear of heights climbs Eiffel Tower to claim visiting rights to see his children), Mum's reaction is always a shrug and a sigh. Dad says it's because her grandmother was Parisian and the French treat love like a sacred god.

'It makes fools of us all,' Mum often says, quietly, sounding just like Nana Jane, who would blush when Papa Tom told her she was beautiful.

'Go on with you!' my grandmother would reply, retying her apron and pushing her hair off her smooth face, a smile playing round her lips, which were always slightly shiny with pale, rose-pink lipstick. I can superimpose her image wherever I look.

'Ow, Possum, don't do that.' He's clawing my hand in

a pummelling action. Usually, he works up such a rhythm that he ends up biting me from over-excitement. I push his paw away and he scratches the air instead. Mental, this cat. His eyes are slits of pure puss-pleasure.

My memory is opening a box sealed four years ago – the last time I was here in the Rainbow Marshes, helping Mum put sheets over the furniture, brushing autumn leaves from the veranda with the wide broom Nana Jane used to shoo Papa Tom's bantams out of the kitchen.

'Pesky creatures!' she would exclaim.

'They think you're a pesky creature,' he would retort, a twinkle in his eye. The only time I ever saw him angry was the day a car hit a swan and left it for dead in the lane by the cottage. Papa Tom loaded it, and me, into his small truck and took it to the countryside ranger on the other side of the marshes. He ground the gears all the way there and kept muttering, 'Damn lunatics,' under his breath.

The ranger told us its wing was almost certainly broken. He and his son, a dark-haired kid who didn't speak, would take it to the bird sanctuary at St Merrion for treatment. The swan would be fine, he thought, and he thanked us for helping. Papa Tom told me afterwards that the ranger had been at school with Mum – 'An admirer, one of many, only this one had a motorbike,' he had chuckled.

It feels like yesterday.

'Miles away?' observes Mum, who has appeared on the

veranda with a glass of mango juice for me from the cool bag we packed at home.

'I was thinking about Papa Tom,' I tell her. 'It's funny here, without him – and Nana Jane.'

'Yes,' replies Mum gently. She sits next to Possum and me on the step. I lean towards her and my nose tingles with her lavender scent. Behind us, I can hear Dad's feet scrunching on the gravel as he unloads the car.

'On your shoulder!' I hear Papa Tom whisper nearby, just as he did when I was about to do something bad, like stick my finger in the jar of chocolate spread (Dad would understand that one, I'm sure!). And he would say it in my ear whenever we said goodbye. It felt nice, thinking that his spirit was watching over me.

And as if she senses my thoughts, Mum puts her hands lightly on my shoulders and gives them a little massage. I close my eyes, breathe in the distinctive marsh air, and let the flood of memories wash through my mind like a fast-moving river.

How strange to think they were all there, in my brain, waiting to be released, revisited, replayed, and all it took was to be here again. But being here is like visiting a stage set, like the ones in Disney World. The filming has finished and the characters have left.

'There's something you can help me with, if you like,' says Mum, when her fingers have finished easing my neck muscles. At that moment, Possum spots a frog in the grass and leaps off my lap in hot pursuit. Mum is standing now and beckoning me with her finger. My phone coughs. It must be Bella, at last.

'Adam having BBQ 4 girls in his ballet class. Pops being v embarrassing – did a pirouette as a dare just now + fell over. Soz u not here. All send our love. Miss u. ☺ xxxxxxxx'

Pangs of jealousy and homesickness hit my chest like arrows finding a bulls-eye, but when I follow Mum into the cottage, I find her holding one end of a sheet round her head like she's a nun, encouraging me to do the same.

We share the sheet and do a little dance round the brown, scuffed leather sofa it was covering, pulling and tugging it away from each other, screeching and giggling like idiots. I decide to let Mum win, so we don't tear it in two (we get *so* competititve sometimes!), and we both end up flopping onto the worn seats, puffed and perfectly happy – in the moment, as Mum always says.

And I'm trying to look on the bright side, hoping I won't need the wind turbines' help after all.

11

'Ready, Jaz?' calls Mum up the narrow stairway.

I'm just tucking in the last corner of the fitted sheet we brought for the double bed in the second bedroom, which is to be my room for the summer. It's larger than the small single room I used to sleep in – under the eaves above the garage. This one faces the sea, instead of north, and through the square, clear panes, the widest sunset I have ever seen is filling the horizon, like strips of pink and orange cellophane layered in a collage over an artist's white board.

Flocks of birds, like distant black dots, glide across the space in seamless symmetry, as if drawn in motion by an invisible pencil. The smell of the ocean is strong and salty, mixing with the incredible aromas of garlic and ginger wafting upstairs from the frying pan of chicken and peppers Dad is tending. I open the chipped, wooden-framed window and take a deep breath, licking my lips and tasting sodium.

'Jaz!'

'Coming!' I call back. I leave the window open to usher in the marsh twilight, throw the duvet onto the bed, flatten it so that the crease by the pillows is straight (a bit obsessive – sorry, Bella!) and walk quickly to the hallway over warm wooden boards, which feel solid and comforting to my bare feet.

In the kitchen, which Papa Tom knocked through into the dining room to create a bigger space, Mum and Dad are already sitting at the table. Tea lights are glowing on the three window sills. A white pillar candle burns between the three plates, which are heaped with rice and Mediterranean sauce.

Dad has opened some champagne. He and Mum have already had a glass, I can tell. They are holding hands over the table like a pair of kids in one of my teen magazines. I can imagine speech bubbles attached to their heads.

Him: 'She's really fit.'

Her: 'Oh no! Did he just say he was an accountant?'

'What are you grinning at?' asks Dad, as I sit down.

'Nothing,' I lie. Dad pours me a little champagne, enough for a toast.

I am about to say something, but Mum interrupts.

'Before you ask, I took my pills. Didn't I, James?' Dad nods. I give Mum a little round of applause. 'I'm going to try to remember, so you don't have to, from now on. So, a toast. To life, love, lipstick and summer in the best place on earth, with the people I love the most in the whole world,' says Mum, her voice steady, her hands shaking slightly. 'And absent friends, whom we miss more than words can say.'

She raises her glass to the room, before clinking it with mine and Dad's.

'Down the hatch!' says Papa Tom, somewhere in my head.

'Yes, down the hatch!' I repeat. Mum and Dad look at me in surprise. Mum's eyes are moist, sparkling in the candlelight. Dad squeezes her hand and no one speaks as we begin to eat. Mum gets halfway through hers before she excuses herself and leaves the table. I rise to follow her to see what's up. Dad touches my arm lightly and shakes his head.

'She's fine,' he assures me. 'It's a big deal, coming back here, after everything that's happened. Full circle. It's the first time she's had to go through something major without Papa Tom being around.'

'I hear her talk to him sometimes,' I say, and then feel guilty, like I've betrayed a confidence.

'Maybe he can hear her. Who knows? It's a comfort, anyway,' says Dad.

'Do you talk to your mum and dad?' I ask, filled with a new recognition that my parents were also children once, vulnerable, needing reassurance. I never knew Dad's parents as they both died before I was born.

'I didn't really talk to them much when they were alive,' he replies. 'Boarding school created quite a distance between us. Often happens to the kids of military men who travel around a lot. I did my growing up in England while they lived in India, Myanmar, Singapore, all over the place. I spent holidays with your Great Auntie Polly and her family in Selsey and wrote to Mum once a month, telling her how I was getting on. They always sent me nice presents at Christmas and for my birthday, and lots of postcards, which used to make my mates jealous. Pretty remote though, when you think about it.'

'Poor Daddykins – all lonely like an ophan,' I say, stroking his rough, stubbly cheek.

'It might have been different if my little sister had survived,' he adds. I had forgotten about Katharine, the aunt-in-the-making who never got past her sixth birthday. 'After she died, my mother just went inside herself.'

'Did Mum do that when she lost my brother?' I ask. Dad looks a little taken aback.

'She was very sad. We both were. But before too long, along came you, like a present for us to share.'

'Did you have a funeral for him?' I persist and immediately realise how stupid that sounds.

'He wasn't born so, no, we didn't,' says Dad. 'But we planted a tree in Regent's Park, when there was a campaign going.'

'Maybe he would have liked hanging upside down from branches, like me,' I suggest.

'Maybe,' agrees Dad, then kisses me on the head as he heads towards the frying pan for a refill.

I wonder suddenly whether he would have been dyslexic too, the brother that never was. I'm playing with my fork, making patterns in the tomato sauce on my plate and Dad recognises this as a sign of sadness (I've always drawn figures of eight in my food when under stress, for some reason).

'Never guess what's for pud,' he says, his mouth full of chicken.

'Hmm. Let me see,' I reply, playing along. 'Yoghurt?' This is Mum's idea of a dessert, but not mine or Dad's.

'Tiramisu with – you guessed it – extra chocolate. Waitrose special,' he says, proudly. 'In honour of our arrival.' He takes a wonderful-looking carton out of the fridge and shows it to me, eyes alight.

'Half each, then?' I suggest, and he nods. 'What's Mum got?'

'Prunes,' he says, pulling a face. 'There's no accounting for taste.'

Five minutes later, the three of us are sitting on the veranda step, watching the last crimson light fade in the west, behind the turbines, whose long sails are slowly turning in the cool breeze that has crept in with the incoming tide. I'm in the middle, although by rights it should be Dad, because he's the piggy.

'You OK?' I ask Mum, who has her arms folded against the night chill. Being so thin, she really feels the cold.

'I'm just dandy,' she confirms, giving me a grin.

We are watching Possum, who is trying to catch dragonflies near the small stream. He keeps pouncing and missing. His fur is flat against his body, which means he must have fallen in at least once.

'He's eaten a mouse,' says Mum. 'I found its innards on the path. He's gone native. Don't suppose he'll eat tinned food again.'

'He might lose some weight while he's here,' suggests Dad.

'He'll be the only one, then,' teases Mum, glancing at our empty tiramisu plates. I admit, eating half was a bit ambitious. I feel slightly queasy when she offers me a prune. I'm still thinking about the mouse's heart, abandoned by Possum on the gravel path.

I wonder if we, like Possum, have begun to change. London seems so far away, already a past tense. I must keep it in my mind every day and speak to all the Chicks, or the memory keepers will pack my city life into sealed crates in some chamber in my brain, and I'll be caught between two worlds, unsure where I belong.

Time feels different here. It's unfolding around us, wrapping us into its rhythm. It seems to be wide and long and deep. Sitting between Mum and Dad, I can sense the length of a minute without having to look at my mobile's clock. And it's like I'm physically experiencing the light disappearing from the sky through my whole body, my eyes wide, my chest open, my breathing deep and regular.

'Look up,' Papa Tom had said to me, the last time I saw him. We were sitting on the veranda during a spring afternoon. He was in his rocking chair, covered in a big blue blanket. I was perched on the wooden balustrade as if it were a thin horse, my legs dangling either side of its spindly limbs. 'What do you see?'

'Soft white balls of cotton wool,' I replied.

'Clumped together or spread about?' he'd asked, his big eyebrows furrowed and almost meeting. He was having problems seeing by then. Anything further away than a metre was a blur.

'Dolloped here and there,' I replied. 'Like messy marshmallows.'

'Cumulus,' he nodded and smiled. 'Our fair weather friends.'

He told me then that ancient peoples used to know what the weather was going to do just by looking at the clouds. They must have sat and stared, just as we're doing now. They didn't know their world was spinning around the sun, that their stillness was a lie.

'They relied on their instincts,' said Papa Tom. 'They needed to, for survival.'

Watching him prance about like an idiot, I think Possum's natural instincts are returning. Maybe mine are too. At this moment, I am safe, sandwiched between Mum and Dad, cosseted in their familiar warmth, protected by their presence. But soon this moment will also be a memory, like the line of fading pink on the horizon, and my life in London. And Papa Tom.

I hug Mum and Dad tighter. Small goose bumps appear on my bare arms and the idea that nothing lasts forever, except maybe time itself, freefalls in my head. My heart tells me I need to locate the rip-cord, to activate the parachute and slow its relentless descent.

Mum spots my sudden cold and rubs my hand between hers. In profile, in the dusk, she looks so much like Nana Jane, only without her double chin. She also seems fragile, like a figurine of fine china, her features chiselled to perfection.

'Penny for them,' she says to me.

'I was just thinking that we're very insignificant,' I reply.

'Speak for yourself,' says Dad, acting put out.

'I mean, compared with all this,' I add, motioning to the darkening landscape which fills our view. 'We're just a blip.'

'Only the gods are immortal,' says Mum. 'That's what your Papa Tom would tell me, when we found a dead rabbit in the lane or one of my guinea pigs snuffed it.' She kisses my head, gently, and exchanges a look with Dad. 'You're shivering. We should go in.'

'Shotgun I don't wash up,' says Dad, suddenly standing and doing a runner indoors.

'Twit,' says Mum, affectionately, over her shoulder. She puts both arms around me and gives me a mahousive hug. 'As if he thinks that'll get him out of it!'

'Love you masses,' I say.

'Love you more,' replies Mum, but today we're not arguing about which of us loves the other one the most. There's a quietness between us – an acceptance that nothing is certain.

'Thank you,' says Mum, looking at me appraisingly, like Tara does with one of her hats.

'What for?' I ask.

'For you,' she says, taking in the detail of my hair, my face, my skin, as if I am a prize exhibit. 'You're going to break a few hearts, Jasmine Ballantyne,' she smiles. I can feel myself blushing. 'Just like your mother,' she adds, giggling, getting to her feet and offering to pull me up. For once, I let her take some of my weight. Her grip is firm and positive. Something in the coastal air is already making her stronger. She is running back to the cottage.

'So, what about all these boyfriends, then?' I call after her accusingly.

She makes a 'they're history' sort of gesture and hops up the veranda steps, happy to have flummoxed me. My mother, the Mata Hari of the marshes.

12

It's Sunday morning. I'm lying in bed, eating a croissant which Mum brought me, fresh from the oven, and Bella is telling me the goss on Adam's barbecue party. Rain is streaking down my window panes and outside the sky is like lead. The bad weather must have sneaked in overnight.

'Yup,' says Bella, and she gulps. She's probably drinking coffee, brewed in the machine by the range cooker in her kitchen. It always smells so wonderful in there in the morning. 'She was doing this *kugh-kugh* thing in her throat – choking – so he put his arms round her and pulled tight and she coughed and a lump of sausage came out at a hundred miles an hour and hit the tree.'

'Awesome!' I tell Bella, my mouth full of flaky pastry.

'So, there's more,' she continues. 'Sausage Girl was the last to go. Her dad came to pick her up and Mum went out into the garden looking for her and she found them.'

'Who?' I ask.

'Sausage Girl and Adam, dur, down each other's throats.'

'Wow!' I exclaim.

'And Meredith is talking to the dad, keeping him occupied, but the dad has looked out of the door and sees Adam, running across the grass with no shirt on.'

'Aaagh!' I squeak.

'Meredith spots Adam, and you'll never guess what he says…' teases Bella.

'What? WHAT?'

'"These young people of ours are very versatile. They treated us to an impromptu performance of *A Midsummer Night's Dream*. Your daughter was a splendid Titania to my son's Bottom."'

I am laughing so hard I have to plunge my face into my pillow to try to subdue the desire to scream.

'Brilliant, isn't it?' squeals Bella.

'What did Sausage Girl do?' I ask eventually, when my eyes have stopped watering.

'Came out from behind the azaleas, said "Thank you for having me," to my mum and breezed into the lounge to collect her dad. Meredith tried to be helpful and told her it was a long time since anyone had tackled the *Dream* in our garden and she actually laughed and said, "Yeah, whatever."'

I love Bella's stories about her family. Even everyday things become an adventure when she describes them, like the time Mowgli went to the vet to have his ears cleaned and was attacked by a large white rabbit in the waiting room. Bella's mum intervened and monster bunny sank its teeth into her leg and wouldn't let go. She needed a tetanus injection after that and four stitches. And every time Mowgli saw Bella's stuffed rabbit on her bed, he growled and showed his teeth.

'So, what's happening at world's end then?' asks my mate.

'It's raining. Dad's cooking a roast and then we're going for a walk,' I reply, my voice falsely enthusiastic.

'Sounds *rivet*-ing,' croaks Bella, doing her frog impression. 'Remember, you have to kiss a lot of frogs to find a prince.'

'How many, exactly?' I ask, picking up the last of my croissant flakes with my finger.

'At least four thousand. And when you find him, ask him if he's got a mate, OK?'

'Maybe. I might be too busy living happily ever after,' I tell her.

There is the sound of scuffling and a disgusted shriek from my friend.

'Oi! Oh, that's SO gross, Adam. STOP IT!' she shouts. Such things are usual in the Farrell household in the morning. 'He's put his socks in my face and they are actually green on the bottom. Ugh, hang on Jaz…putrid Adam wants a word with you.' My breath catches involuntarily at the back of my throat.

'Ballantyne,' says Adam. 'Have you learned how to catch a fish yet?'

'Funny you should ask that,' I reply. 'I was just going out with my harpoon.'

'Most people would use a rod. Why do you have to be so dramatic?'

'Didn't you know they filmed *Moby Dick* round here?'

'Very funny. Have a nice summer, Ballantyne,' says Adam.

'Enjoy your extracurricular Shakespeare,' I smirk.

There is a moment's silence while he takes this in.

'I am now going to kill my sister,' replies Adam – and screams of protest follow for at least a minute.

'OK,' I hear Bella half-sob, half-giggle. 'I'm sorry I told her about Sausage Girl.'

'Her name is Emily,' responds Adam. 'And she is a vegetarian.'

And suddenly the call is cut and the lifeline to my other world recoils and wraps itself round me like a straitjacket, Bella's laughter echoing in my ears, merging into the splish-splatter of the rain as it hits and runs down the wet, wet panes.

As I wriggle down and pull the duvet over my head dejectedly, there is a soft knock on the door. Mum is standing there, in her silky cream dressing gown, with a tray and three mugs on it. Dad is close behind, dressed in a T-shirt and bright yellow shorts (he thinks being here is officially a holiday, so he can wear his most embarrassing collection of surf relics), and soon they are sitting on my bed, babbling about all the possibilities of the day. And they look relaxed and so happy, as if here is the best place in the world to be.

It could just be the shorts, but suddenly the room seems

full of sunshine. We all turn to the window in disbelief. A huge rainbow is arcing over the marshes, like a colossal fairground ride, its colours vibrant and spectacular against the dark clouds. Shafts of light plunge down to earth through the ice crystals, like angelic swords, at the same time as hailstones the size of sprouts hurl themselves with a clatter onto the roof of the cottage.

It's a sound and light show on a scale I've never seen before. The brightness is making me squint, and when I rub my eyes, I notice that Mum is holding Dad's hand, and that there are tears in the corners of her eyes.

13

'*Four serious boyfriends* before you met Dad?' I repeat and Mum nods, popping a cherry into her mouth. We are in my bed with the duvet pulled right up under our chins. Mum offers the bowl to me and I take a looped pair, eating them from the stalks. We throw the stones towards the bin in the corner of the room. None of the three hits its target. They clatter along the wooden floor like stones skimming across the beach.

'I nearly married Ben, number two,' she says. 'It was an impulse thing – my first ball at Cambridge – and he asked me what I was doing tomorrow, and I said, "Nothing," and he proposed, just like that. And I said, "Why not?" and we asked our friends to be witnesses and even got as far as the steps of the Registry Office.'

'What stopped you?' I ask, enthralled at the idea of my mum being so rash.

'It was a mad idea, as full of bubbles as the champagne we'd been drinking. I looked at him – he was gorgeous, gorgeous, gorgeous – and just thought, this isn't what I imagined, such a big decision made so lightly. He was going to be a racing driver – I wanted to join an orchestra. It was too crazy. Although, I might have got my hands on a Ferrari!' she grins.

'What about numbers one, three and four?' I persist.

'Poor Sean. Number three. I was on the rebound, very confused. He was an armchair and slippers sort of person, very reassuring, very good at listening and making tea. He was studying Physics and had the whole constellation in his room. He could tell you precisely all the transits of the planets, but he always spoke in euphemisms about love. "I am beset by problems of Venus," he told me once. I thought it was a medical condition.' Mum sighs. 'He made a lovely lemon drizzle cake, though.'

'Did you dump him?' I ask.

'He dumped himself. He wrote to me saying he didn't think he was good enough to be with a star that was going to "light up the firmament". It was a sweet note. Not long after that, I heard his dad had died, and he left university to help his mother. He probably works for NASA now. I might look him up on Friends Reunited when we get back to London,' she says, adding 'just out of curiosity,' when she sees my brow furrow.

'OK. What's the story on number one?' I enquire.

'Ah. First love. Exceptional young man. Gifted double bassist. Awful mother! She couldn't let go. Kept phoning him up and crying all the time. I think she was an alcoholic. He had to go home a lot. Didn't want me to meet her. I started to feel like the mad woman kept in the attic in *Jane Eyre*. None of his family knew about me. It was my first year and somehow it was all too – heavy.' Mum makes a tragic face at me, then smiles.

'And number four?' I ask.

'Yevgeny,' answers Mum, lifting her eyes to the ceiling. 'The orchestra's visiting soloist, from Russia. I was head-over-heels. And so were most of the other musicians, men and women. He had this incredible, ferocious energy – fantastic to be around. Every cell in your body seemed to burst into flame when he touched you. Such passion, but…'

'Not husband material?' I finish her sentence.

'Nope. Yevgeny just loved Yevgeny. And almost anyone who turned up at his dressing-room door, I found out,' sighs Mum.

'Love rat,' I declare. Mum nods sadly.

'So you chose an accountant,' I grin.

'Well, he chose me, actually,' she replies. 'And I didn't know he was an accountant. Obviously, if I had, I would have run away as fast as my legs could carry me!'

I've heard the story a hundred times before, how Dad went to Mum's first solo performance, was mesmerised by her and waited in the rain outside the stage door, hoping she would sign his programme. It took several dates and a whole year before she returned his affection – her heart was so bruised by the Russian. But having fallen for Dad, she says she has never once regretted it.

'He's the one,' says Mum, simply.

'Are we dressing for lunch?' asks Dad, from the bottom of the stairs. Mum and I look at each other and pull a face.

'Will the restaurant permit pyjamas?' asks Mum.

'Only sexy ones,' replies Dad. Mum looks at her baggy, faded cream and pink two-piece and frowns. 'Oh dear. Plan B then,' she sighs.

'Don't go,' I say, restraining her as she attempts to get out of bed. We've nattered for over an hour.

'Lamb roast isn't so good on a tray,' says Mum. 'Let's throw some trackies on and show willing.' She hops deftly out of bed and moves to the doorway.

'Thanks for our chat,' I say. 'Glad you chose James the Jelly Belly after all that.'

'Me too,' she replies. 'Absolutely the best of the bunch.'

I stretch out in a star shape across the warm space, my head full of images of Mum with all these different men – and just six years older than me when she nearly eloped in a Ferrari. I can't imagine loving anyone the way I love Mum and Dad.

'Are you coming, Jaz?' calls Mum.

'Vrrooooooom!' I reply.

14

'Hey, dude. Howzit comin? ☺'

I'm reading this text from Olly, who is on a family holiday in Bude in Cornwall, and has started to communicate in surf-speak, in between lessons with a Norwegian surf-god called Lars. I'm getting mayo all over the phone, so I stop making sandwiches and wipe my hands on the tea towel with twelve cats on so that I can respond.

'Wore the wellies yesterday. Hail the size of tennis balls. How r u? :)'

'Whooooooah!' comes the reply, in less than thirty seconds. It's Olly's way of saying she's fine. She's not big on using lots of words when one will do, except in her English essays, which are always original and brilliant and pages longer than everyone else's.

Mum is on the veranda, playing her cello. It's a piece by Saint-Saëns and it sounds really haunting outdoors. I'm not sure of the title, or number. I always recognise the composer; I suppose I should do, having listened to so many pieces since I was a baby. I remember watching Mum's bow moving gently backwards and forwards when she played me lullabies in my cot. Some of her pieces are so familiar, they seem like old friends.

She hasn't needed to stop very often, so her fingers must be feeling fluid and relaxed. I know she will have her eyes closed and be breathing hard. Sometimes I've held my hand over her heartbeat when she's finished practicing and it's always racing with the exertion, like she's run a marathon.

Mum's OK, but I've kind of got the Monday morning blues. It might be something to do with the fact that I'm thinking about Olly, Bella and Tash and all the great things they are probably up to. And Lars, balancing on his surfboard, on top of a ten metre wave, his blond hair almost white in the sun, his ultra-white teeth gleaming in a wide smile.

'Daydreams don't get the jobs done,' I hear Nana Jane say.

'Lars is very distracting,' I reply in my defence, as if she's here. It's hard to know what she would make of a surf dude. When she was young, she was very beautiful. Papa Tom told me once she'd had three proposals – one from an American film star.

'I think she probably drew straws,' he said. 'And luckily, mine was the shortest.'

That wasn't quite how it happened. According to Mum, Nana Jane had left modelling to return to Kent and help take care of her mother, who was ill with a wasting disease which left her in a wheelchair. She taught piano and painted a little. One day, she walked past a carpentry studio which had an easel for sale outside. She went inside to ask about it, and met Papa Tom.

She could have lived in Los Angeles in a mansion, with a pink Cadillac and a swimming pool in the shape of a champagne glass. But then Mum wouldn't be Mum. And I wouldn't be here, spreading mayo on brown rolls.

Stuff happens. People make decisions, for better or worse.

We've planned a picnic today – it's warm and windless after the wildness of yesterday. It's as if the marshes have breathed a sigh of relief that the storm's tantrum has passed. Dad pumped up the tyres on our bikes before he left for London this morning. It was so early, I didn't get to say goodbye. I feel really sorry for him having to work all week while we're here. It feels a bit weird to be just with Mum, miles from anywhere. We've still got the car, though, which is great, as I'm thinking Bella could come down soon, maybe with Dad at the weekend, and we could pick them both up from the station.

I've made egg and salad rolls and I'm putting them into our cool bag with some crisps and an apple each. I remember watching Nana Jane do the same thing and Papa Tom would stand in the kitchen doorway, leaning casually on the frame, smiling at her and checking the watch on the cracked brown leather strap on his wrist. When we had plans, like watching the mist-netting and ringing of birds on the marshes, he wanted to get going.

'You can just wait,' Nana Jane would comment quietly,

as she added more and more things to our lunch bag.

'We don't need a thermos, do we, Little Frog?' he'd say, a heavy hand on my head.

'The weather might turn,' Nana Jane would reply matter-of-factly, filling a blue flask with steaming, sweet hot chocolate, made on the electric hob. 'Now, don't you put up with any of his nonsense,' she would tell me, her eyes twinkling, her finger wagging at Papa Tom, who would shrug innocently.

'I won't,' I say out loud, into the emptiness.

'Won't what?' asks Mum, appearing in the doorway, only half-filling the wide space between its wooden architraves. She looks exhilarated and bright-eyed. Her arms wrap round me and she peers over my shoulder into the cool bag, turning her nose up at the sight of the apple and trying to remove it.

'Hey!' I protest.

'Just teasing,' she responds. 'So, are you ready for the magical mystery tour of the marshes?'

'Yup,' I nod, zipping up the bag. 'But first, you've got to have this.' I reach into the fridge for Mum's high-carbohydrate drink, which smells like banana milkshake. She pulls a face, but I ignore this and pour a glass for her.

'You don't need to worry about me,' she says, taking it reluctantly and swallowing a few mouthfuls at once, flexing her left arm like a body-builder at the same time to prove to me that it's having an immediate effect.

'I know you've been good about the pills, but you're supposed to have this too...' I say, trying to justify my bossiness. Maybe the odd day without this gloopy stuff would be OK. Maybe I should lighten up.

'Ah, miracle juice,' says Mum, in between gulps. She may look like Nana Jane, but she is Papa Tom to a T sometimes. She drains the last of the thick liquid, pulls another face, and then grins at me.

'Two Musketeers go out to face another day?' she suggests.

'Two and their faithful mascot,' I reply, pointing to Possum, who has walked into the kitchen rather sleepily, having been out hunting all night. He rubs round Mum's legs, purring softly. She lifts him for a quick cuddle.

'You're one happy chappy, aren't you?' she says, her face very close to Possum's whiskers. He bats her nose playfully with his paw, yawning in slow motion, revealing his yellowed incisors, and a thin, pink slipper of a tongue. His eyes are just slits of half-conscious slumber.

Mum scratches him under his chin. If Dad or I do that, he normally gives us a warning bite.

'Mummy's boy,' I observe. I can just hear Bella telling me I'm also jealous of the family cat. Mum is putting him down on a chair, where he arches his back in a big stretch before curling into a ball, his tail curving round his body like a snake.

'It's a great life,' says Mum, smiling at him. 'Eating,

sleeping, being looked after... He and I have a lot in common.'

'He's rubbish at cello, though.'

'But his catatonic scale is quite impressive,' quips Mum, suddenly meowing her way up a series of discordant notes. Possum raises his head and stares at her, his ears twitching, as if he's aware he's being teased, which makes us both crack up.

'Here's lookin' at you, kid,' she says to him, in her Humphrey Bogart voice, as she leaves the kitchen. *Casablanca* is Mum and Dad's favourite old black-and-white movie. They watch the DVD every Christmas. I've probably seen it at least ten times. Mum always cries at the end, when Ingrid Bergman has to get on the plane. She and Dad can do whole scenes by heart, including the funny accents and fluttering eyelashes.

'Yeah. Here's lookin' at you,' I repeat, slinging the cool bag over my shoulder and following her.

15

'Race you!' I say to Mum, overtaking her on the narrow, hedge-bordered lane which meanders away from Papa Tom's cottage in the direction of the sea.

'I just want to pootle,' she calls after me. 'I'll catch you up.'

It feels good to be doing something physical. I'm missing my training already. I did some press-ups in the lounge this morning, but found it hard to force myself past thirty. The Lioness wouldn't be happy about that. It just didn't feel right, exercising like a lunatic on the rug by the wood burner, surrounded by Papa Tom's old books on the shelves, containing everything you'd ever need to know about the marshes.

And each time my nose came near to the long wool pile it was met by the smell of eucalyptus, which was the oil in the wax polish he used on the floorboards and furniture. My head was so full of images of Papa Tom with his soft cloth, working on the grain of a rich wood with almost loving strokes, that I lost count and rolled over onto my back, staring at the oak beams in the ceiling.

The drawing pins he used to hang decorations the Christmas before he died were still there – quite tarnished, but embedded into the wood. I'd helped him make the long, red and gold loop chain. Each strip of paper had needed licking to make it stick and the glue had tasted horrible. Afterwards, he had fetched a jar of lemon bon-bons and we ate them by the fire, looking at the flames reflected in the shiny circles suspended above our heads.

Papa Tom had a way of making bad things better. Mum must have missed him so much during her illness.

I'm waiting for her at a small crossroads. Our lane carries on in a southeasterly direction towards the wind turbines. Those forking off to the left and right are as narrow as worms. It's lucky there aren't many cars in this part of the marshes. The big four-by-fours Dad calls Chelsea tractors would definitely get stuck.

There's no signpost. These are roads to nowhere.

Mum the pootler arrives, a big smile on her face. 'It's straight on,' she confirms, her eyes darkening a little as she catches sight of the tops of the turbines over the hedgerows in the distance.

We ride in silence, apart from me shrieking when a huge bee flies into my face. Mum tells me to mind where I'm going, which seems a bit unfair, as it was the bee that was lurching, like a drunk on the pavement outside a pub, across my path.

Soon the hedgerows give way to flat, open fields full of sheep, bounded by wooden fences. To the east, the coast curves round and rises gradually towards a series of chalk cliffs. The western skyline is dominated by the turbines, whose sails are barely turning today. Our lane twists past them, taking us within a hundred metres of those at the front of the grid. The site is shielded from trespassers by security mesh topped with barbed wire. Mum stops her bike and stares at the marshes' newest arrivals, taking in the pristine tarmac road which snakes its way down to some low buildings and a car park. I notice that the pink colour in her cheeks has drained away.

'Are you OK?' I ask her.

'I'm glad your Papa Tom didn't live to see this,' she replies.

'He would have hated it,' I agree.

'He always said the marshes were ancient lands, with their own mysteries and rhythms. He saw himself as their protector, I think. He could name all the types of plant and insect you don't find anywhere else in Britain.' Her gaze doesn't waver from the huge, pale structures that rise like fingers boldly out of the earth, casting shadows the size of skyscrapers in their wake.

'But we need wind power, don't we?' I ask.

'Maybe,' says Mum, thoughtfully. 'Dad would probably just say it's not the first time the marshes have been invaded. He was quite a philosopher at heart.' She sighs, quietly. 'I can't believe that two years ago there was nothing here but land and water and sky.'

'And frogs,' I remind her. 'Don't forget them.' I'm alongside her and give her a hug, balancing on tip-toe so my bike doesn't keel over. She is surprisingly cold in the warmth of the morning. She holds me tighter than usual and then pushes the hair off my face, the way she used to when she left me at the school gate, before kissing my forehead.

'You know what?' she says seriously. 'I could eat a horse.' And at that moment, there is a startled whinny from a nearby field. We both laugh out loud, moving off again into the lane, crossing quickly through the chill dark of the turbines' unlit faces.

Mum is pedalling faster now, on a mission to munch. Our small lane ends at a T-junction. The smell of the sea is very strong. We turn left and follow the curving squiggle of uneven tarmac for another mile, passing a small car park and a sign forbidding cars to go further. The grass on either side of us has given way to shingle. The road is now a track. We pass a haphazard collection of single railway carriages that have been turned into homes. Some are their original size and look like troll houses with crooked chimneys. Others have been extended and have double glazing, pretty gardens and white picket fences.

When the track becomes stones, Mum and I push the bikes to the end of the lollipop-shaped promontory. There is no one else here. The tide is lapping around like a hungry mouth as we collapse at last, raiding the cool bag like shipwrecked survivors discovering their first meal for days. The coast stretches away either side of us, to Sussex and the eastern corner of Kent. From here the turbines look like tall thimbles, gathered tidily on a green and brown patchwork quilt.

Mum swallows her tablets without me nagging and looks eagerly at the polythene bag I am holding out towards her.

'Horse roll,' I say, handing Mum the filled wholemeal baps.

'Mmm, delicious,' she answers, sinking her teeth into one hungrily. 'Keep your eyes open for seals. Brown rolls are their favourite.'

I scan the water vigilantly. After visiting Seal World I know they aren't the cuddly things you see in cartoons. Their cute faces hide some mean habits. And they have awful breath. I don't fancy sharing my lunch with one.

'Papa Tom used to call this "Pirates Point",' says Mum. 'It's the southernmost part of the marshes. Quite a shock for my lazy old muscles.' Mum rubs her hip and thigh. 'That's the spire of St Saviour's. The cottage is due south, by about two miles.'

She's pointing inland to the east, to a tall spire that looks like a needle poking through a swathe of yellow material. We've come quite a distance.

'You forget what it's like just to stare into a space without buildings. In London, they frame everything.' Mum breathes in deeply, her chest expanding with the fresh air.

I think about Roxy, who has mountains in her blood, and

who lives in a tall cage in a flat in West Hampstead. I imagine letting her out on this promontory and watching her run free. Her survival would be short-lived, probably. She would make an ideal seal-snack. And chinchillas aren't famed for their love of kelp and sea-grasses. Even clever ones, who can say 'sausages'.

Mum seems quiet. 'Away with the fairies, that one,' Papa Tom would often say, when her eyes were gazing at nothing. I reach into the rucksack and check my phone. No messages. I send one to Bella:

'On beach hoping pirates will kidnap me. Miss u. x'

I press 'send' and see that Mum is watching me. My ears flush hot with guilt. I want to explain that I know she is happy here in the marshes and it is really nice to be with her, but I don't really get her big, empty sky thing, or her need to be quiet and still.

'Shall we get going?' asks Mum, her hand on my arm. I could swear she's a mind-reader sometimes.

'Where to?' I reply. I always like to know where we are heading and, if possible, how long it will take.

'The steam railway for ice creams. OK?' Mum is trying hard. The least I can do is show some enthusiasm.

'Great,' I say and give her a squeeze. I have visions of stealing the engine and driving at full speed back to London. Mum is smiling at me intently.

'What?' I ask defensively. I've probably got mayo all over my chin or something.

'Remember when you started calling me Anna instead of Mum?' she asks. 'You were about six and decided one day that first-name terms would be more – equal.'

'Precocious brat,' I say, apologetically.

'It was just a phase – you wanted to be grown up. Dad and I thought it was funny,' grins Mum. 'It doesn't seem long ago, except there's a young woman looking back at me now.' Mum is giving me the once over again. I feel a little self-conscious. 'A blossoming beauty,' she grins. 'It suits you here.'

I love those rose-tinted specs of hers. Lucky she doesn't have X-ray vision, like Superman, or she would see the calendar in my brain and the crosses marking off the days until we can go home.

16

'And it was a dare so Sibby, that's the bratty one, stuck one of Mum's hat pins right through her left nostril and we had to take her to hospital.'

Bella is recounting the latest adventures from the Farrell household, where her two little cousins from Yorkshire are staying for a week. I'm holding my mobile between my right shoulder and my ear, so my hands are free to drain the rice, which is soft, fluffy and steaming in its boiling water on the hob. As I move it towards the sink, scalding water vapour wraps itself round my wrist. I throw the rice pan into the colander, dropping my phone on the floor in the process.

'OUCH!' I shout.

'Jaz? What happened?' Bell's voice is shrieking into the slate floor tiles.

'First degree burns. Nothing to worry about,' I sigh into the slightly dented receiver. My wrist has red welts across it. In order to run it under the cold tap, I need to scrape up the rice, which has gone everywhere, even up the wall.

'Are you OK now?' asks Bella.

'Think I'll live,' I respond. 'Rice isn't usually fatal.'

'Actually, it is sometimes, if it's reheated,' Bell informs me. She's so literal sometimes.

'Doesn't seem to affect the seagulls,' I point out. A whole generation of them around Trafalgar Square has been brought up on discarded takeaways.

'But they don't microwave it, do they?' says Bell, rather dismissively.

This conversation isn't going anywhere interesting. 'What happened to Silly, or Filly, whatever her name is?' I ask, filling a bowl with cold water and plunging my wrist into it.

'She had this sort of put-on panic attack when the doctor said the hole might never heal up completely. Auntie Rachel was SO mad at Mum, a) because it meant she had to cut short her holiday with Ralph the Rutter and b) she'd said the girls were NEVER to have their noses or navels pierced. And Pops made it worse by printing off a picture of an African girl with tribal spikes through her nose and cheeks and telling Auntie Rachel that a precedent had been set and maybe she should see it as a rite of passage.'

'Sounds more exciting than this end,' I tell her. I'm wondering how I can scoop up all the rice and keep it warm without reheating it. I don't want to kill us with dinner and have Dad find us covered in flies on Friday night.

'At least you went looking for pirates,' answers Bella. 'I spent the afternoon playing hide-and-seek with the pair of them dressed in my old tutus over their jeans.'

There is a smell of burning. The veggie chilli Dad made and froze at the weekend is defrosting and sizzling in the saucepan. I take it off the heat but it's too late. The bottom is black and crusty. I feel suddenly defeated and useless. I just had to reheat the chilli and cook the rice. It's not rocket science.

'Bell, I've got to go,' I tell her. 'Crisis.'

Seconds later I am sending for the cavalry with a six-word text to Dad:

'Pls call me – have toasted dinner'

He's rung twice already today, to check up on us. He spoke to Mum for about twenty minutes while I was eating my ice cream at the steam railway. He tells her funny things about the people in his open-plan office. There's Halitosis Henry, who is the boss; Booby Brad, who is a transvestite at the weekends; Fiddly Phil, who snaps his pencils when he's uptight; and Soggy Simon, who jogs to work and never has time for a shower.

My phone is ringing.

'Hey you,' says Dad, his mouth full of something squishy. 'Who you gonna call? Toast busters!' He starts to hum the theme tune.

'Ugh, gross, what are you eating?' I ask him.

'Piece of watermelon,' he answers, slurping. I just know that drips are running down his chin and his shirt. 'How's it going?'

'Um. Chilli black and crispy. Rice mostly up the wall.

Keen to hear any suggestions,' I confess.

'Scrape off the top layer of chilli carefully. Soak the carbonised bit of the pan overnight. Rice can be rounded up and put in colander and boiling water poured through,' he says, no trace of sarcasm in his voice. I can see why he's the firm's financial troubleshooter. Nothing ruffles him.

'It won't kill us, will it?' I ask, just to be sure.

'Unlikely, unless you add arsenic,' he says, cheerfully.

'Thanks, Dad. Wish you were here,' I tell him, gratefully. 'How's everything at home?'

'Much too quiet. I have to keep opening beers just to hear a noise.'

'James Jelly-Belly.'

'Didn't say I was drinking them,' he adds.

'Very funny.'

'I'm saving them for Stephen. He's coming over later,' he adds.

'Stephen only drinks red wine,' I state. 'He's not a lager lout like you.'

'Oh dear. *Quel dommage*. It would be a travesty to waste them, though, wouldn't it?'

'How many are there?'

'Um. Fifteen. It is *horribly* quiet, you see. I think I am a little traumatised.'

'Hmm. I'm going now. Try to be good, Daddykins.'

'I will, chumpkin. Night night.'

I'm scraping the chilli into another pan and scooping rice

out of the plug hole, wondering how often this happens in restaurants. There must be loads of people with dyspraxia working as chefs, but they probably don't do icing, or cream swirls, or things requiring a steady hand, like lettering. In my case, a two-year-old would probably do a better job. Or Silly and Filly, Bell's cousins.

Luckily, in two minutes, everything looks back to normal and I am lighting the candles on the table.

'Mum!' I yell. 'Ready!'

There is no reply, but five seconds later I hear a terrible crashing noise and a yell coming from outside. I rush to the veranda and see one of the wooden garage doors is open. A moment later I am inside the concrete building and there is Mum, surrounded by packing crates and boxes, yanking at something as if her life depended on it.

'Time this came out,' she says, almost breathless.

I move closer and see that the object of her focus is curved and attached to a frame. It has an arm missing and there are cobwebs across its struts. It is wedged between an old workbench and a chest of drawers that has a Spanish guitar leaning against it, upturned and half-covered in a sheet.

Papa Tom's rocking chair.

I help Mum ease it away from the bottom drawer of the chest, which has collapsed onto the floor, spilling its contents of tarnished silver cutlery. We stand it the right way up in the space near the doors. It moves backwards and forwards slightly, as if in welcome, like an old wounded soldier happy to be reunited with his family.

'We can mend the arm,' says Mum, on her hands and knees so that she can reach under the workbench, where the wooden arm is lying. 'It just needs to be screwed back together. Papa Tom's tools are still here somewhere.'

This is quite an optimistic statement for someone who doesn't even change light bulbs in case she damages her hands.

After some more rooting around, the metal toolbox is located. It makes a grating noise as Mum opens the lid. We peer inside at the selection of instruments, neatly laid in compartments according to size – screwdrivers, a hammer, a knife sharpener, saw blades and packets of nails and screws. She rests her hand lightly on the thick handles for a moment, as if caressing them.

'This one, I think,' she says, lifting a medium-sized screwdriver with a black handle from the second compartment.

'The bit that fits in the groove isn't wide enough,' I point out. 'Try this one.' I give Mum a larger tool with a yellow plastic grip. As she positions the arm over its support, I hold it steady. The screw slots easily back into its hole in the main frame. Mum starts to turn the driver delicately. Half a centimetre down, the screw is resisting and Mum is using both hands to no avail.

'Give it some welly,' I hear Papa Tom say. I close my eyes and I'm five again, trying to mend the wheel of my toy barrow, in which sits, very regally, my favourite white teddy. We are in this same space, using the workbench, which is in the middle of the garage. There is a strong smell of wood varnish as Papa Tom is sealing the doors ready for winter. He is putting his wide, strong hand over mine, and together we are turning the screw which is attaching the wheel back onto the frame.

'Like this, Mum,' I say, laying my hand over her narrower one and adding my strength to the momentum of the turn. The screw spirals down sweetly and the arm is secured. She smiles at me.

'Clever you,' she responds.

'It could do with a rub down,' I suggest, running my hand over the rough edges of the seat. 'And maybe some varnish.'

Mum's eyes are alive with excitement. She is already scouring shelves for sandpaper, quietly humming her all-time favourite song. She starts beating out a rhythm on a can of white paint, the contents of which must have long since gone completely solid. When she gets to the chorus, I join in with a chisel on the side of the workbench.

'She's leaving now, and my heart it is a breakin', like that old fence in the corale,' we sing, much too raucously, a ridiculous inflection on the word 'corale'. It sounds more like a hiccup. Mum carries on, in her best country voice, and I decide to do a harmony for the final line – 'Oh Eloise, don't leave me, precious girl.' Our voices blend and resonate around the damp garage, making the assortment of stacked tins reverberate, sweeping through the old, stale air in damp corners like a fine broom.

We hold the last note until our lungs give out. The sound cascades from the cluttered space, spreading across the marshes into the deep rose and orange horizon. Mum, flushed with exertion, is giving me a nod of approval. It is her highest form of praise – understated, but titanic at the same time.

When we emerge from the garage, dusty and with varnish under our nails, dinner long forgotten, it is almost dark. The last stripes of deep pink light are layered on the horizon. A stiff breeze is blowing through the marsh grasses. Possum, who is already starting to look lean, like a brown tiger, is washing his paws on the veranda. The resident frogs are laughing in monotone like wind-up toys. And in the distance, the sails of the turbines are turning, transforming the wind song into a silent surge of power and stealing it away to some unknown location.

Mum puts her arms round me and rests her chin on my shoulder, watching the silhouetted windmills. I can smell the coconut shampoo and conditioner she uses, tinged with the chemicals in the varnish that now covers Papa Tom's rocking chair. Her breath is warm on my ear. It's making my neck come out in goose bumps.

'I think I'm going to have to eat you,' she states, pretending to bite my neck. I squirm and wriggle away from her.

'Give me two minutes, and dinner will be on the table,' I respond. 'Only this time, please come when you're called.' I wag my finger at her and she looks contrite as she sits by Possum on the veranda and mouths 'Sorry,' at me.

I half-run inside to the kitchen, where my mobile tells me I have seven missed calls – all from Bella, who probably thinks we've been murdered by the marsh monster or something. I send a quick text saying 'All ok, speak l8er' to her, and then fill the kettle with water. It's lucky Dad suggested that, or I would have put the rice in the microwave and it would probably have exploded, knowing my luck.

I turn on the hob and, after a few moments, the salvaged chilli starts to bubble in its new pan. It smells fantastic. The kettle clicks off and I pour the boiling water through the colander. The rice steams invitingly. The plates don't feel too bad, so I decide not to bother heating them. Dad wouldn't approve, so I fold paper napkins with poppies on under our forks in atonement and light new candles. I singe my arm slightly as I put Mum's plate on her mat. The smell of burning hair fills the air.

'Fairly stupid to reach over the flames, dur,' I say out loud, rubbing my arm. Before I call Mum, I survey the scene. The table looks lovely. Just need to put Mum's tablets by her glass. The sink – uh-oh. That resembles the setting for Saucepan Wars – the movie. But if I turn the light off – there – it fades into shadows. Perfect.

I am about to announce that dinner is served when the space is suddenly filled with the deep, mournful sound of Tchaikovsky. I move in the direction of the source. Outside, the night amplifies the haunting melody and the frogs have become silent, holding their breath, an unlikely audience. Mum is sitting on Nana Jane's old stool on the gravel path, her cello clasped closely. In the light from the cottage, her body movements look agonised, tortured, as she works the bow backwards and forwards, lost in the drama of the music, her eyes closed, unaware of the wildness around her.

We are separated by just a few metres, but there is a universe between us. At this moment, she is unreachable, off limits. And so lost in her music, like a string tuned to breaking point. If I touch her, I think the recoil would shatter us both into a million pieces.

17

'Hey Bella,' I say, my voice a bit despondent. I'm in bed with the duvet pulled up under my chin. Outside, the wind has whipped up and is making annoying 'wooo, wooo' sounds through the open skylight window. The floral curtains are flapping, which is quite disconcerting, as if someone is breathing on them from the other side of the glass.

'Hi,' responds my mate, sleepily. 'You do realise it's one am?'

'Were you asleep?' I ask.

'No, I was just doing that thing when you lie very still with your eyelids shut,' she answers.

'Cool,' I say. My brain isn't very dependable at this time of night.

'So what was the big crisis?' she yawns.

'Mum got a bit stuck in the garage. We ended up mending my granddad's rocking chair. It works really well now.'

'Great,' replies Bella, sleepily. There is quite a silence. 'Did you manage to do dinner?' she asks. Bella has an in-depth knowledge of my culinary encounters. We were in the same class for cookery at junior school and she once took the blame for my monumentally clumsy disaster with a porcelain bowl full of sloppy chocolate cake mix, admitting to the teacher, appropriately called Miss Spooner, that she was the one who propelled it over the work surface and onto the floor. I already had five misconduct marks from various teachers – one more and I would have been sent to the Head. Bell always looks out for me, whereas Olly and Tasha often just think I'm funny. That's one reason why she's my best mate.

'Technically, I did it twice. Mum had hers cold in the end. Long story,' I reply, not inviting an explanation, in case it forces me to admit how isolated I feel. 'I've only just finished washing up. I think rice should carry a government health warning. It's not only fatal, but evil. It clumps together on the side of the pan, creating its own glue, which is like slug-slime. No one has invented a scourer which can get it off, unless the Ministry of Defence has but they're keeping it secret, like all the stuff about crop circles and spaceships.'

'We just put the rice pan in the dishwasher,' says Bella, yawning again. 'I think it's the FBI which has all the secret stuff about aliens. Or maybe the CIA. Pops saw a flying saucer once over the Heath.'

'Wow.'

'Mum says he was on some funny medication for his heart and was always having hallucinations. But I believe him. He said Mowgli growled at the spaceship and that's why he's afraid of kites.' Bella is starting to become animated now. 'He was only a puppy then. Mowgli. Not Pops. It could have traumatised him, couldn't it? Mowgli. Not Pops.'

'Maybe that's why he writes about ancient Britain, because it's the other end of the scale from UFOs,' I suggest.

'He says the past and the future are the same thing, just reversed,' says Bella matter-of-factly.

'My head hurts,' I moan. I'm no good at philosophy in the dark.

'It just depends where you are on the timeline,' she continues.

'I'm in the Dark Ages bit, where people and frogs are competing for supremacy,' I say, in between a mahousive yawn. 'If it all goes wrong, the prime minister will be green and will issue a decree that anyone found not hopping will have his or her legs pulled off and deep fried.'

'Maybe the Green Party is just a front,' observes Bella.

'I think we are uncovering a sinister plot to take over the universe,' I say.

'Yeah,' replies Bella, distracted. 'Did you ask when I can come and stay?'

'Nope. Forgot. Anytime will be fine, though,' I lie. Mum is already talking about how great it will be at the weekend when Dad comes and how it might be nice to do the Pirates Point bike ride again. Yay (not). She hasn't once mentioned the possibility of the arrival of my soul mate.

'I'm on a music course next week,' says Bell, who is consulting her diary. 'So it'll have to be after that – and before the week in Italy. I want to meet the frogs! And look for pirates. Sooo exciting!'

When I mention that she and I should definitely do a temporary life-swap, she reminds me that I would have to go to ballet and spend six hours a day for the foreseeable future sight-reading Grade Six flute music in a remote part of Essex.

'In that case, I'll pass,' I say. 'How's Adam?'

'Totally annoying. He keeps moaning about lumps in his neck. Mum thinks he's got glandular fever and insists on juicing special exotic things for him. He still went out with Sausage Girl to see the Indigo Parrots, so he can't be that ill,' complains Bella. 'Pops won't stop making fruit jokes, mostly about kumquats, and Mum laughs at them, which just encourages him. So they're all driving me mad.'

I can picture the scene. Exchanges of banter and insults. Shouting and hilarity. Commotion and emotion. I wish with all my heart that Meredith is right and time travel exists. Maybe the cottage is at the galactic centre of the cosmos, a portal to other time zones and, miraculously, I will at any moment find myself at Bella's, far from the gusting wilderness of the marsh, and the guilty weirdness of being under house arrest with my mother.

18

It's just getting light. The air smells of salt and dew and sheep. The lane near the cottage is damp and covered in snails having a morning drink. I check my watch – it's five am – and do some stretching to warm up my calves. My breath floats ahead of me, mingling with the white old man's beard in the nearby hedgerows.

I've realised that, since arriving in the marshes, I haven't sneezed once.

'Maaaaaaaa!' says a large lamb, startled by my sudden appearance.

I need to run. My head is aching from lack of sleep. My abdomen is aching from period pains. I feel slouchy and grouchy, as Dad would say. I've left Mum a note so she won't be worried. I wanted to put on it that I felt hurt that she didn't come in for dinner and lonely because her music shuts me out. And I didn't mean to grunt at her when she put her head round the door to say goodnight. Instead, I just wrote, 'Gone jogging, back soon xx'.

'Always read between the lines,' says my English teacher, Miss Garnett. Mum would be hard pushed to discover the pain beneath my simple phrase. Maybe she wouldn't even understand. She's gifted and has this other world in her soul. She's never known what it's like to be on the outside, staring in.

I think I'm being really selfish.

I start to jog. My pace is fast, determined and focused. There is an occasional crunch underfoot, and I'm sending mental apologies to all the snails I am despatching.

'Selfish is as selfish does,' I hear Papa Tom say. I see him looking over the rim of his glasses at me. It's what he always uttered when I tried to wriggle out of my chores at the cottage.

'I know, I know,' I reply. I feel my ears flushing hot. 'But she wanted to play the cello instead of eating dinner with me.' God, that sounds so petulant and pathetic. In this landscape, which is opening its huge, hooded eye to the globe of a sun, it is just a random gush of air, its particles dispersing like glitter, dazzling where they fall.

A bird with a red beak, black head and brown and white body flies above me, making a whistling noise. It is keeping pace with me exactly, its large wings labouring slowly between cruising on air currents.

'Hello birdie,' I call, grateful for the company. It feels nice having an escort. Looking at the markings, it could be a duck. It's larger than the ones on the Heath pond at home. There are probably millions of varieties, though. I decide to look it up in Papa Tom's bird dictionary when I get back.

Crunch, crunch. Oh Jaz, look where you're going. That's two more slimy souls on their way to mollusc heaven.

I check my watch. Five fifteen. A cow with pretty eyes blinks at me from behind a metal gate and breathes a heavy greeting, the air from its nostrils rising like two small clouds.

'Moo!' I say in return, already several metres beyond its stare. I'm thinking how brilliant it would be to be able to speak to animals. My blood sugar levels must be very low to be considering this.

On the spur of the moment, I decide to turn round and start running back the way I've come. I've been heading towards the sea, down a myriad of lanes, and if I go much further, finding my way back could be difficult. I'm no good with directions and these narrow, curling wisps of tarmac, with their unexpected T-junctions, all look the same.

'Moo!' I call to the cow, as I pass it again at full speed. This time, it responds with a mahousive bellow.

'Yay! A conversation!' I whoop and give a little jump in the air, which, I realise, is minus mystery bird, who obviously wasn't into U-turns.

My pace is slowing. '*Hana, dool, set, net*,' my brain repeats, regulating my stride and my breathing. I've come a long way. Every so often, when there is a gap in the hedge, I can glimpse the spire of St Saviour's. Behind it are the marsh uplands – a patchwork quilt of golden fields intersected by thin green lines.

Almost back now. And I give an involuntary shriek as something dark and menacing leaps from the obscurity of the tangled elderberry shrubs and tries to cling onto my legs with outstretched claws and wild eyes.

'Possum, you barbarian!' I tell him. (I like using Meredith's words.) My cat has scampered off back into the undergrowth, skittish and kitten-ish, waiting for his next victim. If he were a kid, he'd have a feather in his hair.

Five-thirty am.

I move to the veranda and sit on the lowest step, watching the first light cover the last traces of indigo night. My skin is damp and cool, my heartbeat steady and relaxed. I feel as if I have pure oxygen coursing through my blood. There is salt on my lips.

And stardust in my cells. My head is throbbing with the connectedness of everything. Snails, cows, birds, cats, humans – all cosmic creatures, causing global warming with their methane emissions, according to scientists. Well, maybe not the snails, but who really knows about them? And who would have ears that sensitive?

I need food. My stomach is doing somersaults and tying itself in knots like the Chinese gymnast I saw at the circus with Bella last year. My imagination is creating smells of pancakes with maple syrup and blueberries, and crispy bacon on brittle toast.

'Ready!' calls Mum – surely an ethereal voice from my subconscious breakfast dream? I turn and see a haze of fuchsia and know it has to be Mum's dressing gown and matching slippers.

'You're up!' I exclaim.

'I heard you go out,' she replies. 'And I thought that maybe pancakes would be a good way to say sorry for messing up dinner last night.' She has her hands in her pockets and looks very contrite, pale and about fifteen years old. 'You know your mother is an alien,' she says, as I approach.

'Yup,' I nod, giving her a peck on the cheek.

'Aliens have a funny way of expressing things sometimes,' she adds. 'It's not always in words.'

I wash my hands and sit down at the kitchen table, on which is laid a tempting feast (if you ignore the black tops on some of the pancakes).

'I burned the first batch,' admits Mum. 'Just take the ones from underneath.' She is looking at me as I wiggle three out and put them on my plate. 'You know, it feels so fantastic to be here with you, but emotional too. I'm thinking about my mum and dad and when I was growing up – all the dreams I had. How they've come true, really.'

'Apart from the Ferrari.'

'Yes, apart from that,' she smiles. 'It's not easy to explain, but it's as if all the phases of my life are colliding here – childhood, teens, performing, becoming a mum, then being the mum of a teenager. All the memories keep replaying, wherever I look. I see me fishing in the stream. I see you in your car seat, just a week old. Then running about with that old fishing net. On your red bike with stabilisers. Riding your racer down the lane with Dad. Then me and Dad, on my twenty-fifth birthday, watching the sun set. The years ticking away. I think my brain's on a rollercoaster, trying to come to terms with losing my mum and dad, then getting ill. When I play, it's like I'm travelling to the past and everything is stable and calm. I'm still the girl with the bright future ahead of me, with all those happy times to come.' Mum has tears in her eyes.

'You do have a bright future ahead of you, with us,' I reassure her, my hand on hers. I hate it that she seems so frightened. It makes me afraid too.

'Wouldn't it be great if we could spin the world backwards? Hang onto the people we love just a little longer,' says Mum. I get up and put my arms round her. She is gripping me so tightly, like a climber clinging to a steep rock face.

'I wasn't trying to shut you out,' she says. 'Just to make sense of things, thoughts, worries I've been bottling up. It's hard not to let go, with all this space. No lines, streets, city limits, conformity to keep things orderly, under control.'

We hold each other in silence. It feels like my sensometer, which gauges how she is from the amount of positivity in her voice, is going haywire, trying to get a bearing. It's not calibrated to cope with this level of emotion.

'What's really wrong?' I ask her at last. My heart is thudding in my chest like a woodpecker on a tree.

The pause that follows seems a beat too long.

'I'm being stupid, that's all,' she says, a gesture of her hand dismissing the idea. '"Staring into my boots," as Nana would say.'

'It's OK,' I tell her, holding her gaze. 'You know I'm never letting you go. *Never*. Everything will be all right.' Mum smiles at me, colour returning to the pale moons under her eyes. Her body visibly relaxes. Maybe she just needed some reassurance.

'Sorry Jaz,' she tells me, wiping her eyes. 'God, what a nightmare! A miserable mum and cold pancakes.'

19

I've left a message on Dad's mobile, letting him know that Mum could do with a call.

I'm still trying to understand what happened at breakfast and wishing he were here to lighten us up a little. I haven't seen Mum that bleak before, not even during her chemo cycles. She seems better now, as if a cloud has lifted. But I feel that I'm letting her down, not keeping her cheerful. Maybe having a thirteen-year-old around all the time isn't the buzz she thought it would be?

I feel weirdly drained now, so, as a distraction, I'm looking up my feathered escort from earlier in Papa Tom's bird book, which is so old it has yellow edges to its pages and a musty scent. It's taking forever because I have found, tucked inside, folded notes on lined paper. There are dates and lists of birds – herons, redshanks, gulls, avocets, turnstones, wigeons, teals – and the location where Papa Tom saw them.

One of the pages is headed, 'Seen with Jasmine, while out walking on Starlight Bay'. And suddenly I can smell the rush of the incoming tide and feel the wind whipping my face, as it did that day in August, when I was six, as we watched the yellow wagtails and willow warblers fly overhead – the start of their migration and the long journey south.

I had waved at them and shouted goodbye. Papa Tom told me how many times they had to flap their wings in order to get to their breeding ground. It was something like a zillion.

I run my finger over the spidery words: emerald damselfly, pygmy footman moth, Berwick swans (2), nightingale, pomarine skua (flying east), swifts (migrating), green woodpecker... Papa Tom had stored them all in his memory and recorded them in this very chair with his fountain pen once the sun had gone down. He tried to teach me their Latin names, but I was useless at remembering. The things that stayed in my mind were the noises each one made — especially the 'kleep kleep' of the oystercatchers, the 'plee-oo-wee' of the grey plovers and the 'fraaank' of the grey herons.

I fold the notes together again and slide them back into the front of the book carefully, my throat constricting with the surge of detailed memories. I check the chapter headings and flick through the pages until I find the section which will answer my mystery.

Here he is, my morning companion. He's a shelduck and he lives near coastal sandbars and mudflats. It says he often uses old rabbit burrows or gaps under old buildings for breeding. He can live for fourteen years. That's not long. The pintail on the opposite page can survive for up to twenty-six years.

I am thinking that I am in my fourteenth year and

nowhere near ready to fly the nest…

'Ready?' asks Mum. She is standing in the front doorway, holding the old guitar we found in the garage. I notice she is wearing the orange top I bought her – its first outing. 'Driving into town – remember?'

'Uh huh,' I reply, reluctant to leave Papa Tom's bird bible. I close it gently and place it on the low pine coffee table in front of me. I can still see the faint ring my mug of hot chocolate made, four Christmases ago, even though Papa Tom sanded it down and revarnished it.

'Wood is like us,' he had said to me afterwards. 'Wounds to the body heal, but we carry their imprint in our souls forever.'

I've often thought that's why Mum's cello sounds so sad, carved out of bark and recreated by hand with precision tools. The guitar she is holding looks equally forlorn. Its casing is scratched and battered and it has two strings missing.

'I'm going to get it re-strung,' explains Mum, as we get into the car. 'Give it a new lease of life.'

Mum is to stringed instruments what I am to pizzas. She can't resist them. If a charity wrote asking her to sponsor the rehabilitation of a double bass or a viola, she would sign up immediately.

We lock the cottage door and in another minute are setting off down the lane in the car, which has cobwebs on its side mirrors.

'You can help me choose some scrummy things for the weekend,' says Mum, upbeat. 'I thought we could have a barbecue on Saturday, if I buy one of those instant charcoal things.' She is looking at me for approval. 'And we could get Dad some mackerel, or prawns.'

I'm yawning and Mum is giving me this disapproving look. I quickly cover my mouth. 'Sorry,' I say. Car rides have always made me sleepy.

'And after the weekend, we can talk about Bella coming to stay,' says Mum, glancing at me for my response.

'Fab,' I say, moderating my excitement, trying not to betray my desire to go 'Whoooooah!' and text my mate straightaway.

'I don't think I could cope with Olivia, though,' says Mum apologetically. 'She's lovely, but so loud.'

'It's fine, Mum,' I tell her. 'I know you need quiet time at the moment. Bell and I will be like mice, promise.'

'In that case, I'll probably scream,' grins Mum. She's not a great fan of rodents. I make a mouse face at her and notice the big bags under her eyes, which have deepened since breakfast. Maybe she's not sleeping too well without Dad and his snoring serenade.

We're heading towards Penchurch, a little town by the coast on the eastern side of the marshes. Mum instinctively knows where to go, which is lucky as there are few signs. Every so often, I hear the shrill 'wheep wheep' of the steam train, which trundles every hour between Penchurch and

Salterness, carrying tourists and, in term-time, school parties, which have come to study the rare plants and wildlife.

Soon we are waiting at one of its passing points. Red lights are flashing and there is a one-arm barrier across the lane. It takes four minutes for the train to appear, and when it rattles by, all the kids on board wave at us through the open partitions. Mum waves back with exaggerated gestures. She looks a bit of a muppet. I'm hoping the tractor driver behind us isn't watching.

'WHEEP WHEEP!' goes the train. It's so loud, I jump from my seat.

'Why does it have to do that?' I ask, crossly.

'It's your hormones,' states Mum, which isn't a logical answer. 'They amplify everything. Sometimes I can hear people eating sweets in the audience. They sound like dogs crunching bones. I want to march down and snatch the packets away.'

In another five minutes we are driving along the edge of Starlight Bay, the largest area of shingle in the marshes. A flock of geese is flying low in formation over the salt flats beyond the stones. A man and a small child are digging for worms on the horizon. Two black dogs are running in the soft, water-logged area nearest the beach, ahead of their female owner, who is wearing wellies and shorts.

Everywhere, sky. I press the switch for my electric window, and as it buzzes down, warm marsh air sweeps in and wraps itself around us.

Penchurch is a small town running inland from the bay. Mum turns off the coast road and down a main street with a variety of small to medium sized shops, many selling kids' fishing nets and inflatables. The sight of so many people is a surprise after days in isolation. I was beginning to think we were the only humans in the southern marshes. Looking around, it's busy in a different way from London, where you can sometimes hardly see the pavement for pedestrians. There's no urgency in the way individuals are moving, and no collective direction. We head for the car park at the back of the main food store and pull into one of several spaces.

'It's lovely not fighting for parking,' observes Mum, who seems quite chilled, the opposite of how she is after driving even a short distance at home.

Our first stop is the music shop, which is tucked back from the main street in a small lane, next to a florist. Mum shakes her head as we go by the buckets of flowers on display outside the window. The sign reads 'Chrysanth's'. Mum's got a thing about apostrophes appearing where they shouldn't. It's catching, too. I always triple-check my work because my brain usually sneaks one or two in the wrong places.

A bell rings as we push open the door to Merry's Music. The small space is full of instruments – xylophones, bongo drums, flutes, violins, keyboards, cellos, even a baby grand in one corner with tambourines piled on top of it. There is a strong smell of wood and polish, and the sound of a violin being tuned. I expect a wizened old man in braces to appear through the curtain behind the counter with a bow in his hand. Instead, a young woman's voice calls out, 'With you in a moment!'

I exchange a glance with Mum, who looks like a kid who has entered a sweet shop with unlimited pocket money. She is running her hand over the cellos – gestures of affection as much as professional interest. I watch her hand lightly caress the neck of one like a trainer assessing a thoroughbred. Her eyes are intent and shining, her mouth slightly open in reverence.

She may be an alien, but she is at home here.

'Would you like to go round to the baker's while I sort this out?' asks Mum, sensing my foot scuffing on the ground, a gesture of boredom I've made since I was a toddler. I do a panting dog mime, paws up, so she gives me a ten pound note. 'Choose something for me.'

It's a short jog round the corner, past windows full of fishing tackle and plastic toys, and along the main street to the bread shop, which has strips of coloured plastic over the doorway to keep out the flies. The display facing me is impressive. Cakes, buns, rolls, pastries, all layered in trays. Two enormous gateaux are on raised stands, covered with yellow and pink icing, their middles empty, waiting for special greetings to be squirted in.

Two women, older than Mum, are serving behind the glass cases inside. They wear white aprons over checked shirts and matching hairbands, which look quite odd on faces so lined.

I choose a pasty and a cinnamon swirl for me and an egg sandwich and an Eccles cake for Mum, plus a tea and a lemonade. When I re-emerge through the plastic curtain, Mum is waiting, her mobile to her ear. She's laughing, so I'm guessing it's Dad on the other end, responding to my SOS.

'Jaz sends her love,' says Mum, smiling at me. 'And so do I. Yes, you too. Bye.'

She's almost blushing. Dad must have said something extra gooey. She suggests we walk the short distance down to the beach and, in less than five minutes, our feet are shifting noisily under the weight of our bodies descending the shingle bank and we are sitting down on warm stones.

'Wow!' exclaims Mum, taking in the huge canvas of sky that dominates Starlight Bay. 'Great view.'

'Yup,' I agree, more intent on unwrapping the hot mound of potato and sausage meat wrapped in golden pastry with dinosaur markings down its spine. It has two small gherkin-green eyes – a curious addition, but in keeping with this slightly quirky place.

Mum leans back on her elbows and closes her eyes. It's a bit late for her to be eating lunch and she's tired. I rummage in her bag for her tablet container and lay it on her lap. She sighs, and I'm just about to nudge her into action when a blue butterfly with white-edged wings flutters between us and lands on her cheek.

It seems to be speaking with its wings, which are agitated and moving very quickly, even though its body is stationary. It bows and hovers. Mum is looking at it and holding her breath. It hops onto her nose and flutters some more, before taking off lightly, flying in delicate, broken circles on the breeze.

'The blue ones like that are quite rare,' comments Mum. 'Do you think it's a sign?'

'It was asking you to take your tablets,' I reply.

'Don't tell me the butterflies are ganging up on me too. Grrrrr!' exclaims Mum, in semi-real frustration. I waggle my finger at her. She puts in her mouth two green capsules which contain spirulina – an underwater plant supposed to boost your immune system.

'It's just a cry for kelp,' she says, smugly.

At which point I bury my head in my hands. I'm beginning to understand why Mum and Dad were fatally attracted.

20

'The little trashers have gone!' yells Bella into my ear.

I'm sitting on a grass verge at Lambstreet Station, waiting for Dad's train to roll in. It's Friday evening. Mum and I have made a surprise dinner for him, which started out as a casserole and is now a curry. We're hoping the spices will disguise the taste of the chicken, which we overcooked because Possum dragged a bird into the kitchen and distracted us.

There were flying feathers and yowling and commotion and a chase round the table, which resulted in me grabbing Possum by the tail and Mum catching the terrified grey and white bird, which shot into the sky as soon as they reached the veranda.

'Narrow escape,' observed Mum. We watched it go until it was just a dot on the horizon. 'Wonder if it'll tell its bird friends – "You'll never guess what 'appened to me today." '

'Do birds speak cockney then?' I asked, and Mum gave me a look.

'They all speak like Dick Van Dyke in *Mary Poppins*. Everyone knows that,' she replied, sticking her tongue out at me and crossing her eyes.

By that time, the chicken was black on one side and smoke was rising from the frying pan. Possum, with his tail twitching crossly, was sitting on Nana Jane's stool, eyes wide with adrenaline.

'He thought it was a present,' I said. I was sweeping up feathers with the dustpan and brush and putting them in the bin. Mum was eyeing up a bottle of wine, but changed her mind because she had to drive to the station.

That was an hour ago. Now we're here, calm and collected, showered and fragrant. And I'm sitting away from the car, to get decent reception. Bella is still shrieking at me. Only every other word is coming through.

'Can't hear you very well,' I tell her. There is a stream of expletives. It seems the cousins have killed her iPod.

'...Flushed it down the...told Mum I was bullying... never, never coming to stay...HACKED OFF.' The rant ends in a shriek.

'I can see why you hate them. I'm glad my cousins live in Australia,' I commiserate. Mum's older brother Danny went there backpacking before university and never came back. He still sends a card at Christmas with a photo of the four of them – Danny, his partner Sue (who looks old enough to be his mum), and their sons Rock and Snow, who have a lot of tattoos. Mum said Papa Tom and Nana Jane never really got over it – the fact he went so far away and settled there. But she wasn't surprised. He had always been a wild spirit, she said, happiest plunging down white-water rapids and camping out under the stars.

'So, how are you?' asks Bell, her voice more level.

'Surviving,' I reply. 'I know all there is to know about shelducks. And Mum said you can come – soon, Bella. Please!'

'I'll speak to my mum…call you…' A monotone signals that the call has been cut off. Bella's stress seems a million miles away in an instant. There is nothing but bird song and stillness. Moments later, the expected train makes an entrance, a messenger from the city. It glides in and opens its automatic doors, displacing some of the air-conditioned sterility inside. The carriages are half-full, surprisingly. The marshes must be home to lots of commuters.

Dad appears, a little rumpled, tie loose around his neck, his suit jacket over his arm. Mum is already out of the car, waving at him, looking less like a muppet this time and more like a schoolgirl with a crush. Dad passes through the unmanned ticket barrier, and in three strides is lifting her up off the ground in a hug. And he's kissing her. Yuk, yuk, yuk.

'Hey!' he calls to me, when he gets his lips back. 'Missed you.'

'Good,' I answer. I stroll down the grass verge and then launch myself at him, hugging him so fiercely I feel his ribs contract.

The train is moving away almost noiselessly, like a snake sliding stealthily into undergrowth. The other passengers who got off with Dad have disappeared in waiting cars or on foot and we are alone now, apart from a blackbird, which is putting on a virtuoso performance just for us. We give it a little round of applause before Mum gets into the driving seat and Dad and I have a little mock fight over the front passenger position. (I let him win, of course.)

'What've you been up to, then?' asks Dad, his mouth full of the stale peanuts he's just found in the glove compartment.

'Lots of lovely nothing,' sighs Mum, smiling. Dad turns to look at me and I cross my eyes. He grins.

'We did do one thing,' I say. 'You'll see it when we get back.'

'Any clues?' he asks.

I simulate the sound of Papa Tom's rocking chair, complete with squeaky frame. Dad frowns. 'You've trained a troupe of marsh frogs to sing the *Hallelujah Chorus*?'

'Nice guess, but way off,' I say.

'You've got Nana's Jane's clothes mangle working?'

'Nope.'

'You've constructed and fitted a cat flap for Possum?' Dad knows that the chances of Mum and I achieving such a practical feat are as likely as dogs dancing on the moon.

'Give up then,' he says, closing his eyes in the evening sunshine. Mum has this smug little smile on her lips. I can see it in the driver's mirror. Her right hand rests lightly on the wheel. Her left is on Dad's thigh and his fingers are closed over it. She seems totally relaxed, flowing with the contours of the lanes. It must be the Dad factor.

Nana Jane used to say that he has a good aura. She could see lights around people, or darkness, especially as she got older. I think she's right. He's nice to be around. And he's the one people always approach to ask directions, or the time. Mum and I laugh about it. She calls him the Pied Piper because animals follow him about too, especially big ones like cows and horses. Luckily you don't get many of those loose on Hampstead Heath.

We slow to a stop to let a flock of sheep cross the road from one field to another. They are very vocal, uttering high-pitched 'baaaaa' sounds as if affronted that they are being moved on. It reminds me of the big sales in London, where massive groups of people throng through department stores, bundled together, bags held close to their chests, complaining and chattering.

The sky is full of pink candyfloss clouds. I take a photo on my mobile and send it to Tasha – and then remember she is in Japan, visiting her grandparents, so it will probably cost her a thousand pounds to receive it.

Red sky at night, shepherds' delight.

My gaze rests on the person in a T-shirt over loose trousers and heavy boots, blonde hair tucked up into a baseball cap, ushering the sheep with short, sharp commands. This young, pretty female shepherd doesn't exactly look delirious. She closes the first gate and as she follows the sheep into the field, she makes eye contact with Dad and her face lights up in a big smile. She gives him a little wave as she closes the second gate.

Mum glances at me and raises her eyes. Dad just shrugs defensively as Mum accelerates, quite noisily. I think he must have been the inspiration for that advert where women are driven crazy by a man's deodorant and start chasing him. I glance back down the lane. No stampeding sheep and shepherdess running at full tilt, hair blowing in the wind.

It's a stupid idea, when you think about it.

We pull into the gravel driveway of the cottage. Dad gets out and opens my door for me. Mum nods that I should run on ahead, to introduce our surprise. As I move round the side of the house I can hear a familiar sound, and when I reach the steps I stop dead. Papa Tom's chair is rocking on the veranda.

Mum and Dad, arm in arm, have appeared behind me and are also staring at the empty chair, gently moving backwards and forwards. Mum's hand is on her mouth. Then Possum suddenly runs like a lunatic from under the veranda to a bush, then back out onto the gravel, where he leaps up to try to catch a passing moth, before landing and rolling onto his back, his paws in the air.

'There's your culprit,' says Dad. 'He probably jumped off the seat when he heard the car.'

By this time, the chair has become motionless. On examination, Mum finds some cat hairs, so Dad's theory seems correct.

'Weird creature,' I tell him, stroking his stomach. He purrs and moves his front claws in and out. Dad sits in the chair and pulls Mum onto his lap. He motions for me to join them.

'We've only just mended it,' I protest, but Dad isn't having it and in five seconds I am sitting on his other knee and we are rocking together as if on the bow of a ship on a rough ocean.

'I actually feel sick,' says Mum. 'It's like that day we went to Calais in a force five gale.'

'Only without the throwing-up noises all around us,' I say. Mum cringes at the memory.

'It wasn't that bad,' comments Dad. 'You could still see the cliffs coming home.'

'We all know you've got Viking blood,' says Mum, pinching his nose.

'Which is why you can eat so many puds,' I add, poking his belly.

'OK, OK!' he protests, putting his feet down to stop the rocking motion. 'I give in. How about I have a shower and then I'll sort out dinner and you two ladies can relax?'

'Dinner's done,' I announce proudly. Dad looks surprised and pleased.

'But I'll take you up on your offer,' says Mum. 'I'm going to flop out for a little while until you're ready.' She gives him a kiss on the cheek, then moves off towards the door, swaying her hips like a model. Dad whistles and she throws him a look which says 'out of your league'. He laughs out loud.

'How's she been? Really?' he asks me, when Mum's out of earshot.

'Mostly good,' I reply. 'Apart from the day with the pancakes. She cheered up totally after you rang, though.'

Dad shrugs as if to say 'of course', a gesture which turns into a big, overblown stretch that untucks his shirt from his trousers. He never looks smart for long.

'Glad you're here,' I tell him.

'Very glad to be here,' he replies. His eyes glance up to the bedroom where Mum is taking a nap and I detect a fleeting look of concern.

'I'll see if Mum wants anything,' I tell him, emulating her sexy walk and sending him a Marilyn Monroe kiss.

'You two, what are you like?' he calls after me.

Mum's lying on her bed, her head and shoulders propped up by pillows. Her eyes are closed and she's breathing softly, although I can tell that she's not asleep. Her mouth curls into a smile – she senses I'm here – and her right hand pats the space next to her, an invitation I've loved since I was old enough to escape from my cot and pay an early morning visit.

She opens one hazel eye and looks at me. 'Hey,' she says.

'How are you?' I ask, stroking the hair off her face.

'Amazing,' she replies.

'Hmm,' I say, unconvinced. 'Would you like anything? Glass of water. Glass of wine. Nibbles. Dinner in bed. Dad to do his nude streaker thing?'

She makes a wavering motion with her hand, tempted. 'Glass of water would be nice. Thank you,' she says, sleepily.

There is water in a jug on the pine dressing table and a glass which Nana Jane painted with irises. I fill the glass and put it on the bedside table. Mum pats the bed again and I ease myself onto it. She beckons me closer with her finger, until my cheek is right next to her face. Then she flutters her eyelashes so that they brush my forehead like a fairy's broom. I respond with mine against her cheek.

Butterfly kisses. They have lightly swept between us a thousand times, often the last exchange before sleeping, or the first after waking. It's something Mum and I have kept to ourselves, a coded expression of love. A secret girl thing.

I save the cow kisses for Dad.

'Thank you,' whispers Mum, halfway between here and dreamland. She puts her arms round me and gives me a soft hug. 'Don't let Dad eat all the curry,' she says in my ear.

Within moments, her breathing is deep and regular. I lie in her embrace, feeling her chest rising and falling, her breath softly exploring the contours of my face. I'm sleepy too, drifting with her, my eyelids heavy and sinking deeper towards my cheeks.

A noise nearby reverses the reverie. It seems I've been

here just a moment, but Dad has appeared dripping in the doorway, wearing only a towel. I motion for him to be very quiet, a finger to my lips. He nods and creeps in, opening the creaky pine wardrobe as quietly as possible and taking jeans and a T-shirt off two hangers. These clank a bit, but Mum doesn't stir. He is about to start dressing, but I pull a face. He has been known to hop about and fall onto the bed when putting on trousers. Sighing, he skulks off down the hallway, his feet petulantly floppy and his clothes bundled in his spare hand.

I wiggle out from under Mum's arm and gently slide off the bed. It's evening now, almost dark. We must have been lying here longer than I thought. As I'm taking a folded yellow blanket from the bottom of the wardrobe to lay over Mum, Possum arrives at the top of the stairs. He takes in the scene, saunters to the end of the bed, hops up and makes himself cosy next to the curve of Mum's belly.

I drape the blanket over Mum's legs and upper body, avoiding the interloper.

His superior expression tells me he is the chosen one and he is asserting his right to be nearest to Mum. His fur is full of dust from his escapades in the bushes and he has tiny green sticky balls down the backs of his legs.

'You look like a wild cat,' I whisper, stroking his head. His paw jabs at my wrist, letting me know he's not in the mood for pampering. 'Fine, Ragtag. Just remember who feeds you when Dad's not here, OK?'

Dad, fully clothed, is sitting on the veranda step, drinking a beer straight from the bottle. He looks thoughtful and is gazing far away, towards the wind turbines.

'You should cut your toenails,' I say, as I sit down next to him and lean my head on his shoulder. 'The little ones are totally gross.'

'Let's see yours,' counters Dad. Reluctantly, I take my trainer and sock off. Dad peers down at my purple-painted baby toe, leans forwards to sniff it and then looks at me. 'Horrible. And smelly. I rest my case.'

'You're mean,' I respond, pummelling his arm with my fists. Normally he would wrestle with me until I beg for mercy. But the fight's gone out of him. He takes another swig of his beer.

'I might be growing them for charity,' he says, after a long pause.

'What charity would want them?' I ask, incredulous.

'Save the Nail,' he grins.

'Ugh,' I groan. 'Mum says you're not to eat all the curry, by the way.'

'She needn't have worried. Possum got there first. There was only a bit of green pepper left. He even ate the onions.' Dad's face doesn't crack. 'I'll do us some scrambled eggs when she wakes up.'

'God, it took us ages as well. That cat really freaks me out sometimes,' I seethe, eyes almost instantly filling with tears. Dad looks at me, eyebrows raised in mock offence. I have the capacity to go from nought to ballistic in about two seconds. Better than any Ferrari. 'Sorry,' I say. 'Can we get a takeaway? I just really feel like curry tonight.'

'I'm sorry,' he says, putting an arm around my shoulder. 'Just teasing. Not a very good wind up, was it?'

'Not one of your best,' I reply. 'I'm a bit…'

'Werewolfie?' suggests Dad.

'Yup,' I agree.

'Luckily, I have the antidote,' he says, reaching out to a carrier bag on the veranda. He hands it to me and I open it. Inside is a cream box tied with cream ribbon. It looks dead posh. The lettering is in gold. The words read 'Hammonds of London – chocolatiers since 1892'.

'Hope that isn't the sell-by date,' I grin.

'It's a little thank you from both of us,' Dad states. 'Mum says you've been great.'

'Wow!' I exclaim and, without thinking, give Dad the biggest cow kiss in the world.

21

'Dude, I stood up for the whole wave!' screeches Olly into my ear. 'I've been total rubbish all week but Lars said that if I did it, he'd give me his board (ha ha) and this humongous wave came almost out of nowhere and I was paddling about and caught it and it was like a dream and I was up and riding it like a pro. *God*, Jaz, I *love* surfing!'

'What's that in the background?' I ask her. I can hear something bleeping.

'My hospital monitor,' she replies dismissively. 'Look, everyone falls off at the end. It's not serious. Just bruises. And a bit of concussion. And Lars brought his board in. I've got it here.'

Several slurpy kissing noises; lips on polyfibre.

'OK,' she continues. 'I'm going to take a photo of it and send it to you, so you can see where he signed it. I'll have to call you back. Baaaa for now.' And she is gone. Friendship with Olly is like a pass to unlimited rides at an adventure park. Every encounter is full of excitement, energy and shrieking. Even her parents say they think the nurses forgot to turn down her volume dial when she was born.

The contrast between her high velocity assault on my brain and the tranquillity I'm surrounded with on the veranda is doing my head in. I've still got my mobile to my ear when it sneezes to let me know the surf visual has arrived. It's not just a photo, but a twenty-second film of Olly cuddling the board and pointing to a squiggle, which she is saying is Lars's 'cute' writing. And she introduces me to Dom, the nurse who is acting as cameraman.

'And he's really *hot* too, aren't you, Dom?' Olly is saying, grabbing the phone and turning it on him. 'See? Ha ha ha ha!' There is a glimpse of a dark-haired, thin guy of about twenty, grinning at the floor, then it all goes blank.

She's the only person I know who would have concussion and still be giggling. Maybe it's shock. I send her a text in reply:

'Fab! Thks and get well soon dude!!'

A brown furry creature with a long body suddenly runs along the bottom veranda step and pauses, sniffing the air. I hug my knees up to my chest in case it's some sort of rabid rat. My movement makes it scurry away. It hurries as if it's late for an appointment, glancing back over its shoulder and giving little shudders.

Something else to look up in Papa Tom's flora and fauna library. My new knowledge is definitely going to impress Adam, especially if I can manage to remember the Latin names. Maybe it'll prove I've got a brain after all.

The sky is looking quite threatening, naturally, as we are about to set off on a marathon cycle ride to Pirate's Point and right round to Starlight Bay. Mum insists she's up for it and she and Dad are busy packing a picnic. Laughter keeps spilling from inside the cottage. Making rolls isn't that much fun, in my experience.

There's an ominous rumble from the dark horizon and Possum, who is, as usual, sitting on Papa Tom's rocking chair, stands up abruptly with his tail arched and fluffed up. He jumps down onto the veranda and walks past me haughtily, disappearing inside the front door. The chair's curved runners shift forwards and backwards a few times before coming to a stop.

'Coward!' I call after him. 'The thunder's miles away. I hope.'

Overhead, the sky is still bright blue, with soft clouds dotted about. A pale half-moon, like a mirage, is suspended in the west, amongst them. Maybe it forgot to leave? Maybe the earth stopped spinning and no one noticed. But then the wind would stop, whereas it's whipping up – the washing on the rotary line is billowing and flapping as it turns, like it's performing a mad Russian military dance.

Perhaps this agitated air will blow the storm away. It's quite hard to tell its direction, because the weather vane on top of the garage is locked solid, the metal fox facing forever south. To the west, the turbine sails are circling steadily. They're not quite synchronised. As I'm staring at them, my vision becomes a blur and the sails are circular saws, burning into my brain.

Storms always give me headaches. I'm not very good at dealing with changes in pressure.

'Are the Three Musketeers ready?' asks Dad, who is wearing *those* shorts, a T-shirt and a fleece.

'Look,' I say, pointing to the accumulating funnels of dark clouds to the south.

'Spot of rain,' says Dad, shrugging.

'There was thunder,' I tell him.

'It'll be fine,' he responds. It's the ever-optimistic Venture Scout in him.

'Wales,' I say, eyes narrowed. Our trip to Mount Snowdon when I was eight has gone down in history. Dad is famous for ignoring weather warnings and relying on his instincts. We set out as we would when walking over the Heath, carrying lightweight jackets. No hats or gloves. To be fair, it was warm and sunny at the bottom. But things changed.

We weren't the only family trapped halfway up the slopes that day, in freezing mist that descended like a veil and cut visibility to dangerous levels. There were some smiley Germans in shorts too, who thankfully had come prepared with extra sausages and postage stamps that unfolded into thermal blankets. We sang songs to keep cheerful, mostly from Wagnerian operas, so Mum was OK. Dad and I just 'la la la-ed'.

'It was an adventure,' said Dad, when the mountain rescue team led us down to safety four hours later. Mum and I vowed never to trust him again after that.

'It's going east,' states Dad, after studying the direction of the flapping washing.

We are huddled in an abandoned wooden shack, once used for observing birds, somewhere between Pirate's Point and Starlight Bay, and rain is sheeting in through the open window and the cracks in the rotten door and walls. There is just enough room for us and the bikes. Mum is putting a brave face on, but looks pale and exhausted. When lightning hammered down into the field next to us and the clouds opened, we were moving through open land, with nothing in sight to shelter behind. It took ten minutes of fierce pedalling to reach this hideout on the perimeter of the bird observatory.

'The wind must have changed,' says Dad, pouring Mum a cup of steaming tea from the flask. She takes it gratefully and wraps both hands round it.

'It's a classic Ballantyne picnic,' she smiles, wiping rain drops from her drenched forehead. More bright flashes are followed by thunder rolling overhead, reverberating in my chest.

'I'll go and get the car,' states Dad, brushing some stray strands of hair from her cheek.

'Don't be silly,' says Mum. 'It'll pass. It's like this on the marshes. Things change quickly.'

I unwrap an egg roll and pass it to her. She takes a big bite and ends up with cress sticking out of her lips. I try to poke it in for her because she's still clutching her tea. She tries sucking at the same time and pulls a face. It's so stupid, we all get the giggles.

'You look cress-fallen,' says Dad. We groan. His puns are getting worse.

Five minutes and several rolls and crisps later, sunlight is shafting through the viewing hole and the torrents of water have reduced to a plip-plop on the corrugated roof. There's a strong smell of damp vegetation and the deep drone of a mahousive bee as it begins its pollen-collecting rounds again.

'What did I tell you?' says Mum.

'Safe to set off?' asks Dad, now out of our hut and peering at the receding black clouds. The beam falling to earth in their wake is almost phosphorescent. The wet pasture land around us looks as though it is lit by a thousand camera lights. The sheep have become Hollywood stars. Some of the spring lambs are flouncing about, noses to the wind, sensing a change in the air. Their mums just munch the wet grass greedily.

After packing up the picnic, we push the bikes back onto the lane and start to ride again. Dad's mountain bike doesn't have a mud-guard, so his back is soon spattered with brown water marks.

'Look!' says Mum, stopping for a moment and gazing

skywards. A flock of a few hundred small, brown birds is flying overhead, beating their wings fast and gliding in turn. The sound reminds me of wet sheets being shaken in the wind. 'Swifts,' she says quietly. 'Leaving for winter.'

It's the first of August. A shiver passes up my spine. It suddenly feels like change is sweeping across the marshes with the shadows of the clouds. I notice the first blackberries are in the hedgerows next to us and that freshly cut circular bales are appearing in some of the wheat fields to the north.

'*Tempus fugit*,' as Meredith is always saying. Time flies.

A rainbow arcs across the estuary to the east, where showers are still falling, interspersed with sun. It seems to touch land less than a mile away.

'Let's see if there's a pot of gold,' suggests Mum, starting to pedal.

'I'll have a private jet if so,' Dad calls after her. Mum waves at him in a way that says 'no chance – finders keepers'. He motions for me to speed up so we can overtake her. I point to a red triangle sign set into the verge which warns that ducks may be crossing the road. A few metres further ahead, Dad has to screech to a stop when a startled pheasant launches itself into the air at head height, clucking and squawking in indignation.

'That's fine,' he shouts after it, 'but you won't be so cocky in eleven days' time.' I look perplexed. Dad makes a rifle with his arm and utters a click, click, BANG! 'The glorious twelfth,' he says darkly. 'Not so great if you happen to be a pheasant.'

'That's horrible,' I say.

'It's tradition.'

'Then tradition sucks,' I comment, pedalling again. The lane ahead is empty. Mum is out of sight. She's probably counting her gold already and working out how many cello sanctuaries she can set up.

'You're right. It's fowl,' he calls, in a booming, Shakespearian voice. Dad is definitely becoming more extrovert, as if he's expanding into the space. He is sticking his tongue out as he passes me, crouched low over his handlebars, like one of the racers in the Tour de France, only without the Lycra and the silly helmet.

We pass the entrance to the Glade Observatory. A large sign with a swan on it welcomes visitors to the bird centre and a red arrow points up a long gravel drive towards a low building and a car park. In the distance, beyond the centre on our left, a group of Japanese people with cameras are taking photos of a mist net. Papa Tom told me the nets are used to catch birds so they can be tagged and monitored, particularly at this time of year, when winter flocks arrive and migrating ones leave.

I'm thinking that a photo of a bird trapped in a net wouldn't be my idea of a happy holiday snap, when I notice that the rainbow ahead is fading. All that's left of it is the top of the arc, a downturned clown's mouth, colours smudging into one another randomly.

Dad and I freewheel round a corner, and suddenly we are slamming on our brakes in the same instant, bracing against our pedals to avoid being thrown over our handlebars.

Mum is lying crumpled in the lane, her bike partly on top of her. Her right leg is covered with blood. She isn't moving.

'Jesus Christ!' exclaims Dad and, in a nanosecond, he's on the ground, easing the bike off her limbs, saying her name over and over.

'Hey,' she responds, opening her eyes and smiling at him. 'What took you so long?'

'Don't try to move,' Dad soothes, reaching for his mobile. I've already got mine out, but there is no reception. I notice his hands are shaking. He throws his phone down in frustration.

'Ride as fast as you can to the bird centre and ask them to call an ambulance, and to send anyone with medical training in the meantime,' Dad tells me. 'Mum's going to be OK,' he adds, his voice level and reassuring. I'm already on my way, standing over my pedals to get greater speed. My heart is banging in my chest and my tongue has gone completely dry.

I can't get the image of Mum out of my mind.

It seems to take forever to reach the turning to the centre. My tyres skid a little on the ruts in the gravel on the driveway. I'm biting my lip, and after one of the jolts I can taste blood. If feels as if it's running down my chin. I wipe it carelessly on my hoodie sleeve and notice streaks of red against the blue. The building's in view. Another thirty seconds and I'm running through the open glass doors into a reception area.

There's no one here, just a desk and stands full of leaflets with birds on the front. A phone is ringing. It clicks and beeps, reverting to answerphone. There are voices nearby, though, and looking through the full-length windows ahead of me, I can see the Japanese tourists, listening to a balding man in dark trousers and a blue shirt with a crest on it. To the side of them, there are a few other people in matching sweatshirts – centre staff, probably.

I'm banging on the glass, attracting the man's attention. He motions for me to come through the door at the side of the reception desk. As I appear, some of the tourists gasp and point.

'My mother's had an accident,' I blurt out to the man, whose face looks familiar. 'She's in the road over there. We need an ambulance and anyone who's medically trained.'

'Is she on her own?' he asks me, motioning for one of his colleagues to take over the group.

'My dad's there,' I reply.

'Are you hurt?' he says, taking in my blood-smeared chin and gore-stained sleeve.

'I'm OK,' I tell him. 'Please come now.' My voice is trembling. I must look pathetic.

'I'm Ferdie, by the way,' says the man, 'the countryside ranger for the marshes. And that's my son, Ethan.' He glances back at the black-haired boy of about fifteen, who is jogging towards us. My head is trying to fill with images of an encounter in a small kitchen, long ago, but my brain can't accommodate them. Ethan doesn't make eye contact with me, but when we reach a green Land Rover in the car park, he lets me get in the front passenger seat. In moments, Ferdie is driving fast down the track and turning left into the lane.

'How far down here is it?' he asks.

'About another hundred metres,' I reply. My whole body is shaking now. When we turn the corner, there are Mum and Dad, exactly where I left them. Except Dad has laid each bike about twenty metres either side of them in the lane, to slow any approaching cars.

'Don't worry, we'll take good care of your mum,' Ferdie tells me, as he pulls into the verge and cuts the engine. 'You stay here and keep warm.' He reaches into the back for a blue blanket, which smells vaguely of petrol. But I'm having none of that. I'm out of the car and next to Mum in ten seconds.

Dad is pressing his fleece against the wound on Mum's leg. She has goose bumps on her arms, and her face is white as snow, but she smiles when she sees me. The smile turns to a frown when she notices my chin. She raises a hand to touch it.

'I bit my lip,' I tell her and take her hand in mine. It feels like marble. Ferdie is kneeling next to her now, on the other side. He has a medical kit in a rucksack next to him. Dad is sitting back on his heels, clenching his hands together.

'I'm the local ranger,' he says to Mum. 'Can you tell me what happened?'

'She says she started falling and came to on the ground,' Dad interjects. 'We rode round the corner and found her lying here.'

'That'll teach me to chase rainbows,' Mum says, quietly, and then her face broadens into a grin. 'Hey,' she says, in a completely different tone. 'Ferdie Hartwood!'

'Hello Anna,' Ferdie replies. He gives a little nod to me and Dad. 'Old schoolfriends,' he adds.

He's the ranger Papa Tom and I visited with the wounded swan. I turn to look at Ethan, who is pacing like a wild animal, his hands in his combat pockets, near the car. He has a haunted, lost expression, partially covered by a ragged fringe. He is almost as tall as Ferdie and broad across the chest, his upper arms pushing out of his black T-shirt sleeves.

Ferdie asks Mum several questions before telling her to move her legs and her head. Mum insists on sitting up after that.

'I really am fine,' she states.

'We'll take you to the hospital. They'll want to check you over for concussion and put a few stitches in this cut,' says

Ferdie, wrapping a fresh dressing around the wound. 'Unless you'd rather I called an ambulance? It'll take half an hour to get here.'

'Quicker to come with you,' says Mum. Her bottom lip is trembling slightly.

'Can you get us all in?' asks Dad. I have a sudden vision of being the one who has to stay behind with Wild Boy, who has nothing to say to me.

'Ethan can take the bikes back to the centre for now,' replies Ferdie, who glances at his son. He nods in agreement.

'Thank you,' says Mum. 'Both of you.' She turns to smile at Ethan, who shrugs in a 'no problem' sort of way.

Ferdie brings the Land Rover up close. Dad and I help Mum into the passenger seat. The ranger wraps the blanket round her. Dad leans forwards from the back and holds out his hand.

'I'm James, by the way,' he says. Ferdie responds with a strong shake and a smile.

'Met your dad, a few years back, when this one was small,' says Ferdie to Mum, with a wink in the mirror back at me. He is turning the car round, with easy sweeps of the wheel. Ethan is standing on the verge, holding the two bikes. He nods at his dad and half raises his hand in a wave as we set off.

'Jaz told me,' replies Mum. 'You helped them save a swan. And today, it's me you've had to scrape up. Nothing but trouble, my family.'

'Here on holiday?' asks Ferdie.

'Jaz and I are here for the summer. James is down at weekends. First time for us as a family since we lost Dad. Five years ago now,' says Mum.

'Sorry,' responds Ferdie. There is warmth and compassion in his whole being. If Nana Jane were here, she'd say he has a great aura, I expect. Mum is smiling at him.

'What?' he asks.

'I was just thinking – you weren't exactly Sir Galahad material in fifth form.'

'I went to knight school,' grins Ferdie. 'A-level jousting and then a degree in Chivalry, or Chemistry. I forget. I heard you're famous.'

'Only amongst Radio Three listeners,' says Mum, modestly.

'And what do you do, James?' asks Fergie.

'Number crunching, in the City,' replies Dad. 'And part-time slave to this one,' he adds, pointing at me. The strain in his face is beginning to ease.

We pass most of the rest of the half-hour journey in silence, apart from some bursts of muffled voices through Ferdie's radio handset, fixed to the dashboard. Mum has her eyes closed. Dad and I stare out of the window at the green and gold landscape, which is slowly morphing into houses, flats, shops and the suburbia that tells us we're approaching Appleford, the largest town in the marshes.

My head is full of a hundred questions. Did Mum black

out? Is her blood pressure OK? Has she got problems with her heart? Should we be getting her back to London? Will her leg need plaster? Has the chemo thinned her bones so they snap on impact? What if a car had come along the lane when she was lying there? What if Ferdie hadn't been nearby – would the Japanese tourists have bundled us into their coach?

I feel sick and my pulse is racing. Mum seems to sense this and turns to look at me. She's pale, but calm, and gives me a reassuring smile. The tightness across my chest eases a little. *Hana, dool, set, net…* I focus on trying to minimise my rising panic by slowing my breathing.

Ferdie pulls into a parking space in front of the Accident and Emergency department of the hospital, a white-fronted, two-storey building with a large canopy over its entrance. There's an ambulance there and an elderly person on a stretcher being unloaded by two paramedics.

Dad is already out of the Land Rover, helping Mum. Ferdie is taking an emergency call about a seal caught up in a fishing net near Starlight Bay.

'Guys, I'm really sorry, but I'm going to have to go,' he says, apologetically. 'Will you be OK from here? I can drop the bikes back tomorrow. Just let me take your address…' He is fumbling in his side compartment for a pen.

'Frog Cottage,' I tell him. 'Lullington-in-the-Marsh. First house after the sign on the curvy bend.' He writes this down.

'Thank you so much,' says Dad, shaking Ferdie's hand again across the passenger seat. Mum smiles and gives him a little wave.

'Pop in for coffee tomorrow,' she says. 'Bring Ethan too.'

Noooo, I'm trying to convey by telepathy. The ranger acknowledges this with a nod and a smile. His radio is coming alive again and Dad shuts the Land Rover door. Ferdie reverses, gives us a toot, and drives off at speed. Mum watches the car until it goes out of sight.

'Life's so strange,' she says quietly.

'I know,' agrees Dad. 'Who'd have thought a seal could dial 999?'

22

'Noooo, he's not hot, Bell. He's weird. And silent. And I've got to "entertain" him when he comes for tea today.' I'm tickling Possum's ear with a stalk on the veranda. His tail is twitching. Any minute, he is going to attack.

'Maybe his silence means he's deep and brilliant,' my mate suggests. She is eating her cereal and speaking at the same time. It's making her sound a bit mental.

'Or it could be that he's an idiot,' I sigh. 'Trust me to get the only kid in the marshes who can't string two words together.'

'He's come back into your life for a reason,' says Bella. There she goes again, psychoanalysing.

'Yeah, to get on my nerves,' I say. 'Ouch! You pig, Possum.' His claw has sliced across my fingers, making two of them bleed. I suppose I had it coming.

There is the sound of tyres on gravel. My worst fears are founded. It's the Land Rover. The engine is switched off and two doors open and close.

'Gotta go, Bell. Wild Boy's here,' I say, quietly.

'Call me later. I want to know everything,' she replies in an odd whisper and cuts the call.

'Hello,' says Ferdie, cheerfully. He is pushing a bike in either hand and leans them up against the veranda. I notice he's not in his ranger gear, but a pair of chinos and a loose shirt. 'How's the lip?'

'Much better,' I reply. 'Thanks for bringing the bikes.'

'No problem. How's your mum doing?' he asks.

'Great. Eight stitches. No concussion. She's been resting,' I reply. My eyes are half-looking over Ferdie's shoulder. He takes this in.

'Ethan's just fixing the puncture in your tyre,' he says. 'We carry a kit in the Rover. Tourist season, kids on cycles that only get used once a year, complete nightmare, you get the picture.'

'It was fine yesterday,' I respond, a bit abruptly. I don't want him to think I'm just another one of those kids. Dad has appeared on the veranda.

'Hi!' he says warmly to Ferdie. 'Good timing. The kettle's on. Or I can get you a beer.'

'Beer sounds good,' replies our guest. 'Ethan won't have anything. He just drinks mineral water. He normally brings some with him.'

Great, I'm thinking. He's bound to be a purity-obsessed vegan who doesn't like music, sport or TV either. I would have more fun talking to the frogs.

Dad motions for me to go and find Ethan. I pull a face at him and his eyebrows give me this big telling off, just by the way they arch up and come together strangely in the middle.

I stuff my hands in my pockets and saunter round to the side of the cottage, where the Land Rover is parked.

Wild Boy looks up at me through his black fringe and nods, before bending over my upturned bike again. He has put something that looks like a plaster on the inner part of the wheel and is now using a pump to bring the tyre up to pressure. His hands work deftly and precisely. There is none of the fiddling and fumbling which normally accompany my attempts at maintenance.

A minute later, he is screwing the silver cap back onto the air valve and standing my bike up again, dusting off the seat with his sleeve.

'Thanks,' I say. He pushes it towards me, and when I take the handlebars, he turns and gathers up his repair kit, putting it back into the Land Rover. 'I'll put this away in the garage, then maybe you'd like to come in for a drink?' I ask. Ethan gives a little shrug, which is difficult to interpret. 'See you in a minute, then,' I say, half-hoping he'll get back in the car and lock the doors. That way, Mum and Dad will realise he's weird and won't invite Ferdie over again.

When I emerge from the garage, Ethan is sitting on the bottom veranda step, drawing shapes in the gravel with a stone. There is a flash of blue and we both watch a large dragonfly chase a fly, darting above the overgrown borders near the drive. It closes in on its prey like a heat-seeking missile. The fly disappears with such speed, it's like it never existed at all. I blink in surprise.

'Emperors are deadly,' says Ethan. His voice is deep and gentle at the same time. 'Only to flies and midges, though.'

I'm taken aback at this unexpected conversation. 'It's beautiful,' I respond, a bit lamely.

'One of the largest species in the UK. They're quite rare now.' He starts to draw with his stone again, head bent down towards the ground.

'You must know a lot about the marshes,' I say, encouragingly.

'I help Dad in the holidays,' he shrugs. He scuffs out the pattern he has created with his foot and throws his stone down, hanging his head lower between his knees. He doesn't look like he wants to talk anymore. The silence is making me shuffle from one foot to another. My ears are starting to flush with embarrassment.

'I don't want to be a ranger, though. I like buildings,' he says, unexpectedly. 'And History. I'd like to work for the National Trust or English Heritage one day.'

'Oh,' I reply, taken aback by this revelation. Ethan is checking out my face, to gauge my reaction. 'That sounds great,' I add, more enthusiastically. 'History's my worst subject, though. It just feels like it's full of old, dead things.'

'I like to know what came before – how people managed to build incredible things, like the pyramids and cathedrals and Stonehenge, with such basic tools. A lot of it's down to Maths.'

'That's my second worst subject,' I admit. 'Actually, it ties with English. I have trouble if I have to write words and numbers.' I'm amazed by how easily I've admitted this to him. I never tell people about my dyslexia normally. Ethan nods, taking this in.

'I'm rubbish at languages – and sport,' he tells me. 'Can't see the point of pain. Rugby is torture by another name,' he smiles.

'What's your favourite then, after History?' I ask, sitting on the steps next to him.

'I'm best at Maths. I took my GCSE early,' he says, with a modest shrug. 'Did my AS this summer.'

'What did you get?' I ask, respect creeping into my voice.

'A-star for GCSE. Results for the AS come out on the seventeenth. Maybe–' he hesitates and seems to change his mind.

'Maybe what?' I ask.

'There's a canal that runs across the marshes. It was built in the early 1800s to stop an invasion by Napoleon. Dad asked me check out one of the stretches for leech colonies.'

'Leeches!' I exclaim, pulling a face.

'Yes – they're being used on a medical research project in London to test blood-clotting. So, do you want to?' he asks.

'What? Come leech hunting?' I sound less than impressed.

Ethan drops his gaze and scuffs at the ground with his boot.

'Um. OK,' I find myself saying. 'When?'

'Depends on the weather. We need to go at dusk. Have you got a mobile?' he asks. I give him my number and he keys it into his phone's memory. I notice how nimbly his fingers tap the numbers. 'Good,' he says, and just for a moment looks very deeply into my eyes. A small tremor twinges in my spine and a muscle twitches ridiculously in my face.

'I can make you a fruit crush or something,' I suggest. Ethan is standing up, pacing a little in front of the veranda, like a caged creature in a zoo. 'I'll be back in a minute,' I say, uncomfortable at his lack of response, wondering if I've upset him in some way.

Oh God, Jaz. Boys like Ethan don't drink fruit crush. He's probably into lethal spirits laced with banned substances. He's thinking you are pathetic and immature.

Mum gives me a little wave from the lounge as I move through the hallway to the kitchen. She's stretched out on the sofa, leaning on Dad, and Ferdie is sitting in Papa Tom's armchair. Relaxed laughter, mostly Mum's, ebbs and flows through the cottage; her spirits have definitely lifted.

'Good follows bad,' says Papa Tom, somewhere in my memory. I imagine him standing near the sink and nodding wisely, reassuring me with a warm smile, making whatever it was that had darkened my day recede into shadows. It was a phrase he would state even after the world's worst disasters, like floods and hurricanes, famines and diseases. Mum said he wasn't religious, but he had an unshakeable belief in positive things always coming out of the bleakest times. And in nature knowing best.

I'm not sure the fly would agree with that, as it was golloped up by the dragonfly. I guess it's all part of that annoying 'circle of life' thing they sing about in *The Lion King*. The circle connects the past, present and future like the spun silk of a spider's web. So Ferdie is part of Mum's timeline.

And now, like it or not, Wild Boy is part of mine.

When I return to the veranda, with two fruit crushes in tall glasses, topped with ice cubes in the shape of sea horses, there is no sign of Ethan. Just a dragonfly, drawn in the gravel, and the sharp stone lying by its side.

23

Mum and I are driving along the coast road by Starlight Bay, taking it in turns to do mahousive yawns. It's still only seven-thirty am. We've just dropped Dad at the station; he only agreed to go back to London once Mum persuaded him that she was feeling completely fine. She looks tired but happy, the result of hours of stories about old schoolfriends and Ferdie's late departure at eleven o'clock.

Ethan didn't return. Ferdie said that was normal. He told us that his son found being with people difficult. He had always been quite a solitary child, but when his mum left, he developed a passion for walking and was happiest tramping miles across the marshes, alone.

It was still rude not to say goodbye, I'm thinking.

'That's just so weird!' exclaimed Bella, who couldn't contain her curiosity and called me when I was up to my neck in bubbles in the bath. She had arrived at her residential course in Essex and declared her single room in the converted country house to be smaller than Roxy's cage, with hideous red gingham curtains and a dark brown carpet.

'They've put the strings in the new wing,' she complained. 'They look out over the parkland. I've got dustbins outside my window.'

I told her that creatives famously have to suffer for their art. She took a big bite out of an apple and asked me more about Ethan. It was a conversation that didn't last long, not just because there wasn't much to tell her, but because my phone slipped from my ear into the frothy water and sank like a submarine.

By the time I emerged from the bathroom, wrinkly and cross, all that was on offer downstairs was an animated three-way discussion about the 1980s and the merits of Culture Club versus Wham!, so I took refuge in my room. By midnight, I had concluded that pop songs don't sound great on Mum's cello, even less so when they are accompanied by male falsetto voices. Luckily my iPod blocked out most of the commotion and I drifted off into a fretful sleep filled with images of Ethan singing in a frog choir.

My phone's premature demise is one of the reasons we're visiting Penchurch, which has a small electrical repair shop. The others are a) a cooked breakfast in a café and b) the collection of the guitar, which is ready ahead of schedule.

The fry-up was offered to calm me down after I realised I was now officially cut off from the civilised world.

Turning down the main high street, everywhere looks decidedly shut. There are two cafés, opposite each other, and parking spaces outside both. Mum pulls in and switches off the engine. Apart from two seagulls tearing into a black bin liner on the pavement, we are the only living creatures in the street.

It's like a deserted town in an American western, except there's no saloon and no posts to hitch up your horse. Mum's country compilation is moaning on the CD player. I half expect a cowboy to come bursting out of the off-licence, guns drawn, Stetson tilted on his head.

Hunger makes you hallucinate. It's a well-known fact. Mum has her head back and is snoozing, so there's no sympathy there. I decide to watch the gulls pecking greedily at the assortment of cartons and discarded morsels. I wonder why they aren't obese, living on a diet of fast food. And do the seagull elders warn of falling from the sky with heart attacks if they stray from their natural fare of fresh fish?

Perhaps, in the future, it won't just be global warming and germ warfare we have to worry about, but gulls conking out on the wing. Everyone will have to wear hard hats by law. The UK will suddenly be full of Bob the Builder lookalikes. Tasha would have to wear a pink one, though.

Mum is looking at me, smiling. 'What are you thinking about?' she asks.

'Bob the Builder,' I reply. Mum pulls a face. It's a bit random, but it *is* 7.45.

'We could play I-spy,' suggests Mum, who always chooses the sort of unpronounceable words you get on literary quiz programmes.

I say yes, anyway, just to pass the time, and spend five

minutes trying to guess one beginning with 's' that turns out to be 'sylph', which Mum has chosen because of the nearby logo of a little fairy dancing above the lettering of a combined hardware store and toy shop. She wouldn't allow 'sprite' so I've been racking my brains in silence.

Luckily the café to our left is showing signs of life. A man of about fifty in a blue checked shirt over jeans is bringing plastic tables and chairs outside onto the pavement. He wears a gold chain round his neck and is very tanned. He sees us and gives us a wave. Mum points to her watch and he motions for us to come on in.

Ten minutes later and I am tucking into a full English breakfast, courtesy of Gil, the owner and chef, complete with hash browns, beans and extra fried bread. Mum, on the other hand, is eating toast with butter and drinking a herbal tea. She had trouble swallowing her tablets just now, so I am keeping an eye on her and cutting up bits of egg and bacon for her to taste.

'Don't fuss,' she says. 'I often feel a bit queasy when I've had wine. It was such a nice evening, though. We had a good giggle, the three of us. Poor old Dad had to put up with a lot of talk about schooldays. Ferdie said my favourite Maths teacher ran off to join a Russian travelling circus, calling himself "The Great Numero Uno".'

'Is he going to visit us again?' I ask, squirting more tomato sauce onto my egg yolk. Mum averts her eyes to avoid looking at my plate.

'I hope so,' she replies. I swallow rather heavily.

'You could ask some of your other friends to stay,' I suggest, hopefully.

'I'm not lonely,' she smiles. 'I've got you and Dad. And acres of time to rest and enjoy looking at the sky.' She presses her hand over mine, reading my expression. 'Maybe Ethan could be some company, until Bella comes?'

I shrug, in a non-committal way. He may have taken my number, but, judging by his swift exit, he has no intention of using it.

'I heard you chatting,' says Mum. 'Ferdie said he rarely speaks at all, so you're honoured. Anyway. I told him they were both welcome. They probably won't come. Rangers are busy people.'

I stab the rounded end of my sausage angrily and slice the chipolata into precise, equal-sized chunks. Mum takes this in, clasps her hands together and is about to deliver a little homily about being mature.

'I prefer it when it's just us,' I tell her. 'The three of us. I don't like the way he looks at you.' I can feel my ears pulsing with sudden heat. I didn't mean it to come out like that. I'm just embarrassed about the whole Ethan thing.

Mum is visibly taken aback. 'Jaz, Ferdie is an old acquaintance – not even a friend. He was very kind to me, to all of us. It would be rude not to be friendly. You have no reason to be worried. OK?'

'OK,' I reply, not looking at her, scraping the food I can't eat to the outside edge of the plate in neat piles.

I get the feeling my little outburst has changed the mood of the day. Mum and I visit the electrical shop – where a techie genius manages to get my phone working again – and collect the restrung, retuned guitar from Lottie in Merry's Music, without uttering another word to each other. Mum seems quiet and sad. And I feel guilty that I've upset her.

I've realised silence can be very loud. It is a language all of its own.

Mum turns off her country CD on the way back to the cottage and tunes the radio to a classical channel. It's playing Vaughan Williams's *The Lark Ascending* and the strings rise and fall like butterflies flitting over hedgerows, moving from major to minor keys as easily as changing direction on air currents. Mum's shoulders relax back into her driving seat.

'Your favourite piece,' I say. 'Spooky how that happens. As if the radio knows.'

Mum smiles. 'I see it as a gift – when the universe thinks you need a little lift.'

The lark finally ascends, with the help of dextrous fingering from a violin soloist, and there is a respectful silence during which you realise you've been holding your breath. The presenter makes a link to the next piece of music and Mum pulls a face, reaching for the button on the display.

'Tchaikovsky?' I say, surprised.

'You can't go from the *Lark* to the *1812 Overture*. That's just silly,' says Mum, agreeing with me. And there is silence again, only this time it is tranquil and warmed by sunshine streaming through my passenger window, not tense and prickly with painful feelings and words unsaid.

When I glance at Mum, I notice her left hand is resting on her abdomen, in between gear changes.

'How long has it been hurting?' I ask.

'A couple of days. It's just a tummy bug. I don't think the wine helped,' says Mum, raising her eyes up in self-admonition. 'I feel a bit cold as well.'

I reach across and put the palm of my hand on her forehead. She feels cool. No sign of a temperature.

'I'll probably crash out for a bit when we get back – sleep it off.' She sounds upbeat and positive, so I'm not sure why my sensometer is swaying wildly.

'Have you checked your leg?' I persist.

'My leg's fine, Jaz. Really. And so am I. It's just a blip.' Mum gives me a level stare. I'm not backing down.

'Mr Kenwood said you should ring if anything happens,' I state quietly.

'He'd probably just tell me to put stabilisers on my bike,' says Mum lightly. 'Anyway, I've got my check-up next month. The full monty. So put your mind at rest.' She pats my thigh twice. It reminds me of the two bar lines at the end of a piece of music, signifying the player should return to the beginning. Or, in my case, change the subject. But something is gnawing at me – an unwelcome but familiar companion who took up residence in my brain and claimed squatter's rights a year ago: fear.

'That's six weeks away,' I say gently. The date is committed to my memory, like all of Mum's medical milestones.

'I'll make a deal with you,' responds Mum, at last. 'If the pain doesn't shift in a couple of days, I'll call him. But I can't roll up to his clinic every time there's a bruise, an ache or a hangover.'

'OK,' I agree. I feel suddenly stupid and paranoid. Mum is absolutely right. I wish I could just stop jumping off the deep end every time she has a bad day.

24

I'm doing press-ups in blocks of ten on the small area of lawn in front of the veranda. My arms are straining – I blame the extra fried bread from yesterday's big breakfast. I'm wearing my trackie bums, which are threadbare at the knees, a strappy top with blackcurrant juice stains on the front over an old pink bra, and my hair is scraped back into a ponytail with an elastic that has an orange flower on it.

Bliss!

Mum is having an afternoon nap in her room. Possum is curled up on Papa Tom's rocking chair. The air is warm and sweet-smelling. White, wispy clouds trail across the huge expanse of sky. A line of ants makes its way through the grass in front of my hands, ignoring the elevating and descending giant who puffs and speaks in turn.

'*Tasut, yausut, ilgope, yauldul, ahope, yaul…*'

That's seventy all together. Not bad. I decide to do a headstand to celebrate, being careful not to crush the insects still dutifully parading past me. The great thing about being upside down is the new perspective it gives you on the world. Birds look mad, as does the rabbit which appears near the stream at the bottom of the garden, especially when it hops.

I'm having a good old chuckle and don't really notice the

sound of doors slamming at the side of the cottage.

Suddenly there are two pairs of legs approaching and I'm scrabbling to bring my feet, and my strappy top, back to earth.

'Hello Jaz,' says Ferdie. He's in his uniform, radio attached to his thigh. Just behind him is Ethan, who gives me a fleeting glance before stuffing his hands into his jeans pockets and staring at the ground. My ears have already gone puce – and not just from the headstand. I want the ground to open up and swallow me whole.

'Hi,' I say, trying to be cool, wiping a drip of sweat off my nose. I look worse than a bag lady who has been sleeping rough in shop doorways for a week.

'We were passing by – thought we'd see how you all are.' Ferdie is smiling without any trace of judgement. He doesn't look at all shocked by my appearance. I feel my posture relax a little.

'Mum's resting – but I can make you a drink,' I offer.

'It's fine, but thanks anyway. We'll be doing a seal check later in the week – maybe you and Anna would like to come out on the boat?' he asks.

'Wow!' I say, sounding like a kid in a sweet factory.

'Your Mum's got my mobile number, so just give us a call later on and we can make arrangements,' Ferdie suggests. 'We'll be off then. Enjoy the sunshine.' And he is moving towards the Land Rover in easy strides.

Ethan lingers for a moment, gives me a half-wave and what looks like a gesture of regret, then follows his dad.

OK, I think, *leech hunting is off the agenda*. If he texts me now, I'm just going to delete it – and him.

'Bye!' I call defiantly as they reverse out of the driveway and accelerate away. But Ethan doesn't look at me again.

'Oh, Jaz, that sounds fantastic – you are *sooo* lucky!' breathes Bella. 'I love seals, especially the babies with those cute little faces.'

'Well, Mum hasn't said yes yet, so it's not certain,' I say. 'And I kind of wish Dad could come, so he can be there for her.' (*And a human shield for me*, I'm thinking). I'm sitting in Papa Tom's armchair, his wildlife notes on my lap.

'But you've got a Power Ranger all to yourself to protect you,' responds Bell. 'Is he fit?'

'No,' I snap. 'He's at least forty.'

'What about Wild Boy?' she teases.

'Just shut up about him,' I reply.

'You *like* him!' she gasps theatrically. 'I can hear it in your voice.'

'I really don't – look, shouldn't you be doing arpeggios or something?' I plead.

'I've got my singing tutorial in about five minutes.'

'How's it going?' I'm relieved to be off the subject of Ethan.

'OK. No, great. Sort of,' she says. 'Everyone's wonderful and talented and everything…'

'But?'

'But I'm not sure I want to be here. I can do it, no problem, but I'm not really – loving it,' she confides. 'It's probably just a phase.'

'Hormones!' we say together, mimicking our Pastoral Care tutor, Miss Grimsby, who was a nun until she was forty, when she decided to become a teacher. We burst out laughing.

'I'd better go. Miss you,' she says, blowing me a million kisses.

'You too,' I tell her. 'Remember, smile…'

'And the whole world smiles with you,' she sings, at the top of her beautiful voice.

For a moment, its sweetness fills the room, before vaporising through the open doors and windows into the stratosphere, like a genie escaping from a lamp.

'Dammit!' I hear Mum say from the kitchen. She volunteered to make spaghetti Bolognese tonight. I decide to check on progress and find her chopping onions, tears streaming down her cheeks. When she sees me, she starts to laugh.

'I would never have made it as a chef,' she says, sniffing.

'You don't swear enough,' I agree, offering to take over with the vegetables.

'How's Bella?' she asks, after splashing her face under the cold tap and drying it.

'A bit music-ed out,' I reply. 'She's not sure if she loves it anymore.'

Mum looks thoughtful. 'Maybe it's just a phase.'

'That's what Bella said,' I reply, munching a piece of raw carrot. 'Her mum really wants her to do it, though, so she can be an opera singer.'

'Big decision, either way. She's very gifted,' says Mum. 'But it takes over your life and there are always sacrifices.'

'Did you ever not love it?' I ask. Mum sits down at the table and rests her chin on her hands. Her eyes are glowing and vibrant. She shakes her head and gives me a big smile.

'Not for one minute. I suppose I was lucky. There was never a choice. I knew I had to do it. Your Nana and Papa saw that I had my heart set on a music career and they gave me every support.'

'Are you disappointed that I'm not musical like you?' I ask her and she blinks, as if a physical blow has landed across her nose. I'm wondering if the brother I never had would have grown up to be a concert performer, sharing a bond with her that I can only imagine.

'No, Jaz. Never…' She beckons for me to come and have a hug. 'Music's a language. I think it's in your soul – and we speak it differently, but you feel it deeply too and I love that. And there's a good voice hiding away in there,' she says, proudly patting my chest.

I have a sudden vision of myself, in a mahousive opera gown, singing a duet with Bella on a big stage. We are both the size of Sumo wrestlers. I'm about to convey this crazy thought to Mum, when I notice she has her eyes closed, and is trying to breathe through the pain.

25

It's starting again, the worry-wheel that turns from the first waking moment in the day – slowly grinding away in my consciousness, sometimes gathering momentum and spinning out of control. The stark, massive vision before me mirrors its motion.

Long, tapered blades, like monstrous machetes, are scything through my brain in circular swathes, chopping it into a million pieces, turning it to pulp. My eyes feel as if they are covered with a film of red and orange and are trying to focus under a cellophane sky.

I'm lying on a grass verge, staring up at the turbines towering vertically over my head, backlit by a flaming, volcanic eruption of a sunset. I've left my bike a short distance from the perimeter fence and scrabbled over a ditch and up a bank, scratching my hands on thistles, in order to lie beneath these mechanical giants.

I need to have faith that, if we have the power to harness the wind, we stand a chance of protecting Mum against her hidden enemy.

Tomorrow, Mum will call Mr Kenwood. There will probably be a trip to London and tests and anxious days waiting for results. Hopes will ebb and flow, according to how we feel. The haunted look will reappear around Dad's eyes. I will try to keep our spirits up, and take out my frustrations in the *dojang*. We will all be asking the universe for this to be just a skirmish and not a full-blown offensive.

How is it possible for cancer to return, when the might of twenty-first century medicine and all the love in the world has built a barricade against it?

And why is this happening to us?

'It may be nothing, Jaz. Don't think the worst,' said Mum, trying to calm my growing anxieties. I think she was relieved when I said I needed to let off steam on my bike. 'It'll help keep things in perspective,' she said.

I'm trying. I know I've got to pull myself together. I also know I should have done more to keep her on track with her vitamins and her exercise; maybe with every omission, another cell mutates, and replicates, then another, and another, until a whole mass declares itself and retaliation is impossible.

All of this could be my fault. A shudder of guilt passes down my spine. A sudden gust of chill wind from the southeast turns the blades faster, their frenetic, low 'woo, woo, woo' sounds a soulful lament, almost like the cry of a wounded bird.

A world without her would be like a new ice-age, glaciers covering every corner of the globe, a white shroud under which every living creature is frozen in grief. I fight back the tears, cold as snow flakes, which are forming in the corners of my eyes, wiping them away impatiently on my sleeve.

Your spirit must be indomitable.

I shiver and rub my arms to disperse goose-bumps. Beyond the blades, the fierce red of the sky is softening to deep pink as the sun sets on the horizon. A few breaths later, the turbulent breeze has vanished and the blades are slowing to a stop. The angry vista has become a pastel painting, a still life in soft watercolour.

Maybe that's how it will be for Mum and there will be a new calm after this current unsettled weather. And maybe the sun'll come out, not just tomorrow, but the next day, and the next.

And one day, she and I will lie here under these turbines, telling a story to my kids about one summer that nearly changed everything…

26

'Seal hunting sounds good, doesn't it?' says Mum, suddenly.
We've been riding along the lane in silence, mentally
checking out the hedgerows for signs of juicy blackberries.
Having steeled herself to contact Mr Kenwood first thing
this morning (under pressure from both Dad and me), and
having been given an emergency appointment tomorrow,
Mum went a bit manic, poring through Nana Jane's old
cookery books. Ten minutes later, she announced we were
going to make jam.

'Not hunting, mum. That implies we'll be clubbing them
to death. Ferdie said "checking",' I remind her.

'How do you check a seal?' she asks. 'Do you grapple
with it, turn it on its belly and count its wrinkles?'

'They have to poke out their tongues and say "ah",' I tell
her. She grins.

'Wouldn't it be amazing if there were dolphins, too?
Ferdie told us there are quite a few around Starlight Bay,'
Mum says, almost to herself. She's never really got over Sea
World, where a huge male dolphin 'talked' to her through
the plate glass wall of the outdoor arena, in between
performances. She kept telling him how sorry she was that
he lived in captivity as he turned his beautiful head from
side to side. I think she and Dad still give money to

a dolphin and whale rehabilitation charity at Christmas.

'I'm sure Ferdie could arrange it,' I say. That was as spiky as some of the thorns on the bushes we are passing.

'Jaz…' says Mum, about to give me a lecture.

'Sorry,' I apologise, quickly. 'I do really want to go. And I want you to come, so it can wait until you feel up to it, OK?'

'OK,' she agrees, braking and easing to a stop.

'What's wrong?' I ask her, turning my bike and drawing up alongside. I'm checking her face for signs of exhaustion.

'Nothing. Look!' She points to a tall bramble in the verge, from which dangle clusters of fat, black fruit. 'Bingo!'

I notice that Mum, who is happily singing about broken hearts, is eating more than she is picking. I can only see about ten berries rolling around in her tupperware box. At this rate, we'll be making jam by the thimbleful.

Having plundered the soft treasure, with purple fingers we ride on slowly in the sunshine, side by side. Time, like the lane in front of us, seems to stretch ahead endlessly. We are in the morning, but have no idea what minutes have ticked past which hour. My mobile is switched off. Mum has left her watch at the cottage. We are meandering, without any fear of mad motorists, gently in the direction of what might be the midday sun.

'This looks like a good bush,' says Mum enthusiastically,

braking and stopping. On closer examination, the best blackberries are on the other side of the hedge, which is in a field full of grazing cows. We discover a gate further up the lane and leave the bikes propped up against it. Mum climbs over nimbly, with great purpose.

'Lucky Dad the Pied Piper isn't here,' I say. 'We'd be trampled.'

'They're right over there,' points Mum. 'I don't suppose they'll even notice us.'

The trouble is, not much happens in a cow's day, and I can imagine that small events become very significant – like a fly settling on your nose, or two humans dropping in. It would be intriguing and probably worth investigating.

Mum is determined to reach the ripe, succulent prizes a few feet above our heads. Before I know it, she's got me crouching down so that she can sit on my shoulders, something we haven't attempted before. I am amazed by how easily I lift her. We have become an impressive two-tier plucking machine.

'Right a bit,' says Mum, leaning dangerously and gripping with her feet.

'I'm not a horse,' I tell her, stepping sideways and half-stumbling down a rabbit hole.

It is at this moment that we become aware of a noise like low thunder in the distance. It's something you get used to in the marshes – the weather can change very quickly. But in this case, it has nothing to do with atmospheric pressure. It is being caused by about two hundred hooves, trotting in unison. Towards us.

'I don't believe this,' says Mum, crossly, as I kneel down so that she can get off safely. 'I'm going to clap my hands at them.'

'No, you're not,' I tell her. 'It's a stampede. You're going to run.'

'Not without my blackberries,' she says, pushing the lid onto her tupperware box.

'Mum, *you'll* be jam if they decide not to stop,' I say, my voice going up an octave. 'Come on!'

I grab her hand and we sprint down the field. The bovine chargers are close behind us – inquisitive, clumsy, weighing in at about a thousand pounds each and focused on us. There is no sign of a stile or a gate. When we reach the corner, I cup my hands together to make a stirrup and tell Mum to put her foot in it for a leg up.

'They look so much bigger close up,' pants Mum, staring back at our pursuers.

'Just do it!' I command, as she starts to remonstrate. She shrieks as she rolls over the top of the hedge, propelled by a rather enthusiastic push from me. I jump and grab the undergrowth, jamming my feet into the woody structure within. I follow Mum over the top just as the brown and white rebel horde arrives, amid a mass of mooing and snorting.

Mum and I are leaning on the opposite side of the hedge,

scratched, cut, bruised and grazed. We look at one another, taking in the dishevelled hair and the snagged clothes. Mum holds up her full tupperware box triumphantly.

'A fruitful adventure,' she proclaims. And we start to giggle. And the giggle becomes a chuckle. And the chuckle becomes a knees-bent, chest-heaving wheezy thing that totally creases us up. And when an old man cycles past, touches his hat and just says, 'Good morning, lovely day,' we roll onto our bellies and cry with laughter.

27

We're in the reception area of the Oncology Unit at St. Belvedere's Hospital in London. Mum, Dad and I are staring at framed colour photographs of countryside scenes from around the UK. There's a Scottish castle by a lake, long boats on a canal in East Anglia and the cliffs of Dover. I look at the cloud formations in each and feel something unexpected in my heart.

A pang of sadness.

Four hours ago, Mum and I were surrounded by sky. We ate breakfast on the veranda and watched Possum chasing moths. He was still pretending to be a hunter-gatherer when we drove away from the cottage, which we left locked for the weekend, with enough cat food in dishes to sustain the furry member of our family while we were gone.

Despite the situation, Mum looks radiant today. She's wearing a pink jacket over white jeans and pink lipstick 'for luck'. Under the artificial lights, she looks thinner in the face, though. Maybe all the exercise is burning up too many calories. We need Dad to bake us some of his chocolate brownies with masses of nuts. Each slice has about eight hundred calories.

I would give anything to be able to say, 'There's been a mistake. She's fine. Sorry to have wasted your time.'

We've been here so often, wishing with all our hearts that the symptoms are just false alarms.

'Mrs Ballantyne?' A nurse appears in the doorway of reception and smiles at Mum, who is having a blood test before her chat with Mr Kenwood.

'See you soon,' she says, squeezing my knee as she gets up. She gives us a little wave and is led away through double doors and down a carpeted corridor. Dad runs his hands through what's left of his hair.

'You OK?' he asks.

'Yup,' I lie.

Dad nods, gets up and starts to pace about, his face thoughtful. His shirt is loosely tucked into his work suit trousers and is ballooning a bit at the back. He resembles an ice cream on a blue cone. Aw. I fumble in my bag for my phone, which shows I have two text messages. The first is from Olly:

'Whoah dude – let's have a Chicks night out piggin pizza. Wot u fink ☺☺☺☺☺☺'

The second is from Bella:

'Soooo happy u home! C u 2nite? x'

I didn't tell either of them why we were back in London so soon, just that it would be great to get together for a Friday feast (and to hear all about Bell's week at music prison).

I notice a polite sign asking patients not to have their mobiles switched on in this area, so I slip mine back into my bag and reach for one of the glossy magazines on the low table in front of me. It's like a hotel here – quiet and efficient with an exotic flower arrangement on the reception desk.

I've skimmed through about ten magazines on beauty, antiques and living in France and Dad has worn a hole in the carpet by the time Mum returns. My stomach is making yowling noises, similar to Possum when he's preparing to have a scrap with another cat.

'Anna,' says Dad, slipping an arm round her waist.

'Hey,' says Mum, brightly. 'All set?'

Dad and I exchange glances. Normally Mum asks us to be with her when she has a consultation. We had expected to be ushered into Mr Kenwood's office after her blood test.

'I need to pop back for a scan tomorrow,' she tells us, taking my hand. 'And for the blood test results. Today was just a quickie. Mr Kenwood was due in theatre at two so he squeezed me in for a speedy examination.'

A moment later, we're walking down the corridor leading to the lifts. There are wide windows on our right revealing the other wings of the stone building and, beyond them, a thousand roofs over which the London Eye arcs like a metal rainbow.

I'm giving Mum this look which says I'm not fooled by her cheerfulness. Scans are hugely expensive and they only do them when there's a good reason.

'It's just a few weeks earlier than it would have been,' says Mum. 'I told Mr Kenwood I've got a concert scheduled for late September. I thought I might give him two tickets.'

She and Dad are looking intently into each other's eyes. It's *Casablanca* without words. I notice the rims underneath his are quite red. I don't think he slept much last night. And he wasn't the only one.

'So where would you two ladies like to have lunch?' asks Dad, pressing the button for the lift. I know exactly what Mum is going to say.

'Home, James,' she answers, grinning and resting her head on his shoulder.

I'm sitting in our garden, close to the lantern lights, watching Mum and Dad smooching round the kitchen to a Nat King Cole number. Finkie is watching me from his balcony, his ears pricked forwards. I give him a little wave and he answers with a manic yap. Then I am suddenly sneezing, eight times in a row. Some things don't change.

The day's events have made me close down, like the Thames barrier. I couldn't face seeing my mates and trying to be jolly. I told them I've gone down with a lurgy. I don't even feel like hanging from the tree. I'm just sitting here, like a gargoyle, my head in my hands, watching the light drain from the sky.

'Crumble and custard is served,' calls Dad from the kitchen.

My stomach has clenched like an angry fist. Five minutes ago, food was top of my agenda. There's only one emotion flowing through me now. It's like a freak tide crashing up on an unprotected shingle beach, dragging the stones back into the sea, drowning any living creature in its path. It may be invisible, but it has a name.

Panic.

28

Mum is lying on her back, disappearing slowly into a large tube, like the Eurostar into the Channel Tunnel. Dad and I are watching through the window of the radiographer's room, where the data from the scanning machine is fed back onto computers for analysis. Mum's a bit claustrophobic. I can see her hands are clenched.

As the machines begin to map her body, I can read her mind. She's wishing the capsule could make her vaporise and reappear in the past.

It will be a few days until she gets the scan results. A whole team has to look at them. Mr Kenwood will contact us, but he's not here again until next Friday, as he's going away to Canada to be a guest speaker at a cancer conference.

Good follows bad. Yes, Papa Tom. Maybe it's nothing. Maybe luck will be on our side.

An hour later, the three of us are sitting in Mr Kenwood's office. I notice his potted palm has grown another big leaf since we were last here. Mum is holding Dad's hand. I'm staring intently at the consultant's face for positive signals. He looks tanned and healthy, his blue eyes clear and focused. The two small children in the photos on his desk have his exact same smile.

'I'm afraid the blood test showed the tumour markers

have changed, Anna,' he says, without preamble. 'It may be nothing, or it may be we're looking at a recurrence. We'll know more when the scan results are through. I was hoping to give you better news. I'm very sorry.'

Mum is nodding, taking this in. Dad clears his throat. My brain attempts to tell me that the markers are substances in blood which react to altered body conditions.

'If it's back, you said that more chemo was out of the question,' Dad says, 'but that there may be other options.'

'I suggest we have that discussion after next week, when we know what we're up against,' replies Mr Kenwood.

'She can have radiotherapy,' I state. My mind is scrolling through the hundreds of pages I've read on the net. The words and statistics are a blur. I feel quite nauseous.

'Possibly,' he says, gently. 'But let's get all the facts before us. And in the meantime, try not to be downhearted. The markers can change for other reasons, remember. We might need to be good detectives,' he says to me, smiling.

I'm running, arms clenched into my side, pushing in and out like pistons. My trainers are pounding the tarmac path under my feet. Behind my dark glasses, my eyes are streaming, and it's not just the proximity to the trees on this part of the Heath. My phone keeps sneezing. I'm ignoring it for once. It could be the Prime Minister giving me a three-minute warning to announce that aliens have taken control of the earth. It couldn't matter less.

Then again, it might be Mum. When I left the flat, she was crying, in great big, heaving, anguished sobs, on Dad's shoulder. He motioned for me to leave them alone for a bit. His face looked as grey as stone. I've never heard Mum break down like that before. When I put my runners on, my hands were shaking.

I slow my pace, pull my phone out of my pocket and press 'view'. The message that pops up is so unexpected, I do an emergency stop, almost gasping from the cumulative exertion.

'Hi, how r u? Leech convention gathering 2moz. Go on bikes? Meet at yours b4. OK? Ethan'

No explanation about his silence, no apology for hurting my feelings. So why am I not pressing the delete key? And why are my ears flushing hot?

There's a second message. This one's from Bella, who is worried about my prolonged lurgy and the fact I've told her I need to remain in quarantine.

'Soz u still sick Jazeeeee. C u, wouldn't want to b u xxx'

No, Bell. You wouldn't want to be me, for sure. But I wish you were here, right now, and could hold me tight, because the whole world is shaking.

29

Sunday morning, eleven am, and we're pulling into the drive at Frog Cottage.

Possum springs out of the undergrowth, leaves in his fur, and greets us, and Mum in particular, with an unusual amount of affection.

'He's starving,' says Mum. 'I feel so guilty.'

'He's fine,' Dad reassures her. 'Cats are hunters. Look at his belly. He's probably got a dozen mice in there.'

Dad and I are unloading the car and Mum is given strict instructions to sit down. She completely ignores these and wanders down to the stream, where I find her trailing her fingers in the sparkling water, causing ripples across her reflection.

'It's good to be back,' she says, wrapping her other arm round me. 'Oh, hello, you.'

A small blue butterfly, just like the one from Starlight Bay, dances in front of our faces, before fluttering away across the fields.

'Wonder if it's the same one,' says Mum, her hand shielding her eyes from the sun as she watches it go. 'Wouldn't that be funny? Maybe it's adopted us, Jaz. Our little guardian angel.'

We both stare until it's out of sight. Mum sighs. Tension

seems to be leaving her body, eased away on the currents of the warm marsh wind. After a couple of minutes, she gives me this 'spill the beans, something's up' sort of look.

'OK.' I find myself taking a deep breath. 'If someone older than thirteen asks someone younger out, is that a date?' I ask.

'Do I take it the "someone" is a boy?' enquires Mum. I nod. 'And how much older is he?'

'Two years,' I say. She nods thoughtfully.

'And the invitation is to do what?'

'Count leeches,' I reply.

'Hmm,' says Mum. There is a smile playing round her lips, but she keeps her face serious and thoughtful. 'That's quite unusual – and intriguing,' she comments. 'And is the young person who has been offered this opportunity keen to go?'

'She's not sure. She's worried the leeches might be more fun than the boy,' I reply cryptically.

'I see. Well, if I were her, I would risk it,' says my mother.

'Really?' I ask. 'Even though it means she wouldn't be around to be sous-chef for supper duty?'

Mum is beaming at me, brushing the hair out of my eyes. 'Once in a lifetime opportunity,' she points out. 'I've never met anyone else who has gone leech counting in the Rainbow Marshes.'

So it's down to Mum that I'm in a wooden boat, somewhere on a stretch of canal, sitting opposite a dark-haired boy who is rowing with strong, even strokes, and looking everywhere but at me. I'm hoping the leeches have got a good selection of one-liners, otherwise I'm in for a dull time. There are wide pink and orange bands across the sky. The water ahead of us looks like a rose-coloured ribbon, laid flat.

'Are they frightened of noise or something?' I ask at last.

'Who?' Ethan replies, mystified.

'The leeches.'

'They don't have ears,' he says.

'So there's no reason why we shouldn't speak, then,' I state.

'Sorry,' he says. His eyes scan the river bank, the tall grasses, the lapping water round the oars, the sunset. I give him a little wave.

'You asked me to come with you,' I remind him.

'Yes.'

'Are you always this quiet when you take girls out?' I ask.

'I don't,' he answers.

'What?'

'Take girls out. I haven't...you're...' he says, with difficulty. 'Sorry,' he repeats, shaking his head and putting more effort into rowing. The muscles in his forearms are flexing with each stroke.

'Look, it's no big deal. We can just chat, like we did the

other day. It doesn't have to be a girl–boy thing,' I say, proud of myself for sounding so mature.

'You start,' he suggests. This is so weird.

'OK. Um. What do leeches look like?'

'Slugs with suckers. And teeth,' he replies. 'We've got the biggest colony of the medicinal kind in England.'

'Oh God! Are we counting all of them?' I ask. 'I'm no good past a hundred.'

'Don't worry,' he reassures me, letting the oars rest a moment. Then he motions for us to swap seats.

'You have a go,' he says. 'It's about another mile and we want to be there in ten minutes. No pressure or anything.'

'What happens in ten minutes?' I ask, moving the oars in their locks and lowering them into the water, determined to rise to this challenge.

'You'll see,' says Ethan, and refuses to be drawn further. He is watching the bank again and the playful games of two furry creatures, rolling and tumbling into the water.

'Water voles?' I ask. He looks impressed and gives me a silent clap. It soon turns into a Biology lesson, with him pointing at creatures and me trying to guess their species.

'Lizard,' I say, when he points to an ancient-looking reptilian creature loitering on a large leaf.

'Great-crested newt,' he corrects me. 'Specially protected, so don't whop it with the oar.'

'Dragonfly,' I say with confidence, as one wafts across our boat, landing on the water's surface.

'Ah, but what variety? Red-veined darter, lesser emperor, red-eyed damselfly...'

'I'm not an encyclopaedia,' I respond, a bit huffily.

'It was an unfair question,' he concedes. 'There are twenty-two different ones to choose from. And that's just in the marshes. I don't know about worldwide. How are your arms holding up?'

'Fine,' I reply. I don't mention that my back is starting to feel like it's on a rack, being stretched to the point of snapping. 'How much further?' I must have been rowing for at least ten minutes by now. My forehead is prickling with perspiration. I let the oars trail in the water for a moment.

Ethan stands up, making the boat rock violently, and looks around in all directions.

'Hey!' I shout, grabbing the left oar as it starts to slide out of its lock.

'This is OK,' he says, sitting down again.

'What? We're here?' I ask. This part of the canal doesn't look any different from the section we have just travelled along: about ten metres wide, steep grassy banks, and, on either side, fields stretching as far as the eye can see. Which isn't very far, as the light has faded quickly and night is approaching across the horizon.

We sit in silence for at least a minute. There is the occasional plip-plop of a frog, or a fish, and the honking of geese flying in formation in the distance. I jump as a bat flits across my face, but manage to stop myself screaming.

'I don't see any leeches,' I state, suspiciously. An involuntarily shiver moves up my spine as cold mist rises from the canal and sweeps like smoke across the boat.

'Wait. They're very shy,' Ethan says, putting his finger to his lips. I've decided he really is one of the most irritating people I've ever met. If we're counting slimy creatures, we're going to need a torch.

I've got goose bumps on my arms now and make a point of untying my hoodie from my waist and yanking it over my head, punching through the arms. My teeth are chattering. It's almost dark, but I can still make out that Ethan is smiling at me, for some reason.

'Look around you,' he says softly.

Amazing! As far as my eyes can see, there are hundreds of individual, twinkly white lights, like fairy lanterns, illuminating the entire length of the canal bank. Moonlight is pouring onto the water like liquid silver. It's a fairy footpath, leading to the stars.

'Glow worms,' says Ethan.

'Wow!' I whisper. 'Do they do this every night?'

'Just during summer. The females light up to attract the flying males. After they mate, she turns off the light, lays eggs and dies,' he explains.

'That's rough,' I say, my teeth still chattering. Ethan nods. He's smiling at me again. Luckily, he can't see my ears changing colour under his gaze.

There is a pause, which hangs heavily in the air. The marsh frogs and crickets have struck up their nightly noise contest, filling our silence.

'We should get back,' he says. 'Before you get hypothermia.'

'What about the leeches?' I ask.

'It's physically impossible to count them,' he replies, his face quite serious. 'Especially in the dark.'

'Oh boy,' I sigh, well and truly had.

'Let's swap seats. You've done enough work for one evening,' Ethan suggests.

'Hmm. Well, maybe we can both row,' I tell him. When he sits next to me, my body tightens down one side, and there are strange, tingling sensations in the arm nearest him. I wriggle a little so we're not touching. He glances at me and I notice how long his dark lashes are. Bella would kill for those; she always buys false ones for parties.

'Thank you,' I say. 'It was fab, even if you can't recite all twenty-two species of marsh dragonfly.'

He shuffles a bit and takes his oar before saying, 'Good.'

'Yes, good,' I repeat, as we start to pull our oars in synchronicity, big smiles stretching across both our faces.

30

It's midnight. I'm under my duvet and I'm texting Bella:

'Went rowing. Saw glow worms with Wild Boy! ☺☺☺'

Then I remember I'm supposed to be ill. I delete the message, turn off my mobile and hold it close to my chest, my mouth set in a permanent grin. Tonight was the sunshine between the showers, the rainbow bridging the storm. Ethan didn't realise I was thanking him for more than the glow worms. I can feel hope returning. Whatever tomorrow brings for Mum, Dad and me, I'll be better able to face it now.

🦋

'Autumn chill,' says Mum. 'It's come early this year.'

We're waving Dad off in his taxi. He's going to tie up an audit at work and then take some extended leave. Halitosis Henry has been very understanding, apparently. Dad is disappearing into the mist, while Possum presses up against our legs, asking for his breakfast.

'Why don't I make us some pancakes?' offers Mum, when we are surrounded by silence again.

'Hmm. Why don't *I* make us some pancakes?' I counter.

Mum laughs and slips her arm through mine. 'You could have a shower,' I suggest.

Five minutes later, I'm squashing blueberries with a fork. Deep purple juice is oozing from their punctured bellies. Oil is sizzling in the pan. The batter is made. Sunshine is filtering into the kitchen and the woman on the radio says it's going to be a fantastic day.

With all my heart, I want her to be right.

🦋

Mum is brushing her wet hair, sitting at the dressing table, when I take the tray of pancakes and orange juice upstairs. She is wearing a towel and the white-gold necklace Dad gave her for their fifteenth anniversary. She looks frail and vulnerable, although the reflection in the oval mirror is smiling warmly at me.

'You *are* spoiling me,' Mum says, hopping back into bed and pulling the duvet up over her legs.

'Glad you noticed,' I tell her, and she flicks her hair back over her shoulder like a model.

'I don't think they should actually be completely blue,' I say, prodding a pancake with my fork. 'Maybe I shouldn't have squashed the berries, after all.'

'Blue food is very therapeutic,' states Mum. 'And they are delicious.' She dabs her mouth with a paper napkin which has a poppy on it. She is holding my gaze, eyes bright with mischief.

'It was your favourite book when you were little,' she says.

'What was?' I ask.

'*Tales from the Riverbank.*' Oh no, here go my ears.

'Nothing happened,' I protest. 'It was just nice and he was just…'

'Nice too?' Mum holds my hands. 'That's great,' she says and pretends to zip her lips. I flop down on her lap and bury my head. She strokes my hair and softly sings, in an exaggerated Texan accent:

'And she dreamt by night of rainbows
Of a time when darkness ends
And she saw the morning glory
Through the light a rainbow sends.'

I lift my face out of the duckdown and smile at her. I can't count how many times that song lulled me into a nap when I was small.

'I didn't want there to be any shadows this summer. Just sunshine and blue skies,' Mum says, quietly.

'I know,' I reply and squeeze her hand. 'It's going to be OK. The butterfly was a sign.'

Mum nods, lying down next to me.

'Are you seeing him again?' she asks. Our eyes are just centimetres apart. Hers are sparkling, the shades of green and brown quite distinct.

I reach for my mobile and show her the text message

from Ethan which has already arrived:

'Want to watch the birds fly south 2day?'

Mum has a look of mock shock on her face. 'What have you replied?' she asks.

'I haven't,' I half-mumble, embarrassed. 'I'm looking after you, remember?'

'I think I can spare you for a couple of hours,' she says. 'You should go.'

'I told Dad I wouldn't leave you,' I state.

'I'll be very good. I could make us a cake for later. And I might do some practice – outside. It's a perfect day,' Mum enthuses. These sound like positive options. The idea of the cake is also quite persuasive. When the cottage is full of sweet, spongy scent, it's the best place on earth.

But a promise is a promise. 'No can do,' I tell her, flatly.

'What if I text you every half hour?' she persists. Role reversal feels strange. Normally it's Mum and Dad deciding the ground rules for me. 'Hmm, possibly lemon drizzle, or maybe a chocolate torte…'

Naughty Mum. She knows how to break down my defences.

'Are you totally, one-hundred-and-a-half-per-cent sure?' I ask, butterflies beginning to swirl in my belly at the thought of another outing with Ethan.

'Yes, ma'am,' she drawls, in Texan.

31

'There!' Ethan says softly in my ear. 'Do you see it?'

He's standing behind me in the hide at the observatory, helping me focus the lens of a pair of powerful binoculars on a blue-grey bird with what looks like a black moustache, flying low along the shore of the estuary. My vision is filled with mid-afternoon sun filtering through a blanket of high cloud, the shafts piercing the earth in a fan pattern, like spokes from a wheel.

'It's a peregrine falcon,' he whispers. 'He's looking for lunch. Watch him closely.'

The falcon gains height suddenly and starts to weave and turn, in pursuit of a smaller bird. The gap between them narrows, despite great agility from the victim, and seconds later, strong talons pluck it from the sky.

'They're ace hunters,' explains Ethan. 'The gull didn't stand a chance.'

I give the binoculars back to him and lean my chin on my arms on the ledge of the open hide window. Witnessing the ending of a life, with such swift dedication, has made me feel sad.

'You OK?' asks Ethan, sitting astride the wooden benchseat and looking at me intently.

I shake my head. Suddenly my eyes are hot and stinging

and I can feel my lip quivering. *Jaz, you are* so *not going to cry*. I dig my nails into the palms of my hands in the hope that a rush of pain might prevent catastrophe.

'We had some bad news – about Mum.' Ethan nods. He doesn't press me to say more. His face is full of concern and kindness. After a while, he raises the binoculars and scans the horizon. He passes them to me and gently tells me to look east. There's a group of maybe one hundred small birds moving across the skyline.

'Swallows,' he says.

'Where are they heading?' I ask.

'South Africa. They know instinctively when it's time to leave. They're early this year,' he comments.

'It's so brave to go all that way,' I say, as we watch them cross our line of vision and become nothing but tiny dots going west.

'Maybe if our climate keeps warming, they won't need to go,' suggests Ethan. 'Everything keeps adapting. The frogs came here from Hungary – just twelve of them in the 1930s. Now they're everywhere! There are twenty species of orchid in the marshes, including the spider orchid, which is incredibly rare. Do you like marshmallows?' he asks.

'Random, but yeah,' I reply. He disappears out of the hide and doesn't return for at least five minutes. I'm wondering if he's just gone walkabout again and whether I should think about heading back to the cottage, when I hear footsteps, and Ethan appears with a small, white flower in his hand, which he presents to me.

'Marshmallow flower,' he says, proudly. 'It's almost extinct now, but the plant thrives here.'

'What are you saying?' I ask, not getting the point. He puts his hands on my shoulders. I am surprised by the lightness of his grip.

'Survival is the strongest instinct,' he assures me. I'm nodding, exposed by his ability to see right through to my inner fears. Something in his steady gaze stops me from dissolving completely.

'And good follows bad, right?' I say, my voice a hoarse shadow of itself. Ethan folds his arms round me and holds me tightly. I take that as a 'yes'.

32

I'm sitting on the veranda steps, the rescued guitar across my lap, and I'm plucking at strings and attempting to find some chords.

'And she dreamt by night of rainbows
Of a time when darkness ends...'

My voice leads my fingers. It doesn't sound completely like Mum's song, but I'm surprised how many notes are recognisable. The tone of the instrument is mellow and deep – its vibrations resonate across the garden, along with my discordant harmonies.

Better this noise than the silent tension of waiting for a phone to ring. Mum has sat with her mobile all day.

Maybe no news is good news. Perhaps Mr Kenwood has nothing to say, so is leaving Mum's call until last.

'That's great,' says Mum, who is leaning against the front doorway and has been listening to my unofficial concert.

'Oh no!' I cringe, embarrassed by my lack of musical ability. 'How long have you been there?'

'About two minutes,' answers Mum. 'You've got a natural ear,' she says, impressed.

'Really?' I ask, disbelievingly. Mum nods and smiles.

I suddenly feel six feet tall.

Dad's in the kitchen, opening a bottle of red wine. We've made chicken fried with peppers and herbs for dinner, but none of us is very hungry, so we left it simmering gently.

It's 9.15.

Mum's been playing scales on the cello in the lounge – up and down, up and down. It sounded as if the instrument were crying. If she's not careful, she'll wear her bow out.

'Shall we eat?' asks Dad, from the doorway. Mum and I exchange glances and shrug a half-hearted 'yes'.

'Not much for me,' says Mum, as we enter the kitchen, which is aglow with candles on all the sills and worktops. Dad's a star, trying to keep our spirits high. We all end up with sparrow's portions on our plates. Mum waits until we are sat down before she raises her water glass in a toast.

'Life, love and lipstick,' she says, mustering a smile.

We clink our glasses together. Dad winks at Mum. Just at that moment, her mobile starts to ring. We all stare at it for a few seconds. Then Mum picks it up and leaves the room. We hear her close the lounge door. Dad puts his fork and spoon down and runs his hands through his hair.

I'm watching the long hand on the wall clock as it moves steadily towards the half-past point on the floral face. Its ticking seems as loud as a hammer banging in a nail. I glance at Dad. He is staring at his glass, barely breathing.

At 9.45, he pushes back his chair and walks towards the lounge. He pauses a moment before opening the door. I hear the catch click softly as he closes it behind him.

I watch the clock hand move through twenty more minutes before my legs feel strong enough to hold my weight. I put down the fork I've been holding and move towards the lounge. The house is silent. Through the open front door, I can hear the marsh frogs having their usual nightly gossip.

Part of me wants to run into the open space and feel the rush of twilight air envelop me. But I'm already turning the handle on my right.

'Hey,' says Dad from the sofa. Mum is curled up on his lap, her head against his chest. She doesn't look up.

'Hey,' I say, quietly. As I approach, I can see that Dad has been crying. Mum's face is ashen and impassive. She doesn't look at me.

'Not good news, I'm afraid,' says Dad, trying to regulate his voice. I sit down on the floor by his knee and take Mum's hand. She squeezes mine, but her grip is weak and fleeting.

'The cancer's back,' he continues.

'Where?' I ask. It's hard to speak. My throat is closing up. Dad nods.

'Lungs, pancreas and spine,' he says. Mum closes her eyes and presses her head harder into his chest. Tears are pumping out of my eyes silently and cascading down the sides of my paralysed face.

'No,' I say, bitterly. 'He said he got it all out.'

'It spread through the lymph nodes. There was always

that possibility,' Dad tells me, his voice almost a whisper.

I feel dizzy suddenly. Waves of nausea flow through my body. I get up and run outside onto the veranda, down the steps and right to the bottom of the garden, where I think I'm going to be sick. Instead, I crouch down low and rock wildly, my feet gripping the wet grass. And it takes a while to realise that the voice yelling across the marshes like a wounded wild animal is my own.

33

'I shouldn't have made her run,' I say, when Dad touches my shoulder and sits beside me on the top step of the veranda. It's about three in the morning and neither of us is in the mood for sleep. My duvet is wrapped round me, like a fat cocoon, and my breath trails up into the night sky like gossamer.

'This isn't your fault, Jaz,' he says gently. 'It isn't anyone's fault.'

Stuff happens...

'It isn't fair,' I state.

'No,' he agrees, simply.

'Now she's got to go through loads of treatment again,' I say. 'And more surgery.'

Dad takes my hand. 'There may not be that option,' he tells me. 'Because of the spread. Although the spots are small, for now.'

I take this in. 'There must be something,' I manage to utter. Dad is very quiet. 'I want you to tell me exactly what Mr Kenwood said.' Dad breathes out heavily. 'I want to know, Dad.'

'Mum could have some different chemo for the lungs, but there are some bad side effects. He wants to talk to her about radiotherapy, but he's saying that even with luck, given the advance of the tumours, it will probably only give her a bit more time.' His body is shaking. I can feel it through his hand.

'But there are other things – herbs and holistic centres – all that stuff I found on the net before.'

'It's Mum's decision. She'll need a little while to come to terms with all this,' he replies. Even in the faint light from the hallway, Dad looks broken. I put both arms round him and squeeze him tight. His eyes are staring across the marshes, almost unblinking. 'We need to try to be strong for her,' he says quietly, as if to himself.

I don't respond. Dad seems lost in a reverie. I gather up my duvet and trudge back inside. The night air no longer holds any comfort, the sea of blackness mirroring the dark void in my heart. I want to lie down to ease the ache in my stomach, a mixture of anxiety and protestation that the dinner on my plate didn't actually make it to my mouth.

I climb the stairs, trying to avoid the wooden parts which creak. Tiredness has turned me into a blundering tortoise, my duckdown shell on my back, and I manage to trip halfway up and create a racket when my big toe bends too far the wrong way.

'Jaz?' Mum calls softly from her room.

I pad along the corridor and poke my head round her doorway. She is horizontal under the sheet. There is a dark brown blob by her stomach – Possum. She is holding her arms open in invitation. I climb across the bed, avoiding the sleeping cat, and snuggle down next to her, pulling my duvet on top of me.

'You're so cold,' comments Mum, wrapping an arm round me protectively.

'I love you,' I tell her. She doesn't say anything in reply. I think she's holding her breath.

Her bed feels warm and safe. In moments, I am drifting away, my thoughts suspended in the relief of oblivion.

When I open my eyes, sunshine is streaming underneath the pulled curtains in the bedroom. I feel like I've been sparring with a dozen tae kwon do partners. My body is aching and I can't remember why. Responding to my wakefulness, my brain does a quick recap and I feel my chest tighten as the events of last night become reality and zoom into sharp focus again.

I'm alone in the bed. There is no sign of Mum and Dad, or Possum. When I glance at the alarm clock, it reads eleven am.

I pad downstairs and find Mum in the kitchen, sitting at the table, still in her dressing gown, drinking coffee. Dad is on his mobile in the garden.

'You slept a long time,' says Mum, smiling. She looks very pale, but peaceful, somehow.

'How long have you been up?' I ask.

'Since about six,' she replies. 'Dad and I watched the sun come up.'

I nod and move to the worktop to cut a couple of slices from the loaf on the board. They end up too wide at the bottom and I have to stuff them into the toaster. I know what will happen – smoke and charcoal – but I can't be bothered to take preventive action. Things feel surreal. My limbs are performing in slow motion. I busy myself picking up crumbs with the tips of my index fingers and putting them in piles of ten.

'Would you like me to tell the Farrells?' asks Mum.

'Not yet,' I reply. A plume of black is rising from inside the electric bars. I flick the handle up and my toast appears, the top half underdone, the bottom burned to a crisp. I spear both slices with a fork and wiggle them out of the machine. I'm panicking at the thought of Bella knowing. Once the news is out, it's real and irreversible. But at the same time, I don't know how I would tell her myself. I've never cried in front of her, not even when Mum had her surgery. But now, even the thought of seeing her makes me want to start blubbing.

The Farrells felt like a big, solid, colourful island when the last storms came. Now Mum, Dad and I are on a life raft; their island is within reach, but the tide is pulling us further away – casting us adrift. And as the waves get larger and the swell increases, it's harder and harder to see land.

'By the way, Bell, Mum's dying.'

The words keep repeating in my head, with each scrape of the knife against the blackened bread. When it starts to resemble toast again, I spread on butter and marmalade and sit down opposite Mum, whose eyes are bright and clear, although framed with dark circles.

'I'm never letting you go, remember?' I tell her. The words sound a little hollow now, somehow. Mum's chest rises as she takes a breath and her eyes become like liquid glass. She gets up slowly from the table, kisses my head and moves silently to the kettle, bare feet hardly making any impact on the floor.

'As soon as we get home, I'm getting onto those sites about natural treatments,' I say.

'I *am* home, Jaz,' she replies, closing her eyes and letting cold water gush into the kettle.

'Let's go look for newts,' says Papa Tom, in the doorway. He is beckoning me with his hand. I am seven and Nana Jane is sitting at the table with Mum, who has just returned from performing in Moscow and is nursing a terrible cold. In front of her is a steaming bowl of soup, full of spinach from the vegetable garden. And round her neck is a lavender bag, which Nana Jane told me to heat for two minutes in the microwave. Mum is making Nana Jane laugh with her imitations of the Russian conductor. The soup spoon is her baton, which she waves wildly in the air, a cross-eyed look of rapture on her face.

'I'll make you spinach soup for lunch,' I suddenly announce, and Mum raises her eyebrows. She is about to ask me how I plan to do that, but I am already padding out of the cottage and down the veranda steps.

Dad, who is still on his mobile, gives me a questioning look as I half-run along the gravel path leading to the far side of the garage. I am still in a T-shirt and cropped pyjama bottoms with dogs on. My bare feet are complaining about the sharpness of the white stones.

There's a small wooden gate leading to the vegetable garden and as I open the catch and push it open, I'm met with a wilderness of green and a variety of sprouting flower heads, prickly stalks and foliage, which spill over the central grass pathway and the four areas on either side defined by low, rectangular plank boxes.

There is a sinking feeling in my stomach. The whole area is chaotic. I lift leaves and stems and peer underneath, but there is no sign of spinach. I remember that Esme was the last person to grow things here. She was a keen gardener and the vegetable plot was one of the main reasons she chose to rent Frog Cottage, Mum had said. It's as if nature has claimed back its space gleefully, removing all traces of human hands.

Bees are buzzing between flowers quite happily. They have no idea of the urgency of my quest. I'm holding my face in a silent scream – like that painting by Munch which was the inspiration for our Year Seven art project.

'Whatever it is you need, we can get it at Tesco's,' says Dad helpfully. It's the one time I'm grateful for him being a townie.

34

'How r u?'

I'm staring at my mobile, wondering how to answer this text from Ethan, which arrived half an hour ago, while we were having dinner. Mum managed some of the spinach soup, made with veggies bought from Penchurch, which is where Dad whisked me when I started to lose it amongst the triffids in Nana Jane's patch this morning. I told Mum and Dad I would wash the dishes while they went for a walk up the lane. Dad thought the fresh air would do Mum good. I think it's a euphemism for 'adult' talk.

There are texts from Bella, Olly and Tash too, full of smiley faces and exclamation marks. My eyes read the words, but their meaning doesn't sink in.

By the way, guys, my Mum's dying.

My fingers start to tap the keys.

'Mum's cancer's back. World shaking'

But I change my mind, press delete and watch the letters disappear. Instead, I find the 'call back' setting, and two seconds later there is a ringing tone.

'Hello,' says Ethan. He sounds pleased I've rung.

'Hi,' I respond. 'Thanks for your text.'

'No problem.'

Silence. This could be the shortest mobile call in the history of time.

'What have you been up to, then?' I ask. My voice sounds flat and weird.

'Helped Dad on some guided walks,' says Ethan. 'Mended some wire fencing at the observatory and fixed the hinges on the doors in a couple of hides. There's a storm expected tonight. What about you?'

'Um. Not much, really.' My throat is tightening and an isolated pain is throbbing in one temple.

'We're probably doing another seal check next week,' he says. 'Maybe you could come, if your Mum's not up to it.' He's guessed how ill she is — I can hear it in his voice.

'Yup. Maybe,' I answer. 'I wanted to ask you something.'

'OK,' he says.

'Do you ever think about finding your mum?' I ask.

Silence.

My head is throbbing. I feel totally embarrassed. Of all people, Ethan doesn't want to have a heart-to-heart about mothers. Relief sweeps over me when I hear voices outside — Mum and Dad are returning.

'Gotta go,' I gabble, abruptly. 'See you around?'

'Yes, see you,' he says, sounding perplexed and offended. The line goes dead as my parents come into the kitchen. Mum takes in the pile of unwashed plates and pans and the fact that my mobile is in my hand, its screen illuminated.

'Could you turn your phone off a minute?' asks Dad. I shrug and press the key that starts the shutdown. 'Goodbye,' says the display, before going dark.

She and Dad exchange glances and then they both sit down with me at the table. Mum holds my hand in both of hers.

'I want you to know that you and Dad mean everything in the world to me,' she begins. 'And if there was the slightest chance that treatment would make a positive difference, I would go for it. But Mr Kenwood says the disease is in too many organs.'

'No,' I say quietly, shaking my head. Mum grips my hands a little tighter.

'So I've decided to forget about hospitals and pills and tubes and be here with you both until I need special care. And we'll take each day as it comes and be there for each other – and still do the things we promised ourselves we'd do, like watching the seals.'

'I can't believe you're giving up,' I say to Mum. I feel angry but my voice is almost a whisper. 'The chemo made the cancer go away last time.'

'It just kept it at bay. The sort of drug cocktail I'd need would be so severe, I'd have to stay in hospital most of the time. This way, I can be with you both, for as long as possible.'

Too much information. I can't take it in. My whole body

is trembling. It feels like the walls in the room are pressing in on me. My chest isn't letting in air and I'm looking down a tunnel, which is narrowing with every second. With a swift, sharp gesture, I'm taking a plate from the rack and throwing it at the wall, wincing as it shatters into a thousand pieces.

35

I'm riding against the wind, pushing down on my pedals from a standing position. The effort has made sweat beads form on my forehead. My hands are aching because of the tightness of my grip on the handlebars. I didn't stop to switch on my lights when I grabbed my bike from inside the garage and headed off into the night. There's no moonlight – banks of dark clouds are hanging low over the marshes – so it's hard to see far ahead.

Thunder is rumbling in the distance, low and threatening, like a tiger's growl.

Mum and Dad didn't try to stop me, although I heard Mum call my name as I ran out of the cottage. They'll be mad I haven't got my mobile with me. And I don't have a coat or my safety helmet.

None of that seems important. I'm moving at speed, crouched in racing position, putting every ounce of energy into covering distance so that the words in my head and my rising panic are diluted by adrenaline.

Gusts of wind are whistling through the hedgerows. An empty plastic sack, like the ones Dad buys at the garden centre, flies across my path – a magic carpet with no passengers. It does a loop-the-loop and lands in a field on my right, where a mass of dark bovine shapes lie in a huddle, braced against the weather.

I'm taking turnings I don't recognise, leaning into corners, willing myself to go faster. The lanes feel strange and uncharted, a labyrinth as twisted as black spaghetti. I'm afraid to stop, afraid the family truths I've left behind will catch me up and tear me apart.

The tiger is prowling nearer now. Maybe it's standing on Pirate's Point, roaring at the sky, daring the wild sea to approach.

Suddenly, the horizon in front of me explodes with jagged light and a deafening bang and I am braking and shielding my head with my arms (how stupid is that?), and when I look up, the massive turbines of the wind farm are almost on top of me, their sails moving like propellers, their eerie woo-woo-woo a mass tribal lament.

And as the lightning flares and illuminates the landscape intermittently, I see a large shape in the lane ahead – something or someone lying motionless. My heart pounds as I ease my bike forwards.

The tiger roars again and this time I scream as the sky fills with a billion volts and I throw myself down onto the tarmac, curling as small as I can and pressing my head down. An electrical smell which reminds me of the labs at school fills my nostrils and I lift my head, expecting to be in the centre of a circle of fire.

A surge of wind, almost as loud as the thunder, sweeps through the turbines, hitting my body like a clenched fist.

Two seconds later, droplets of water the size of small marbles begin to splatter onto my already-damp back and hair.

I open my eyes cautiously and see that the mound lying not far from me is white and large and very still. I move on my hands and knees towards it, too wobbly to stand. There is blood spreading out from under it in a circular pool. As the rain starts to pelt down heavily, the blood disperses across the lane.

I'm staring at white feathers and an open belly exposing flesh and bone and an outstretched wing, limply trailing. I feel the chest, which is soft and warm, searching for a heart beat, and look at the eye staring blankly. The beak is fixed slightly open, rigid and unresponsive.

The swan is dead.

'Sorry, sorry,' I murmur, stroking its head. I'm crying now, my tears mingling with the shower, washing the bird's wounds.

'Papa Tom, what shall I do?' I yell, above the noise of the gale.

'Too late, Jaz,' he seems to say. I shake my dripping head in defiance.

'Woo-woo,' shriek the sails in reply, gathering more momentum, working themselves up into hysteria.

My drenched clothes are clinging to my body as I gather the creature in my arms and try to lift it.

'Your spirit is strong,' I hear the Lioness say, and a cry

comes from somewhere deep inside as I raise the broken body, move slowly back to my abandoned bike and lay the swan over the handlebars.

I turn on my two lamps – their lights are weak against the onslaught of the torrent from the sky – and within moments I am riding again, the weight of the lifeless creature in front of me slowing my pace, the rumbling behind spurring me to struggle on.

I leave the perimeter fence of the wind farm behind and head for what I hope is east, deeper into the tangle of lanes. It's impossible to see further than a few feet ahead. I don't recognise where I am. The hedgerows all look the same and there are no sign posts. It's like being lost inside one of the nerve pathways inside your own head. If only the rain would stop, I could scan the fields for distant lights and signs of life.

'*Hana, dool, set, net…*' I'm counting in groups of four to keep a rhythm going, my eyes almost closed against the sheeting water.

Another unnamed crossroads looms and I turn right, my tyres making a 'swish-swish' sound as they cling to the tarmac, which is now hidden under a running river. I'm feeling exhausted, cold and disorientated. I could be riding in circles, and the idea of that makes me lose concentration. I'm freewheeling and making little progress.

Another flash rips down into the fields nearby, and I glimpse a track and small structure on my left. I turn the bike and start to bump up the uneven surface. The swan's neck bounces about, as if it's doing a weird dance. A mahousive rippling bang, like a thousand glass boulders being dropped into a giant jar, crashes overhead.

'Leave me alone!' I'm yelling at the invisible tiger that is playing games, reaching for me with his outstretched paw.

When I realise the low building I'm approaching is a hide, I start to sob with relief. I open its wooden door and push the bike inside, leaning it gently against a wall. Everything inside is wet, but the three solid sides provide protection from the wind and, if I tuck into a corner, I can avoid the horizontal rain entering through the open window space.

It feels familiar, this damp box in the centre of a maelstrom. I suddenly realise it is the hide I shared with Ethan, just a few days ago.

I stroke the swan's head again. Its eyes stare into the darkness, unseeing.

36

'I've found her. She's in the Clearwater hide at the Observatory.'

When I raise my right eyelid, I see Ethan, mobile next to his ear, looking at me anxiously. My next sensation is aching pain, running the length of my body. I am horizontal, lying on something very hard. I push myself up onto my elbow and realise my arm is completely numb.

My gaze takes in the inside of the hide – my bike supporting a huge, limp swan, with angel wings dangling to the ground. My jeans and trainers and hands, stained with dark blood. Early morning light, streaming through the observation hole.

'Are you hurt?' asks Ethan. I shake my head. 'She seems OK,' he relays into his phone before pressing a key and putting it back in his pocket. He looks ragged, with dark swathes under his eyes, and patches of stubble like a black shadow up to his cheekbones.

He helps me sit up on the bench and gives me a drink of water from his bike flask. I take several gulps, even though the coldness makes me shiver.

'Thanks,' I say and manage a smile.

'We've been out all night, looking for you,' he tells me.

'I got lost in the storm. We both did.' I nod to the swan.

'Where did you find her?' Ethan asks. It's a girl.

'On the lane near the turbines. She was already dead,' I reply. 'But I couldn't leave her. She was still warm.' My voice starts to crack as the memory of Mum's words floods back into the analytical space in my brain which sleep successfully numbed.

We'll take each day as it comes...

'My Mum's dying, Ethan,' I whisper.

He nods and pulls my head gently onto his shoulder, at the same time folding his arms around me. He smells of the dawn – a mixture of dew and grass and salty air. There are no tears. My eyes feel empty, even though my heart is pumping pain like an artery.

The sound of an approaching engine fills me with apprehension. My body tightens and flinches as I hear the opening and closing of a car door.

'It's my Dad,' says Ethan, holding my gaze.

Ferdie appears in the entrance to the hide. He's not in uniform, but still has his radio strapped round his waist. Moments later, I'm being helped into the Land Rover and Ethan is loading my bike and the swan into the back. I'm eating a chocolate bar and feeling drowsy under the blanket tucked around me. And my vision is becoming as blurred as the mist rising above the marshes, made iridescent by the first rays of sun.

'Hey,' says Mum, as I blink my eyes open. I'm lying on the sofa in Frog Cottage. There's a fire roaring in the grate. Mum is kneeling next to me, stroking my arm. I'm still wearing my clothes from the night before. I don't remember coming back, or being carried to this makeshift bed.

'The swan died,' I say to her. 'The turbines…'

'I know,' she soothes. 'Nothing you could have done.'

I blink again. Dad is coming into focus. And behind him, rain is lashing down the window pane.

'Sorry,' I say to Mum. She puts her finger to her lips.

'You're in shock,' she says. 'We all are.'

Memories of the phone call and all the tears are coming back to me now. I long for deep, unconscious sleep to reclaim me.

'You had us worried,' breathes Dad, shaking his head. He is tousled and unshaven. I realise neither of them has been to bed.

I hold my arms out to Mum, who cradles me in a gentle embrace, and strokes my hair, while a confusion of despair and relief gravitates up from my stomach and finds its way out of my aching, shaking frame in big, uncontrollable sobs.

37

Mum and I are sitting by the stream in the garden, eating ice lollies. We made them earlier by pouring orange juice into moulds and popping them in the freezer. The kit, complete with plastic handles, was a present when I was six. We've used it every summer since. After this one, I've decided I'm going to throw it away.

Mum's wearing jeans and trainers and a long-sleeved top, which is a bit excessive in the midday heat. She's losing weight and is chilly most of the time now, but today she has make-up on and a necklace and bracelet. It's the first time she's dressed up since before Bad News Day, and she looks pretty and not really ill at all.

We've spent every hour together since Ferdie brought me back to the cottage more than two weeks ago. Mum told me I could ask her anything I wanted, so I've written lists and lists of questions about her favourite things: colours, flowers, food, hit singles, authors, painters, politicians, musicians (living and dead), dancers, clothes – everything. We've been sitting back to back while she's been answering them, leaning on one of Papa Tom's bird books.

'That's so difficult,' she keeps sighing. 'Can I choose three?'

'Nope,' I say, unfairly. 'You can put the others in brackets if you want,' I concede.

'With music, it depends how you're feeling – and with flowers, oh gosh, there are so many beautiful ones,' says Mum. 'How on earth can you decide between sunflowers and stargazer lilies?' She sighs again and keeps scribbling.

Possum is stalking flies in the long grass and providing a comic crouching and leaping act for us to enjoy, and every so often Mum puts her pen down and laughs at his antics. I record a burst of his clowning on my phone, just so that I have a record of her voice, happy and bubbling with joy.

Dad's in London today, sorting out bills at the flat and packing more things for an extended stay in the marshes, including a prescription for painkillers in the form of patches from Mum's GP, who will take over her care now. He doesn't think she'll need them yet, but it's good to be prepared, he suggested.

Mr Kenwood said that Mum may have several more months, or even a year, to live. When the tumours have grown too big and her body starts to fail, there will be a place for her at a hospice in North London and she will be looked after and made as comfortable as possible. She can also decide to stay at home. I think there is only one place she'd like to be at the end of everything – right here, where it all began, thirty-eight years ago.

I can't let myself think about endings all the time she is here with me. Life without her is unimaginable. Whenever the fact creeps into my consciousness, I get an acute pain in my stomach that makes me double up and want to be sick.

Looking at her, giggling and drawing butterflies on the lined paper, all of this seems unreal. I want this moment to last until the end of time.

The sound of a throaty motorbike engine turning into the driveway of the cottage makes us both look up, me with surprise and Mum with a wide smile on her face. I give her a questioning look. She just taps her nose and keeps grinning.

'Twenty years late, but madam's Harley-Davidson has arrived and is at her disposal,' says Ferdie, in full leathers, removing his helmet. Riding pillion is Ethan, who is now handing Mum his helmet and black jacket. It's a conspiracy.

'Surprise!' says Mum to me, as she pulls the headgear over her small features and pushes the visor up.

'Don't worry, I'll go slowly,' Ferdie assures me.

'No you won't,' says Mum. 'That's no fun.'

I look at Ethan and he just shrugs. I'm wishing Dad were here to add a voice of reason.

'Dad knows,' Mum tells me, doing that spooky thought-catching thing. That's that then. Mum is zipping up her protective armour. Her body looks huge now compared to her thin legs. She's giving me a little wave and is almost skipping next to Ferdie as they move towards her dream machine.

Ethan and I follow. I can't believe the person sitting astride the black and shining chrome beast behind the driver is my mother. When Ferdie kick-starts the engine, it sounds like a rocket preparing for takeoff at Cape Canavral. Mum gives a little whoop of excitement as they turn a half-circle and pull out of the driveway, and a thumbs-up as the machine accelerates ridiculously fast up the lane.

'How long have they had this planned?' I ask Ethan.

'Since yesterday,' he replies. 'He's never taken time off in the summer before. And he hasn't ridden the bike for months.'

'Sorry you got dragged along – guess you're my official company while two go mad in the countryside,' I say.

'I offered. Wanted to see if you were OK,' he replies, looking at the ground.

'Breathing. Surviving,' I respond. 'Thanks.'

There's a long pause. Ethan kicks at the gravel with his boot.

'I've decided to talk to my mum,' he says. 'After what you said. Dad doesn't know where she is, but he's got a friend who's still in touch with her. I'm hoping she'll meet me, or at least talk on the phone.'

'Big step,' I respond. 'Proud of you.' I don't know what's come over me, but I'm squeezing his hand. He looks mahousively embarrassed and pleased at the same time.

He seems to be on the point of saying something else, when suddenly a blue butterfly with white-edged wings is flitting between us.

'Hey you,' I say to it, sadly. 'Meet my guardian angel,'

I tell Ethan. 'Mine and Mum's, actually. It's been following us about all summer. Turns out it wasn't much help.'

Ethan's face is clouded with a mixture of seriousness and awe.

'You look like you've seen a ghost,' I tease.

'It's an Adonis Blue,' he answers. 'The rarest butterfly in the marshes.'

38

Mum and I are on the veranda, munching toast which Dad has cooked to perfection. Since he's been here full time, he's dedicated himself to his new role as superchef, using locally sourced, organic food. We always wake up to the smell of freshly baked bread, straight out of the oven. As a result, breakfast lasts at least an hour. We just take our time and have a good old natter about our plans for the day.

Mum's rocking gently in Papa Tom's chair. We've added a pillow to the seat, as she's lost all padding and gets uncomfortable sitting. Possum is right next to her in the sun, washing himself and purring.

My phone is jangling in my room. I run upstairs and get to it just before it switches to voicemail.

'Hey Bell,' I say. 'How are you?'

'Good, thanks. We all wanted to say have a fantabulous day,' she says. Since Mum spoke to her parents a while ago, things between us have been a bit strained. We've texted every day, but this is the first time we've had a conversation. I can tell she's nervous; Mum told me my friends will find it very hard, because they know words won't really help.

They do, though. Just hearing her voice, I can feel my spirits lifting.

'Oh, and Pops said to send you his *seal* of approval,' she

adds. I give a little chuckle. Meredith is such a sweetie. 'And he hopes you fulfil the *porpoise* of your trip.' Groans all round. 'That was terrible, wasn't it?' says Bella.

'Yup,' I agree. 'Wish you were coming,' I tell her.

'So do I, you're so lucky,' enthuses Bell, and I can hear the catch in her voice as she regrets any reference to luck.

'Yeah, it's going to be great,' I reply, choosing to ignore the slip.

'Take lots of pics,' she says. 'Especially of Wild Boy.'

'He won't be up for that,' I say.

'Do it when he's not looking, Jaz. Pleeease…?' begs Bella.

'No promises,' I reply. 'Anyway, you'll meet him. We've invited him and his dad to London for a weekend. I'm going to take him round some old buildings.'

'Aaaaaargh!' exclaims Bella. I have to hold the mobile away from my ear. It's the sort of response I would have expected from Olly, who has been surprisingly quiet and sensible since she heard my news. 'Wild Boy in the city – wow!'

'If you're expecting a cross between Tarzan and Crocodile Dundee, you're gonna be disappointed,' I say. 'He's just like us, Bell, except he understands animals and weather and stuff.'

'*Soooo* excited you're coming home,' she states. My lovely mate.

'Aw, thanks,' I tell her, even though I can't contemplate

the end of the summer and leaving Frog Cottage. 'Big hug. Call you later,' I confirm.

'Ta-ta, love you lots,' she half-sings, and the electronic tone tells me that the call has ended.

'Look, Jaz,' smiles Mum, when I arrive back at the veranda. Our favourite member of the lepidoptera family is fluttering around her head. As I kneel down next to her, it settles on her hand. Its beautiful wings pulse up and down silently.

'It's an Adonis Blue,' I tell her. 'You were right about it being very rare.'

She looks impressed.

'Then we are very honoured to see you again,' Mum says quietly, raising it to eye level. It shows no desire to fly away, but its wings move doubly fast, as if it's having a conversation.

Mum brings the butterfly close to her face. It flutters responsively, brushing against her skin. A mahousive smile ripples round her mouth. She motions for me to come near and its wings whisper across my cheek.

'A true butterfly kiss,' she beams.

In a moment, it is dancing in the air in front of us, looping, turning, gliding. And just as Possum begins to show an intense interest, with a twitching tail and a hunter's stare, it flits away over the balustrade of the veranda and is whisked upwards by an air current, high into the cobalt-blue sky.

'That's all the magic I need for one day,' sighs Mum. 'Although seeing dolphins leap out of the water would be the icing on the cake. You'll have to send them my love.'

'Leaving in ten,' calls Dad from the kitchen, where he is packing up a wonderful picnic of salad and salmon panninis and chocolate brownies.

I help Mum out of the rocking chair and give her my arm. Her touch feels as light as the furry thistle seeds blowing about in the garden. When I glance at her face, I notice that all the colour has drained from it. As we enter the cottage, she holds onto the doorframe. Dad appears and takes this in.

'Come on,' he says, putting an arm round her waist. 'You need to sit down.'

'Stupid,' she says, cross with herself, as Dad and I help her into the lounge and onto the sofa. 'I was fine first thing.'

'Maybe eight pieces of toast was overdoing it,' teases Dad. She tries to hit him, but can't reach.

I tuck a rug round Mum. 'Wish you were coming,' I tell her. 'I'll miss you.' I give her a big, gentle squeeze.

'You too, pretty girl,' she says, holding my face in her hands and gazing at me for a moment, before crossing her eyes and kissing my nose.

'Love you,' I tell her, giving her a wave from the doorway.

'Love you more,' she responds, waving back.

'Back in an hour,' Dad tells her, putting her mobile on the table in front of her. 'Be good,' I hear him say, as I'm hopping down the veranda steps. I can imagine Mum's response to that, and it probably wasn't polite.

We get into the car, which is steamy hot, and Dad turns on the ignition so that we can get the windows down. Cooler air isn't the only thing to rush in as the glass descends. Loud strains of a Bach cello sonata, emanating from the cottage, mingle with the fresh marsh breeze. I look at Dad and he raises his eyes to the ceiling.

'I should have hidden her bow. What is she like?' he sighs.

'Disobedient, creative, brilliant and the best mum in the world,' I answer, grinning.

39

Ferdie and Ethan are waiting for us on the jetty at Starlight Bay. We've texted ahead about the situation with Mum, so they are only expecting one passenger. Dad and Ferdie have a quiet word and I see them shaking hands. I'm glad they get on OK. It's cheered Mum up, being able to talk about old times and go for the occasional roar around the marsh lanes.

She would have loved this adventure, the sea wind blowing through her hair. I feel empty without her, disappointed and sad that we're not going to share this special day.

I'm going to try to remember every detail so that I can recount the story later – the sounds, tastes, images and feelings, so that she can be here with me, in her imagination at least, when she closes her eyes.

Waves are slapping playfully against the jetty, whipped by the wind. I can sense myself responding to the energy of the elements all around. My ribs are expanding as my chest takes its fill of air. My shoulder blades are easing back towards my spine, relaxing. I want to pretend that everything in my world is wonderful and visualise all the painful, collective truths of Mum's situation spiralling skyward, in the updraft of a gull's wings. A long-forgotten lightness rushes in to fill the void. It's as if rays of sunlight are piercing my heart.

It's so unexpected, this momentary lifting of grief. I want to cry and laugh at the same time.

'Arms up,' instructs Ethan.

I'm doing a little jig on the spot as he tries to put a yellow life-jacket over my head.

He's looking slightly smug as he zips me up. We're standing very close. My ears are tingling, which means that they will soon resemble two tomatoes.

'I wasn't expecting to go *swimming* with dolphins,' I say, my voice half an octave above its normal tone, as I watch the white tips on the tide rolling into shore. I pull a face at Dad.

'Have fun,' he says, as Ferdie helps me down the metal ladder into *Persephone*, a twenty-seater wooden craft with a downstairs galley and a covered area over the wheel. The Rainbow Marshes Country Park logo covers the stern. There's a winch on the back and several life-belts attached to the sides.

Ethan unties the rope securing *Persephone* to the jetty and jumps down onto the bow. Ferdie starts the engine, which splutters into life and fills the air with the smell of fuel.

'Tell Mum I'm filming it for her,' I call to Dad, waving my mobile phone. 'And tell her I love her!'

Dad's giving me the thumbs up and waving. In moments we are slicing through the choppy water, leaving the bay and the diminishing figure of my father far behind.

Salt spray is crusting around my eyes and a cool wind whips my hair across my face. Ethan has joined me on the padded seat facing over the winch and we're watching the white wake divide like an unfolding fan behind us.

Noisy gulls hover behind us, occasionally diving for fish into the surf frothing from the back of the boat.

'The mackerel are in,' Ethan shouts back to his dad, who nods and smiles, his hands firm on the wheel. He motions at me to come close.

'Want to take it?' Ferdie calls. My heart skips a beat.

'Yeah!' I say, jumping up and grabbing the small steering mechanism.

'We're heading southwest,' says Ferdie, pointing to dials on a display in front of me.

I'm surprised by how sensitive the boat feels under my hands. Even small movements with the wheel send us immediately to the left or right.

'Ahoy there!' I shout, as an almost-full tourist boat passes us on its way back to Starlight Bay. It gives us two honks on its warning horn in greeting and there is much waving from its deck, which we return.

'Shall we hoist the mainsail?' asks Ferdie.

'Yes, Mr Hartwood, without delay,' I reply.

'Hoist the mainsail, you scurvy rat!' shouts Ferdie to Ethan. 'Cap'n Jaz's orders.'

'Aye aye, cap'n!' he responds, disappearing down into the galley and reappearing with a flag celebrating the tenth anniversary of the Rainbow Marshes Countryside Park. He secures it at the stern of the boat, where it billows out over the water.

'Hove to, me hearties,' declares Ferdie, helping me bring the wheel round and cutting the engine until it's just turning over. We are bobbing on the water like a cork. Waves slap the side of the boat. The gulls circle us, making a 'kew-kew' noise. When I lick my lips, they taste bitter. When I breathe in, my head almost buzzes with the freshness of the air. My cheeks feel battered by the elements and my brain is saying 'whoooah!'

I'm grinning from ear to ear. Ethan must think I'm a right idiot.

Ferdie is using binoculars to scan the water all around us. Land is still visible, but distant – about three miles away now. I can make out the wind turbines to the west and, more clearly, the cliffs to the east, but the marshes are just a thin line between the two.

'We're going to head out a bit further,' says Ferdie. 'You might want to put on a couple of layers and have a bite to eat. It's going to get a bit breezy.'

I nod and follow Ethan down into the galley, where I take off my life-jacket and pull on an extra fleecy sweatshirt. It's hard to stand upright with the swell of the water, but somehow Ethan is managing to make tea. I take a mug up to Ferdie, clinging to the side of the steep stairs with one hand.

We share our picnics – Dad's brownies receive ten gold stars – and the greedy gulls get the crusts from Ethan's ham sandwiches. I make Ferdie and Ethan pose for some live action footage. *Persephone* ploughs through the waves steadily, passing south of Pirate's Point.

'Know what's down there?' asks Ferdie, pointing ahead at the open skyline to the west. I shake my head. 'Africa,' he says, with a grin.

'Wow!' I shout, elated. The force of the wind and ocean in my face is infectious – I feel like I could climb the highest mast and do a headstand on the top, especially when Ethan puts an arm round me to help keep me anchored down.

Ferdie slows the engine and does another surface check through the binoculars. He takes *Persephone* in a grand loop so that we're facing east, his eyes scanning the water for any sign of a nose or a fin.

'Pod's law,' he shrugs, disappointed. Dad would approve of that pun.

'I'm having a totally brilliant time anyway,' I tell him, glancing at Ethan, who blushes and decides it's probably a good time to make more tea. He disappears into the galley.

I'm peering down the steps, reminding him I'd like two sugars in mine, when Ferdie calls: 'Seals to starboard!'

We rush to the side of the boat in time to see two grey-brown, metre-long mammals streaking through the water, breaking the surface for a moment, then disappearing into the depths. Their speed, agility and focus is awesome. Compared to the seals at Sea World, who clap their fins and bellow for fish on command, they're like Olympic athletes.

'They're hunting,' says Ferdie. 'Probably part of a larger group.'

Our visitors aren't playing ball. After a five-minute wait, staring avidly into the ocean, my phone's camera primed, we decide it's time to move on and *Persephone* accelerates away, heading home. Ethan and I keep our eyes peeled for signs of whiskers in the wake, but it seems the seals are long gone.

The wind eases and the swell reduces the further towards land we travel. Ferdie is taking us in close so that I can get a good view of the coastline, which looks so different from the sea. Ethan tries to point out the estuary and the location of the hides belonging to the Observatory, but the strong lens of the binoculars and the motion of the boat are making me feel quite green, much to his amusement. He takes the wheel when Ferdie offers to make hot chocolate in the galley kitchen and looks completely at ease (and totally fit). I click off a sneaky pic on my phone when he's not looking – but the image is mostly a blur of dark, windswept hair and a big red jacket.

Ferdie re-emerges with drinks and fruit cake, which we devour. I'm seriously wondering how the Vikings managed to row to Britain in longboats without so much as a bread roll on board.

Late August sun is filling the afternoon sky and casting a blanket of light across the ocean. I bring my knees up under my chin and try to save this view in my memory, pixel by pixel, frame by frame. I rehearse in my head how I'm going to describe all this to Mum: how the waves lap with a hollow clonk against *Persephone*'s belly; how the gulls rest on the tide and dip their heads completely under the water (doesn't it sting their eyes?). And how, for one magical moment, the seals came.

The water's much calmer now, and I'm leaning over the side, with my hand washing in the spray. Ethan's got the wheel and Ferdie's doing some maintenance on the winch. We're about half an hour from the jetty, he says. When we get back, the plan is to get some fish and chips from Penchurch and take them to Frog Cottage. Dad told him Mum would like to see us all.

'Shouldn't you be scrubbing the deck or something?' Ethan asks me.

I pull a face at him. He grins and offers me the wheel, which I'm eager to take. I can see Ferdie smiling, out of the corner of my eye, and suddenly there's a flash of grey and a mahousive thud and two dolphins arc across the bow of the boat, at least six metres in the air.

'Bottlenoses!' shouts Ethan, taking the wheel again and keeping *Persephone* on a steady course. I'm filming them and screaming at the same time.

The dolphins, the larger of the two about three metres

long, keep pace with us in the water, like steel spears slicing through air. I'm trying to keep my phone steady and not jump up and down with excitement.

'It's a mum and baby, probably a month old,' says Ferdie. 'They're in good condition.'

Another huge thud and the dolphins leave the water just ahead of us, propelled so fast they appear to be flying.

'Whoooah!' I yell.

Mum, this is sooo amazing…

I'm dancing round Ethan, being a pain. He laughs and just shakes his head. 'I know you've probably seen a million dolphins, but this is my *first time*, OK?'

'They're pretty cool,' he says, calmly.

'Not cool. *Mahousive*!' I correct him. The last time I was this excited, I had just been given my blue belt in the *dojang*. (But this is ten times better.) I'm watching their fins, side by side, now on our left, and am breathless at their speed and agility. They're passing under the boat and then appearing ahead – definitely playing with us.

They leap again in perfect synchronicity and flip over, landing with a graceful dive.

'This is just so…*brilliant*!' I exclaim.

'That's it, folks,' says Ferdie, watching them veer away towards the deeper ocean, their fins finally submerging in the surf. I'm hoping I've managed to capture some of this magic for Mum to see.

'Thank you, thank you, thank you,' I say, giving him

a hug before rushing to the stern and waving for all I'm worth. 'Bye, dolphins, bye…'

It's not Sea World, I'm reminding myself. They won't wave back.

The three of us are singing an old sea shanty about rum and treasure as we approach the jetty. The afternoon sun is reflected in wide iridescent circles on the water. Ethan scrambles onto the bow, ready to do his rope trick. Ferdie turns *Persephone*, cuts the engine, which splutters and dies, and lets her drift alongside.

I'm climbing up the horizontal metal ladder. Ethan offers a hand to help pull me up the last bit. I give him the biggest hug when I reach solid ground. I think this experience has been one of the very best of my life.

I'm looking around for Dad – I'm like a champagne bottle about to pop its cork. The whole afternoon wants to come pouring out of me in a rush of bubbles and foam.

But there is no sign of him, just the sound of Ferdie's mobile, its ringtone insistent and loud across Starlight Bay.

40

The Land Rover is pulling into the driveway at Frog Cottage. Our car is there, together with another that I don't recognise. Ferdie hasn't said much on the journey back. From the moment he spoke to Dad, the mood changed and I felt the brightness of the day fade. The waves slapping against the jetty had suddenly seemed much too loud in the void that followed.

The three of us have navigated the winding marsh lanes in near silence. I've tried to speak to Dad, but his phone's off. And I've texted Mum, telling her something wonderful happened. She hasn't replied.

When I asked Ferdie what Dad said to him, he just answered that he needed to get me back to the cottage as quickly as possible. There were no more details.

Something inside me has become as heavy as an anchor. I think it's my heart.

I'm stepping out onto the gravel, its familiar crunch echoing in my churning brain. Dad is approaching, his hair sticking out at angles after several assaults from his hands. The sockets round his eyes are sunken. He wraps his arms round me without any words and we stand, locked together, as his tears come and we turn to a stalactite of salt.

'Mum!' I say, half calling out, breaking Dad's grip and

running to the veranda steps, taking them in two jumps, entering the cottage, rushing through the doorway into the lounge, where Mum's cello is lying on its side, her bow on the floor next to it; then, instinctively, up the stairs, along the corridor, into her room, where a female stranger in a smart suit is standing by the window, a briefcase on the ground by her feet, a stethoscope in her hand. I start at the sight of her, and in the same split second my eyes find Mum, who is resting, her eyes closed, the duvet pulled up to her chest.

'Hey,' I say, quietly, moving forwards to sit beside her.

'Jaz,' says the woman on my left, stepping forwards. My body language tells her not to approach further. I'm taking Mum's hand. It feels cool. I'm looking to see if her face has registered my touch. Normally, she senses I'm there and the corners of her mouth begin to rise – the first sign of a smile.

There's no movement. 'Mum?' I say, squeezing her fingers a fraction harder.

'She's sleeping, Little Frog,' says Papa Tom, by my shoulder.

I have no thoughts in my head, just blackness, and a tidal wave surging up through my abdomen and my chest, which is starting to heave up and down. The stranger is kneeling next to me now, her mouth making shapes from which words are emerging, very slowly.

'Your mum had a heart attack, Jaz. It was very unexpected...'

'Get out!' I'm yelling at her. 'Get out, get out…' And she's moving out of the room and I'm slamming the door so that its latch jumps and I'm crawling onto the bed next to Mum, a stricken cub, my face really close to hers, wrapping my arm over her and turning her a little towards me, pushing stray locks of auburn hair off her tranquil face.

We're alone, Mum.

'Where've you gone?' I trace a finger down your cheek. My voice is trembling, although my body feels calm, curled beside you, like it's been a thousand times before.

'Are you here with me?' I ask, silently begging the universe for a miracle, a sudden gasp and exhalation through your pale lips, a flutter of your lashes as they open and the green of your eyes sparkles like the damp marsh grasses at sunrise.

But there is just stillness. I fold your hand to my lips and kiss your fingers, the instruments of your talent. Your skin smells of royal jelly – the lotion Possum gave you for Christmas. I inhale deeply and breathe you in.

The light is fading outside the window and there are soft shadows stretching across us now.

'Are you cold?' My hand feels comforted by its contact with the outline of your body and the action of tucking the duvet into its contours and around the curve of your belly, which was once my home. 'Better now,' I whisper. 'I'm not leaving you. We can stay like this forever.'

I'm holding you tighter, entwining myself round you,

wrapping myself in your embrace, my tears snail-tracking softly down your smooth temple.

'There's something you should know, Mum. The dolphins came – a mother and baby, and they leaped out of the water three times – look.' I reach for my mobile and in a moment the clip is playing. But I can't bear to look at the images, or hear the childish voice shrieking at fever-pitch.

'Your wish came true,' I whisper, kissing your forehead, curling up against your chest. But your heart can no longer soothe me with the beat of its love.

41

Here with me.

I would give anything – my breath, my body, my soul, my life, to reverse time; to hold the world with both my hands and spin it gently backwards on its journey round the sun. I would stop it on its axis at the time I am tiny, curled up on your lap while you read me stories about heroines and happy endings in the heat of the day. You hold me until my eyes close, lulled by the rise and fall of your words on the warm summer winds under the shade of the apple tree.

I want to be your heroine now. I would do anything – walk a tightrope over an abyss of fire, wander in frozen wastes without hope of reaching home, sail through unending storms with waves skyscraper high, leap from the Empire State Building, crawl through trenches of mud and blood, allow doctors to dismantle me to donate my organs, immerse myself in liquid nitrogen, drink a potion like Juliet, to change the clock, to disable its momentum.

We're moving slowly through traffic and I'm not taking my eyes off you. On the other side of the glass, which is separating me from the normal world, pedestrians, kids in buggies, dogs, toddlers, stiff mannequins in shop windows, a man slumped in a doorway, half in a sleeping bag, pass by in the soft focus of my outer vision. Some people stare in our direction. Others look away, not wanting to intrude. Many don't see us at all, their faces vacant, minds on a mission to avoid body contact with anyone else.

Only you are in focus, a short distance ahead, smiling at me, throwing your head back, laughing, surrounded by lavender and sunflowers. The sound of your voice in my ears takes me by surprise, makes me catch my breath. The heavy thing that sits inside my chest, as solid as tree bark with twisted roots, is suddenly pushed up my throat, through my mouth and out into the world. Shards of pain shoot down my abdomen and up my spine.

'Jaz, it's OK.' Dad is holding me tight, trying to soothe me. I am rigid, like a feral creature, trapped in an alien environment, barely breathing, my heart at the point of explosion. My body softens under Dad's touch. The dam behind my eyes breaks and my tear ducts are pumping pure sea water.

'Cry Me A River' is one of your favourite songs. I remember that humans have the same water-to-salt ratio as the sea – nine parts to one. Today, I am your river flowing into an ocean, washed away by the pull of the tide.

I thought if I were strong, strong enough for two, even three, we would win. The brave and valiant Ballantynes. Dad calls us 'the Three Musketeers'. No matter what confronts us, we always 'ride out to face another day'. We're the three permanent sides of the triangle, but the damaged angles have skewed and flexed and changed the shape of us.

Dad must think of a new name now.

We've driven down this road so often, you and me. We usually turn left just ahead and pull into the pay-and-display car park, the start of a shop-fest (if I have my way) or a book-fest (if you have yours). If I close my eyes, I can hear our indicator ticking, like a metronome, keeping time with *The Lark Ascending* on our CD player – your favourite classical piece. I'm longing to feel a swerve as the wheels change direction, to hear you hum the melody, but today we continue onwards, past the round sign displaying a capital P and two more sets of traffic lights. The engine is so quiet, it feels as if we're in a bubble, blowing through other people's lives. Unreal, surreal and real relentlessly entwined.

'Nearly there,' says Dad softly, kissing my forehead. The thorn from the yellow rose I am holding is scraping my skin. The flower is from our garden, freshly picked.

Time is moving us forwards, Mum. There is something else I want to tell you before the bubble bursts and it's no longer just the three of us. When I close my eyes, I am standing in your marshes, under a wide, sun-streaked sky, singing a single note for all eternity.

I am calling you. And you are here with me.

We've reached the crematorium, a low building set in wooded parkland with well-tended flower borders and an air of tranquillity, away from the town. Our car pulls up behind

Mum's and, as we get out, there is a sea of colour (no black, Dad has stipulated) and faces – friends, orchestra colleagues, distant relatives, and Father Andrew, our local minister. Mum wasn't religious, but she's played several concerts in his church and he asked if we would like him to take her service today.

Bella appears and gives me a big hug. Her family is close by – her mum's wearing a beautiful pink hat. Meredith is sporting a tie with violins and cellos on it and has trimmed his beard. Stephen is crying on his new boyfriend's shoulder. The Dobbses are holding hands, standing a little way apart from the crowd. My breath catches a little when I notice Ferdie, with Ethan next to him.

'Hello,' I mouth at Ethan, silently. He gives me a warm smile. I'd like to run and bury my head against the shoulder of his smart jacket. I want his arms to close around me, their familiar strength shoring me up. My legs feel weak and unreliable. I am gripping Dad's arm for all I am worth.

There is a hush as Mum is lifted out of the car. Dad squeezes my hand and then moves forwards with Stephen to the front of the coffin, where they take its weight with the other four bearers from the undertakers. A moment later, Ethan is at my side and Bella is holding my hand. Somehow I manage to put one foot in front of another.

I am following you, Mum, and will keep following you, to the end of the rainbow.

Slowly, we begin to process into the wide hallway and through to the room where the ceremony is to be conducted, where a grey-haired woman in a brown dress is handing out the orders of service Dad and I designed and made.

A Saint-Saëns cello sonata is playing as we enter – Mum is the soloist and the recording was made in London about five years ago. We've chosen all her favourite pieces from those she included on my questionnaire.

Mum is laid on a raised dais in front of the congregation. I'm looking at the slender box in which she lies and I still can't take it in. Anger and emptiness and a black hole have taken the place of all hope and joy.

Dad is next to me now in the front seat. Ethan and Bella are behind us, with Ferdie and Bell's family. Mum has united us all.

She is smiling at us from the cover of the programme – her beautiful face full of Florida sunshine. A moment after the photo was taken, Mickey Mouse pinched her bottom and she chased him towards the Magic Kingdom with the light sabre I'd just bought in the Star Wars shop.

'Today, we are here to celebrate and give thanks for the life of one of the brightest stars in our earthly firmament.' So begins Father Andrew, who welcomes us and tells us about Mum's exceptional talents and qualities – her love of music and her drive to achieve perfection in her performance; her fulfilment in family life and the tranquillity she found in the marshes of her childhood. He ends by speaking of the terrible loss of a young and wonderful person, prematurely taken from us by cancer.

It wasn't the cancer, though, was it Mum? It was your heart that couldn't take the strain of the growing tumours. The GP at Frog Cottage said the sudden ending was a 'small mercy' for you. But how could it be, when we didn't get the chance to say goodbye?

We sing 'Morning Has Broken', accompanied by one of Mum's colleagues playing a Yamaha keyboard. He plays beautifully, which makes up for the poor quality of the voices. There are prayers about eternal life and another hymn, 'Hills of the North Rejoice', which was Mum's favourite from school and talks about restless waves, southern seas, valleys and lowlands, and a 'warring breeze'.

When I glance to my left, at the far end of the aisle, I see two whiskered noses poking out from inside Mr Dobbs's jacket. Roxy, and her new friend, Pipkin, have come to say goodbye to my mum. How totally brilliant.

We sit down and Stephen is the first to speak. He tells us about Mum's commitment to the orchestra's education programme, her voluntary work in schools to 'give the gift of music to children everywhere'. And he reminds us of her love for life, love and lipstick, and how, even in a Moscow blizzard, with the temperature minus thirty, she insisted on stopping in the snow to put on her 'lippy' before entering a concert hall. After that, Stephen can't speak anymore.

Dad moves forwards to comfort him and to say a few words. He speaks clearly and well. I'm so proud of him. His voice is fading in and out of my consciousness, even though I'm trying so hard to concentrate.

'Every day, Anna made me laugh and brought me joy.' Dad is looking at his notes, composing himself. 'From the day we met, she turned my life upside down and was the best thing that ever happened to me. She gave me a precious daughter, Jasmine, and more happiness than I could have dared hope for. "We've been so lucky" was one of her frequent phrases, meant with all her heart…'

I'm sorry, Mum, I don't agree.

And now it's my turn. Every part of me is shaking, even my bum muscles, but I want to do this, just in case she's watching. In case she can hear me.

The piece of paper which carries my words vibrates in my hand. It's hard to see the words through the mist over my eyes.

'Hey, Mum. There are so many things I want to tell you and I've made a list, like I asked you to do at Frog Cottage. It would probably go on for ever, so I've just included the ten most important. I'll read them as I've written them here.

"I love you
I'm so proud of you
You're my best friend
I want to be like you
You inspire me to try harder and to be better
You make me laugh and give me the courage to be true
    to myself
You make me feel safe
Through you, I've come to love the marshes

You're the best mum in the world
And I will miss you until the end of time."'

'Don't leave me, Eloise' fades up as I return to my seat and rest my head against Dad's shoulder. My eyes are closed but I can't contain the tears. They're splashing down his sleeve like a burst water main.

'She's leavin' now and my heart, it is a breakin'…'

There's a final prayer and then the first few bars of *The Lark Ascending*, which is my cue to put the yellow rose on Mum's coffin. I lay it gently and have a sudden urge to sit down next to her and pour out my heart, as I always did every morning. But Dad is waiting in the aisle, so I touch the casket for the last time before turning and taking his hand.

The open double doors lead us to a pretty garden with a fountain. A raised wooden platform contains the flowers from each service, with the name of the deceased on a label. By the time we reach Mum's area, her sunflowers have arrived.

There are no other arrangements – she had told Dad she wanted people to donate to the orchestra's education fund instead if they wished.

The note attached, clipped into a plastic case, looks stark, written in a stranger's hand. Staring at it, I realise deep in my being that this surreal, sad situation belongs to me and Dad and not to a terrible dream. It's there, in black and white.

'Anna – forever in our hearts, with all our love, James and Jasmine xxx'

42

'Make a wish,' I say. 'Don't tell me what it is.'

'Er. OK. Now what?' says Ethan.

'You wait for it to come true,' I reply.

'How long?' he asks.

'As long as it takes,' I answer, shrugging my shoulders.

We're on a cruise boat, travelling under Southwark Bridge on the River Thames, and I've remembered that Mum always used to grab my hand and run with me over bridges, telling me to make a wish on the way. So it's a family tradition, of sorts. And, as luck would have it, there are several bridges on our journey.

Ethan is staring at the Tate Modern, which stretches behind us on our right. The October sun is making him squint. He reaches for his new shades, which I bought him for his sixteenth birthday and are dead cool.

For my fourteenth, last month, he gave me a fantabulous book about dolphins and a framed photo he'd taken of a sunset over the marshes.

'It's a lurve thing,' the other Urban Chicks sang, teasing me, when I arrived at our first proper girl-band rehearsal last week. I'm the lead singer – and I'm playing acoustic guitar. When term started, one of the first things I did was to sign up for singing lessons.

We're working on a folkie version of Mum's lullaby – I've written the music, with Bella's help. Maybe we'll record it one day. I'd be dead proud if we did.

'Awesome!' exclaims Ethan, taking in the architecture of London Bridge up ahead. As we pass into the shadows underneath and the engine noise echoes along the ageing structure, I close my eyes and ask for this day to never end.

A minute later, the recorded commentary tells us that we are approaching Traitor's Gate, where those condemned to die were brought by boat. And next to it is the Tower of London, the site of countless executions of nobles and commoners. Ethan's mouth is partly open. Olly would describe him as 'gobsmacked'.

'Mind you don't lose your 'ead as we pass,' warns the commentary darkly, and there are chuckles of laughter from several passengers on our open deck.

'Thanks, Jaz,' says Ethan. 'This was such a great idea.'

'You can't come to London and not do a river ride,' I tell him. 'It's a Ballantyne rule.'

The boat turns a slow circle by the Tower and begins its journey back to Westminster, where I've promised Ethan a tour of the Abbey and the Houses of Parliament.

As we approach London Bridge, Ethan looks at me, an unexpected seriousness clouding his face.

'I'm not sure how the second wish will work out. It's about my Mum. I'm meeting up with her next month,' he tells me.

'Hey, that's fantastic,' I respond.

'And I've decided – I'm not going to wait,' he says, leaning forwards and kissing me gently on the lips.

'For what?' I ask, eventually.

'For my first wish to come true,' he grins.

We're running up the steps of West Hampstead Tube Station and out onto the pavement, laughing like lunatics. For some insane reason, Ethan thought I'd look nice in an 'I love London' baseball cap, but changed his mind when I put it on and is now wearing it himself, back to front. I keep trying to grab it off his head, but so far he's evaded me, which is a bit cheeky, as I'm on the way to my red belt now.

Anyway, there's nothing I can do to prevent this being the first image my fellow Chicks Olly and Tasha have of my boyfriend. We arrive outside Guido's restaurant in the High Street, puce, dishevelled and giggling.

Olly is pointing to her watch sternly. 'Sorry,' I mouth through the glass. We're ten minutes late and the girls are already eating dough balls. Then they start squealing, like teens before meeting their pop idol.

All very embarrassing.

'Hiya!' they shriek, as Ethan and I make our way to their table. They take it in turns to kiss him on the cheek, which he's really happy about.

'Hi again, Bella,' he says to my best mate.

'Hi, Wild Boy,' she replies, giving him five. Ethan raises his eyebrows at me. He doesn't look exactly put out about this description.

'I'm Tasha,' says Olly, shaking his hand.

'Hello Olly,' says Ethan, sussing her straightaway.

'*I'm* Tasha,' says my shy, oriental friend. 'You've got great hair,' she says, admiring his shining black mop as he takes off the cap. 'Do you have Japanese relatives?'

'Not that I know of,' replies Ethan.

'Would you like one?' she asks innocently, and I wag my finger at her. The quiet ones are always the worst.

Our soft drinks arrive and I raise a toast.

'To life, love and lipstick,' I say and we all clink our glasses together. Ethan squeezes my hand under the table, reassuringly. We eat mahousive amounts of pizza and gossip about school, the merits of doing AS Maths a year early (Olly is already calling Ethan 'Geeky Boy'), our plans for the rest of half term (including a return to the marshes for me and Dad), and our band's fictitious forthcoming tour of America. We've appointed Ethan as our roadie, by unanimous consent.

He isn't saying much – he can't get a word in – but he's making approving noises in between munching his dinner. My mates are a bit of a handful en masse. I'm really proud of him for agreeing to spend an evening with them.

Just as we're leaving the restaurant, Bella takes me to one side.

'If you ever decide to dump him, you'll tell me first?' she whispers, grinning. I waggle my finger at her. And there go my ears... Bell gives me a mahousive hug.

'Thanks, Jaz,' she continues. 'What you said at your Mum's funeral, about being true to yourself – it helped me make up my mind. I don't want to be an opera diva. I've told my parents. I want to be open to new things, like you are. You're my role model.'

Change blows in, when you least expect it.

'Your mates are OK,' Ethan comments, as we wave them off in the Farrell-mobile. 'Bright, noisy, quite good-looking and totally insane.'

'Which one's quite good-looking?' I ask, my fist in front of his face.

'They've all got their good points,' he answers diplomatically.

We're walking along the High Street, heading in the direction of home. Ethan's looking up at the night sky, whose stars are diffused slightly by the amount of local light pollution.

'Don't look for comets,' I tell him, holding his arm, bringing him back down to earth.

'Why's that?' he asks.

'Because you'll walk into a lamppost, country boy,' I tell him, manoeuvring him round a metal pole on the pavement. He's grinning at me strangely.

'What?' I ask. I've probably got spinach stuck in my

teeth or something gross.

He turns me round and points to the display in the hardware shop window nearest us. A line of flashing creatures is strung across it. The empty box lying underneath reads 'Garden Glow Worms'.

'Let's count them!' I tease him. We start laughing and give each other the biggest squeeze, so tight it's possible our bodies will burst.

43

Dad pulls into the driveway of Frog Cottage, switches off the engine and takes my hand. We haven't spoken since we dropped Ethan home. The prospect of returning has loomed for several weeks, and now that we're here, there's no escaping the rush of memories as we step out into the evening air of the marshes.

The wide October sky wraps itself round us like a cool blanket, shot through with strands of orange, red and pink. I breathe in and let my lungs fill and expand. A small purple-bordered Fritillary butterfly pirouettes across my path, a Pygmy Footman moth dancing attendance in its wake.

Possum is yowling in his cat transport on the back seat. He can hear the frogs and is working himself up into a frenzy at the thought of unlimited snacks.

I let Dad worry about unloading him and our two sports bags, which contain enough clothes for our three-day stay, plus the box of groceries packed at home in London.

My hands are already full. I'm carrying the special blue glass jar with Mum's ashes in, returned to us by the undertakers a week after her service. And I'm holding it so tightly my hands are aching.

There are brown, crunchy leaves strewn over the veranda

and fine cobwebs across the front door. Papa Tom's chair is in its usual place. The varnish Mum and I put on has faded a little and it has an air of neglect about it.

Dad opens Possum's prison door and he shoots out like a bullet, straight towards the stream, where he ploughs into the long grasses and crouches down, ready for his hunting games to begin.

'Crazy animal,' says Dad, unlocking the door and pushing it open with our kit bags.

The cottage feels sun-warmed, although it smells slightly damp – the heating hasn't been on yet. Dad's going to fix a timer to the system during our stay.

I'm standing in the hall, rooted to the spot. Every inch of the space is full of my past. Each room is a memorial, each piece of furniture a reminder. Everywhere is full of ghosts.

Dad is at my side and together we open the lounge door, treading carefully, reverentially, as we enter the room. Mum's cello is exactly where it fell, when her heart finally faded and stopped. Her bow is on the floor. Despite this still-life scene before us, the air feels expectant, as if we are waiting for a performance. Any moment, I expect to see Mum breeze in, take her seat and begin to play.

I place the glass jar on the mantelpiece and Dad and I just look at it for a while. There are no words to fill the silence, which feels eternal and fathomless, like infinity. Our brains are reeling, trying to make sense of this great loss, trying to accustom us to being two, not three; to Mum's spirit being everywhere, and nowhere.

I bend down to lift the cello carefully and place it back on its stand. Inadvertently, my hand brushes over the strings. The sound echoes round the room, discordant and mournful. Dad bows his head a little, fighting back emotion. I know he lifted Mum from this floor and carried her lifeless body upstairs. And then forbade anyone from coming in here. He touches the instrument with reverence and tenderness.

We hug, saying nothing, for several minutes. Then Dad puts his hands on my shoulders. 'You hungry?' he asks.

'Yup,' I answer, glad that he's rescued my consciousness from its free-fall.

So, before long, we're sitting on the veranda steps, plates on our laps, tucking into fajitas with sour cream, chicken and salsa, shivering slightly in the cold, but content. With emotions so strained, dinner round the table in the kitchen wasn't an option. Eating outside is a great idea – if we run out of things to say, we can just look at the view.

The last vestiges of orange light are fading, like low flames, in the west, behind the turbines. I recognise a formation of white-fronted geese making its way across the horizon.

'They're back from the Arctic,' I say. *Like us, Mum. They're coming home.*

'Hey, Dad. Wakey, wakey, rise and shine.' I'm delivering a mug of steaming coffee to the table next to the double bed. Dad is spread-eagled across Mum's side, too.

'Must be a mirage, you, up early,' he observes, rubbing his eyes. I'm showered and dressed, but, owing to a slight problem with the microwave, resulting in my porridge exploding, I haven't had breakfast yet.

'Big day,' I reply. 'And you know what, it's raining.'

Dad pulls a face, swings his legs out from under the duvet and pulls back the curtains. Low cloud lies like a soggy fleece across the countryside. Water drizzles down the window pane. A black and white avocet, with its long, upturned beak, flies by, making a mournful 'kleep-kleep' cry.

'It might brighten up,' says Dad, ever positive. 'What was it Mum used to say about the marshes?'

They're never the same for a minute...

'We can't do it if it's like this. She'll get soggy,' I tell him. Dad agrees and, after finishing his coffee, pads off downstairs to the shower. I snuggle into the warmth his body has left behind in the bed, pulling the duvet up round my chin.

'Miss you, Mum, sooooo much,' I hear myself saying, to the space on the pillow next to me where her sleepy head should be.

The rain answers me with a gentle pitter-patter and streaks of droplets. I'm counting the rivulets in Korean, trying to ease the pain across my chest and silently repeating the Lioness's words:

Your spirit is strong, Jaz. Your spirit is strong.

My mind is full of images; of Mum smiling at me from the sofa ('Love you more'); of dolphins skimming through the ocean; of Dad hanging me upside down from his shoulders; of Ethan, the first time I saw him; of glow worms; of Mum playing the cello in the garden; of the dead swan in the hide; of the Adonis Blue, fluttering against her face.

It's a sign.

I open my phone, find the key accessing my video footage and press 'play'. There's Possum, rummaging in the undergrowth. Mum's laughter spills out of the tiny speaker and fills the room, and there is the briefest glimpse of her happy face, bathed in summer sunshine.

I must have played this, and stroked the picture on the screen, a million times.

Downstairs, there is an exclamation of 'Oh, what?' followed by the sound of running water and the mop hitting against chair legs.

'The microwave's vomited,' Dad calls up the stairs, a few minutes later. His matter-of-fact tone dilutes my sadness and delivers me back into reality. His voice is strong and steady. I feel suddenly reassured. I know there is no crisis he cannot cope with, no tragedy he cannot overcome.

'Everything's OK now. I called International Rescue,' he adds. 'It's safe to go back in the kitchen.'

We're in the garden of Frog Cottage, Dad and I. The rain has become a fine mist and the low cloud has lifted, revealing bursts of blue. A warm breeze is wafting the white ice crystals west at speed. Gulls and ducks are zooming about, gliding on air currents. It looks like it's rush hour in the sky.

I'm holding Mum's jar of ashes. The blue glass reminds me of the present Stephen gave me last Christmas – organic Turkish delight from some posh emporium in Knightsbridge. Mum would smile at that, being put in a sweetie jar.

We've decided that now is the time. The forecast for later isn't good and we're both uptight, waiting for the event. It's weird, planning a ceremony for someone who isn't here, with just two of us attending. Well, three if you count Possum, who has followed us through the wet grass gingerly, trying to avoid getting his paws soaked.

Dad and I weren't sure what to wear. It's been a major topic of our conversation for the last week. We've discussed everything from party dress and white tuxedo (which Mum loved), down to jeans and jumpers – marsh-trekking uniform.

'She'd want us to be ourselves,' I suggested. So we agreed that however we felt on the day would dictate the outcome and that we would pack for all eventualities.

I'm wearing my best jeans tucked into the leather and suede boots Mum bought me in the spring and a blue

T-shirt dress over the top. On my wrist is my silver heart bracelet. Dad's in a pale lemon shirt over blue chinos and Italian loafers. He had his hair cut in the week, to tame the fluff at the back (which Mum didn't like). I've used some of her green eyeliner and, of course, a touch of her rosy pink lipstick.

Possum has a flowery ribbon round his neck and looks quite put out. I told him he had to make an effort, just this once.

We're by the stream and a frog is hopping about on the water's edge. Possum is watching its every move, weighing up whether he can be bothered to stalk it.

Dad is looking at me expectantly. 'I think you should say something first,' I say, quietly, so Mum can't hear. He nods and clears his throat, while I open the catch on the jar. Shafts of light suddenly beam down between the clouds, silver bright, scything into the earth of the ploughed fields to the north.

'What?' says Dad, noticing that I'm staring at him and giggling.

'You've got a halo,' I say. The vapour round his head is shining and small droplets on his lashes gleam like baby pearls.

'First time you've noticed?' he responds, smugly. 'Anyway. Um. We're gathered here today…'

'Nooo,' I say. 'Not like that.'

Dad is looking at his shoes and swallowing hard. I can tell

he's too upset to speak. The enormity of what we are about to do has caught up with him.

'OK, Mum,' I begin. 'We know this is what you wanted, to be free forever in your favourite place. We want you to know that we're keeping Frog Cottage, so that we can always be near you and be true to your memory. And so that you can maybe see my kids playing here one day.' Dad raises his eyebrows at this. 'We wish you peace and joy, and wherever you go, we're sending our love with you.'

Dad nods at me – his eyes are glassy like the stream. I tip the jar forwards and let the ashes start to fall. They scatter over the long grass and some of the dust catches in the wind and is whipped skyward. We watch it disperse intently, dazzled by the sun.

'Meeeoow!' complains Possum, as something hard lands on him from a great height.

And then, as if from nowhere, hailstones the size of golf balls hurl themselves down on our heads and clatter around us, starting to lie on the grass like a crystal carpet, crunching underfoot as we run to take refuge in the cottage.

We reach the veranda, breathless and a little bedraggled.

'Thanks, Anna,' says Dad, pulling a pretend cross face at the sky.

And as we watch the ice shower pelting in a wave across the landscape, shielding our eyes against the luminous vibrancy of the light, a transformation is taking place.

'Look,' murmurs Dad softly, pointing to the east.

A double rainbow is arcing across the horizon, bridging the boundaries of the marshes, connecting the earth with the sky, the two semi-circles of colours becoming more defined and distinct, like separate instruments building up to a crescendo. The hard crystals continue to fall in a frenzy of hail.

It's your special show, Mum, and the clouds are applauding.